THE UNDYING FIRE

The Undying Fire

Copyright © 2013 by Steven Thorn

First edition published in 2013

Second edition published in 2017

Cover art by Daniel Kordek

ISBN-13: 978-1544236612
ISBN-10: 1544236611

ALSO BY STEVEN THORN

BOOKS IN THE PHOENIX GUARDIAN SERIES:

The Phoenix Guardian
The Undying Fire

SHORT STORIES:

The Vines
Waldo Reed and the Totem Mountain
Waldo Reed and the Weird Sisters

POETRY:

Dear God: My Grief Observed

In loving memory of
Dr. J. Rufus Fears, Carmen Thorn, and Jimmy Brown,
who each passed away during the writing of this book
in 2012-2013

Resurgam

THE
UNDYING
FIRE

CHAPTER 1:
SUPERNOVA EN ROUTE TO WORMHOLE

The heating element ignited with a burst of flame that licked the ceiling.

"Damien!" Nestor thundered from the front of the trolley, his gray beard shaking under his immense cap. "Are you trying to set my trolley on fire?"

"I don't want to hear it!" Damien twisted a series of knobs and glared at a teapot. "I know what I'm doing."

He strode up the aisle, ducking his head to avoid the low ceiling. After shooting an annoyed glance at Nestor, he turned to face the passengers. He stroked his fuzzy brown mustache absentmindedly. In front of him was a motley group, but that was normal for a trolley flying through this part of space.

A chubby cherub in a booster seat sat next to a blonde fairy with glistening wings. Two dwarves sulked across the aisle. The dwarves had black leather gauntlets on their broad forearms. Their untidy black beards fell across sleeveless, black t-shirts that depicted chain-mailed, axe-wielding dwarves. Behind them was a short gnome with a thick beard. He sat next to a pale banshee, whose dark blue hair flowed over her shoulders and into her lap. A muzzle was clamped over her mouth. The gnome kept glancing nervously at the banshee. She stared straight ahead without blinking.

One passenger that caught Damien's attention was a red-haired girl in a yellow raincoat and shocking white rain boots. The ensemble made her look like a walking candy corn.

Damien adjusted his flimsy glasses and twirled his fuzzy brown mustache nervously. "We're, uh, making our approach to the wormhole. Would anyone like a cup of tea?"

Tea? Natalie sat up straight in her seat. *Do I like tea?*

A memory stirred in the foggy depths of her mind. She liked tea, right?

Or...did she really, really *dis*like tea?

Natalie frowned. She might as well try it.

She raised her hand along with a few other passengers. "I'd like tea, please."

Damien walked back down the aisle, his lanky arms swinging by his sides. He crouched next to the teapot and pushed his floppy cap back.

"Not sure why it's acting up...thought I fixed it before we left the junction." He pressed a button and turned one of the knobs again. "There we go!"

Natalie watched him for a while as the tea began to brew.

Tea wasn't the only subject on which her memory was deficient. She also couldn't remember if she liked to travel through space by interstellar trolley.

She prodded her crimson seat cushion. The trolley was quaint, which she liked—but "quaint" was one of those words that people threw around without knowing what it meant, just like "nice" and "interesting." People said something was "nice" because they couldn't actually think of anything nice to say. And "interesting" was a dismissive way of saying, "I'm too polite to say what I really think, so I'll withhold my opinion and substitute a vague application of the word 'interesting.'"

At least, that's what Natalie thought about the words "quaint," "nice," and "interesting." They were interesting and nice in their own way, but their original meanings were rather quaint, so no one used them properly anymore.

"Tea's ready!" Damien called a few minutes later. He wiped sweat from his brow, staring at the passengers and looking confused. "Er, who wanted tea again?"

Natalie raised her hand, and Damien gave her a steaming cup of tea on a little plate. She raised the drink to her lips, pausing to savor the pleasant aroma. Then she took a generous gulp of the very hot, freshly-brewed tea.

Fire poured down her throat. Her eyes watered. She slapped her knees, feeling the horrible heat flow down to her stomach and incinerate her insides.

"Aaah! Aaah!" She gasped as the unbearable sensation swept through her chest. The shock of the moment caused her to spill the very hot tea onto her blue jeans.

Natalie gave a little scream. Her yellow raincoat was waterproof, but her denim jeans were a less-than-satisfactory protection.

A few surrounding passengers gave her irritated looks. The cherub made a high-pitched grunt of annoyance. Then he and the others shook their heads and returned to their own cups of tea, which they sipped in quiet dignity.

Natalie blinked her eyes, which were streaming with tears. She glared at the cup as if it had betrayed her.

"You should be careful with that tea. It's...quite hot."

Natalie looked across the aisle to see a tall, thin elf staring back at her. The elf's pointy ears stuck out between long braids of blonde hair. He regarded Natalie with an expression of condescending amusement.

She faked a gracious smile. "Oh, *thank* you! I shall try to be more careful."

"Sipping tea is really more proper than...gulping." The elf smiled, raising his cup to his lips and sticking out a dainty little finger.

"I suppose it is."

"You suppose...correctly."

Natalie's lips twitched into a frown of their own accord.

The elf's manner of speaking was very annoying.

And he stuck out his little finger when he drank tea.

And he had brought his own teacup. It was decorated with water lilies, and it had a tiny handle that curved so much it looked impractical *and* dangerous.

The elf mistook Natalie's disgust for interest.

"Do you like the teacup? It was...my mother's."

"Oh. Yes. It's...beautiful."

Natalie could have kicked herself. Now *she* was talking with a pause.

The elf indicated the book in her lap. "What are...you reading?"

Natalie looked at her leather-bound journal. The brown cover contrasted with her yellow raincoat. There was a young red bird with bright, shiny plumage on the cover.

"Oh, nothing." She held the book self-consciously against her chest. "Just a journal."

"Introspection." The elf nodded approvingly. "That is an...admirable trait in any young person."

"Oh. Yes. Thank you." Natalie gave an exaggerated smile.

"Perhaps you could journal that sipping tea is much safer than...gulping it. Aha. Ha." The elf laughed. It was an annoying, sickly-sweet sound, like the tinkling of tiny bells.

3

"Mmm." Natalie nodded half-heartedly and turned away, hoping that he might stop talking if she looked out of the window long enough.

That star looked interesting. Natalie would just stare determinedly at it and the elf would realize she didn't want to talk—

"My name is Telesto, by the...way."

Sigh...

"Natalie." She turned around and extended her hand.

Telesto arched an eyebrow at her hand but did not take it.

"Yes...indeed. You have quite a beautiful hand for such a young girl."

"Oh. Thank you." Natalie blushed at the elf's snub. She dropped her hand, pretending to brush her knees.

"I must confess that I am not used to seeing...humans on the trolley."

"Do you see one?" Natalie's eyes widened. She turned around and scanned the passengers.

"No, I meant...you."

"Oh." Natalie settled back in her chair. "I'm a phoenix."

Telesto's face betrayed surprise.

At the word "phoenix," a few passengers turned around to sneak a glance at Natalie. The cherub stood to look over the top of his chair. He stared at Natalie, a monocle in one hand and a newspaper in the other.

"Indeed? A phoenix?" the elf repeated. "Then I am quite sorry to have confused you with...a human."

"It's not a problem." Natalie shrugged. "I look like one."

"Yes, although I should...have known." Telesto crossed his legs and smiled indulgently. "It is very rare for humans to travel on *our* transportation. Not many of them know that other races...exist. They are a very narrow-minded, self-centered race. Quite arrogant, don't...you find?"

"Some of them, yes. Not so different from other races in that regard..." Natalie trailed off, looking Telesto up and down. He had a deep blue jacket with golden buttons and trim. The long tails of his coat were tucked neatly beneath him, and they trailed over the seat edge.

"Are you a performer?" she asked.

"A performer? Aha. Ha. Oh...no. I am a journalist."

"A journalist? For what publication?"

4

"*Faerie Interest.*" Telesto managed to stretch a good three syllables from "in-ter-est."

Up ahead, the dwarves snorted in amusement.

Natalie's face was blank.

"You have never heard...of it?" Telesto asked, ignoring the dwarves.

"I must confess I haven't."

Telesto chuckled. He looked around to share the joke of Natalie's ignorance, but no one else was laughing—except for the dwarves, who giggled in a manner that defied their intimidating appearance. Telesto shot them a derisive look.

"Well," he sniffed proudly, "the *Faerie* is a very prestigious publication based in Calypso. It is currently distributed in over...twenty-one solar systems. I am out here writing a period piece about the worlds that were...destroyed during the War of Chaos."

"Really?" For the first time in the conversation, Natalie felt a spark of interest.

"Yes, we are doing a feature on...the Desolation."

"The Desolation?" Natalie raised her teacup to her lips, testing the warmth again. But there wasn't much tea left that she hadn't already spilled. She put it back down.

"The Desolation was a patch of space particularly devastated by the War of Chaos. We are...at the edges of it now." Telesto indicated the stars outside. "We have been in it almost since we left...the junction."

Telesto set his teacup aside, stood up in the aisle, and pointed over Natalie's shoulder. She noted the collection of ruby- and emerald-encrusted rings on his outstretched hand.

"That is Ophelia, the star for which this system is named. The inhabitants of this...system, however, typically call it the Sun. It is—"

"*Sun* is a good word." Natalie interrupted the elf. "It's like an affectionate term for *your* star, the one that gives you light and life."

Telesto frowned. He stared at Natalie, momentarily nonplussed. "Well, I suppose so. I have never really...thought of it that way."

"It's like *mom.* There are countless mothers in the universe, but every child thinks the woman who gave birth to him or her is the most important. *Mom,*" Natalie drew her legs up onto the crimson seat cushion, "and *Sun.*"

5

"Yes." Telesto cleared his throat. "Well, they call it the Sun—or perhaps I should say...they *called* it the Sun."

"Called?" Natalie pressed her hand against the cold glass.

"Yes. Do you see that planet orbiting Ophelia? That is Mneme. It is...uninhabited."

Natalie looked at the fiery planet. Red clouds swirled like ink stains in the orange atmosphere.

"Why?"

"War," Telesto answered simply. "All life on Mneme was...wiped out during the War of Chaos. There used to be some other planets here, but..." He waved his hand vaguely.

For the first time, Natalie noted other stellar bodies in the distance. The light from Ophelia reflected off their irregular shapes.

"Those are *planets*?"

"They *were* planets. Now they are just asteroids and...debris."

Natalie felt a sinking feeling in the pit of her stomach. Billions of people had died here. All that remained of their worlds were charred fragments drifting through space.

She looked at the Sun, Ophelia, which seemed to shine brighter the longer she stared at it. She held up her hand to the window, framing Ophelia against her thumb and index finger. From this distance, it was about the size of her thumbnail.

"At least Ophelia is still here. She's so bright and beautiful."

Ophelia seemed to respond to her compliment. The Sun burst forth with a dazzling display of light.

"Wow. That's beautiful!" Natalie gasped. "It's almost like she knows we're talking about her."

"Oh, my. That is not...good."

Natalie glanced back at Telesto, who had gone pale.

"What do you mean?"

"I mean that looks like...a supernova." Hands trembling, the elf pulled a small telescope out of an inside pocket and looked through it.

"But stars twinkle, don't they?"

"Not like that! Driver!" Still looking through his telescope, the elf fumbled for a cable above his head. When his hand finally found it, he pulled sharply. A horn blasted.

"What? What do you want?" Nestor turned in his squeaky swivel chair to glare at Telesto.

"Supernova!" Telesto pointed a shaking finger at the right side of the trolley.

Everyone in the trolley turned to see what Telesto was pointing at—everyone except the banshee, who continued to stare straight ahead.

Nestor pushed back the bill of his cap, revealing small brown eyes.

"Sweet Soul of Sol, save us all."

"Oh, dear," Damien moaned from the back of the trolley. There was a scraping noise as he shoved the cooking shelf into the wall and stowed the teapot away.

"Here, let me see!" Natalie took the telescope from Telesto's shaking hands. The elf was too petrified to protest.

Natalie adjusted the lens and peered through the telescope at the Sun.

Ophelia was more than twice the size that it had been a moment ago. Natalie's eyes watered at the Sun's intense brightness. But that wasn't the worst of it. A tremendous shockwave shot out of the star's center—a rippling sphere of energy that grew larger and larger.

Natalie watched the expanding wave crash against Mneme. The blast hit the world, and the surface peeled away under the crushing heat. A moment later, the planet's core exploded, and the shattered pieces of Mneme joined the older planetary debris.

The shockwave grew larger—and closer.

One of the dwarves waved to attract Nestor's attention. "Oi! How far are we from the wormhole?"

"Erm," Nestor squeaked. "Just two or three minutes away."

"Two or three minutes?" Telesto gasped. "Do we have enough time to get out of the way?"

The supernova blast was expanding, trailing fragments of the planets that had once belonged to the Ophelia system.

Natalie watched the shimmering wave of heat come closer.

"What happens if it hits us? This trolley is made for interstellar flight, isn't it?"

"Sweetie, nobody engineers a trolley to withstand a supernova." The cherub squinted at Natalie through his monocle. "Our only hope is to make it to the wormhole and jump outta this galaxy. But he," the cherub jerked a chubby thumb at Nestor, "says he can't get us there for a few minutes. Well, I don't know if that shockwave is gonna give us a few minutes!"

Natalie bit her lip. "Can't we increase our speed?"

7

"Oh, be realistic!" Telesto wrung his hands, his voice rising to hysterics. "This is just a trolley! How can we possibly outrun that?"

"Excuse me, sir, but if you will please sit down." Damien took Telesto by the shoulders and planted the elf firmly in his seat. "We cannot outrun it, but as it explains in your safety pamphlet, the aisles must remain clear for trolley employees during in-flight emergencies."

Natalie examined the trolley's wood paneling. "What makes this thing go?"

The panels didn't provide an explanation, but Damien did.

"Rays of starlight, of course!" He pointed to pairs of lanterns at the front and back of the trolley. "The lanterns harness the starlight and power the engine."

"So shouldn't the starlight from the supernova increase our speed?" Natalie glanced at both sets of lanterns. "That's a lot of light."

Damien looked dumbfounded. He twirled his fuzzy mustache thoughtfully.

"Well, naturally, it..." he stuttered. "I mean..."

"Harness the supernova, eh? It's worth havin' a go." Nestor cackled loudly, causing Natalie to jump in surprise. "All right, Damien, open the lanterns and let's take advantage of the light before it washes us out."

"Washes us out?"

"Wipes the floor with us!"

"The floor—?"

"Just open the lanterns!"

"Right, right." Damien pushed his slipping glasses up and stumbled to the back of the trolley. He opened a small overhead compartment and pulled out a drawer, which popped open to reveal a series of levers. He started to pull each one.

The lantern windows opened. The glowing orbs burned brighter as they caught the light from the supernova.

"All right, everyone, we don't have any seatbelts on here. But you best take your seat." Damien raised a warning hand—a little too late, as it turned out. The trolley shot forward and Telesto face-planted against a headrest.

"And hold onto something," Damien added. "The trolley's about to go really fast."

"But will it be fast enough?" the cherub asked grimly.

Natalie braced herself against the seat in front of her and held onto the golden railing overhead.

She glanced over her shoulder at the advancing shockwave. Planet shards and amber gas clouds swirled in a growing wall of fire.

Natalie let go of the railing with a gasp. It was getting hot. She tapped the window with her hand and drew back. The glass was getting warm too.

The shockwave was getting closer.

So was the wormhole.

And the trolley was going faster.

Natalie leaned into the aisle and looked ahead to see the wormhole. It was a swirling vortex of blue, purple, and white lightning. Nebulous clouds crashed against each other as the maelstrom beckoned the trolley forward.

Natalie slouched in her seat, blocking the wormhole from view. She clutched her journal and Telesto's telescope.

Wormhole before me...

She glanced back.

Firewall behind me...

Above her, the golden railing glowed with heat.

"Thirty seconds till we enter the wormhole!" Nestor shouted.

"Twenty-three seconds until the shockwave incinerates us all!" Damien countered from the back.

Nestor lifted his cap and shot an annoyed look at Damien.

"Twenty-three seconds? How in the Aeon can you be so precise about the shockwave?"

"How in the universe can *you* be so precise about the wormhole?" Damien retorted. "Ouch!" He jumped away from the back of the trolley and sucked his hand, which had been resting against the rear window. "It's getting hot back here!"

Damien scurried to the middle of the trolley, and the passengers sitting in the back followed his example. They scrunched together in the aisle between Telesto and Natalie.

"I thought you were supposed to keep the aisle clear," Telesto sniffed.

"Hey!" Damien glared at the elf. "No disrespecting trolley employees during in-flight emergencies!"

Natalie stole a glance backward—and saw the shockwave envelope the entire rear view of the trolley.

She quickly turned away.

Instead, she would focus on...the furious lightning storm around the whirling mass of the wormhole.

Oh, dear.

Natalie blinked, having finally resolved her previous question about travel by interstellar trolley. Taking the trolley itself wasn't too bad. Parts of it were quaint, nice, and interesting.

But the supernova and the wormhole would have to go next time.

And the tea. The tea would have to go too.

If there was a next time.

"Oh gods! It's gonna be close!" Damien crouched in the aisle, covering his eyes.

Natalie noticed that the banshee continued to stare straight ahead. She didn't get fazed by much.

"Why journalism?" Telesto rocked back and forth in his seat. "Why journalism? I'm sorry, Mother! I'll go back to school and become a civil engineer! I'll live close to home just like you told me too!"

The shockwave was far too close.

The heat was stifling.

Natalie took deep breaths, feeling the panic grow in her chest.

The rear of the trolley glowed red, and something sounded like it was hissing.

Or singing.

Was the glass melting?

"Hold on!" Nestor shouted, gripping the trolley controls.

Natalie closed her eyes. This was it.

Boom!

A high-pitched squeal.

BOOM!

Then everything got very, very hot...and very, very bright.

They were either dead or through the wormhole.

Maybe both.

CHAPTER 2:
IMMIGRATION

It turned out that Natalie and the other trolley passengers were not, in fact, dead.

They had passed through the wormhole while Natalie closed her eyes and hugged herself tightly. And the whole time she had listened to Telesto's panicked, girlish screams.

She probably shouldn't have judged Telesto's girlish screams, because he was an elf.

But still, it was a little embarrassing.

Natalie took a deep breath, letting her legs gently back onto the floor. She noticed deep crumples in her jeans where she had gripped them.

Telesto let out a deep breath.

One of the dwarves sniggered. "Exciting ride there, eh, pretty boy?"

Telesto didn't respond. He just sat quietly with his hands folded in his lap. The braids of his hair had loosened, scattering blonde strands across his face. Natalie handed him his telescope. He accepted it wordlessly.

"Ladies and gentlemen, we have come safely through the wormhole!" Damien grinned in triumph. He ran to the front to high-five Nestor. "Just another day on the interstellar trolley, eh?"

He clapped his hands, filling the stunned silence. "We're only an hour away from Arcadia now, and we'll be entering the Aeon soon. Sit back and enjoy the rest of the ride."

"The Aeon?" Natalie looked confused. "What's that?"

"Why, it's right ahead, miss." Damien pointed to the front of the trolley.

Natalie leaned into the aisle and saw a magnificent spiral galaxy straight ahead. She would have enjoyed it more if her heartbeat could slow down to an acceptable level. But the Aeon was still a magnificent sight.

A radiant celestial disk stretched out before them. Seven arms curled out from the center, and billions of stars blurred together, forming a cascade of light.

Damien walked over to Natalie's seat.

"Good thought you had, miss—harnessing the starlight." He tipped his hat to her. "You're a sharp one and no mistake."

"Of course she is!" The cherub with the monocle gave Natalie a wink of approval. "She's a phoenix!"

"Oh, thank you." Natalie blushed. She turned away from the attention and looked at the colorful dust particles as they entered one of the Aeon's spiral arms. The bright wisps of cloud brushed against the trolley windows, bathing the interior in luminous purple light.

"It's lovely, isn't it?" she whispered.

"Indeed it is, miss." Damien nodded, clasping his hands behind his back.

The trolley flew out of the nebula. It was like the lifting of a veil as the Aeon's center came into clear view—a colossal cluster of stars shining against velvety black. The hair rose on the back of Natalie's neck.

"It's never looked so beautiful." Telesto's voice cracked. They were the first words he had spoken since the wormhole. "And to think...we almost died and missed it."

Damien nodded wisely. "Yeah, we could have died."

Telesto wiped his eyes with a handkerchief. "It would have been so dreadful."

"It would have," Natalie agreed. "I just died a few weeks ago. I have no plans to do it again so soon."

Damien and a few other passengers laughed heartily at the apparent joke. Even Telesto managed a smile.

But they fell silent when she saw Natalie's earnest expression.

"Oh, right." Damien cleared his throat. "You said you were a phoenix."

*

When Natalie stepped off the trolley onto the station platform, she realized that she didn't have a clue where to go. She turned around aimlessly in the crowd of people, each walking to their known destinations.

She looked up at the huge hole in the roof to watch red trolleys come and go on distant rays of starlight. Lanterns ignited on each trolley, and then the cars slowly rose into the air and out of the station.

By the time that Natalie looked back to see her own trolley, it was moving down the platform toward a covered dock. Damien and Nestor waved at her from inside the trolley.

Natalie smiled and waved back. Then the lanterns on the corners of the trolley flickered and died. The trolley stopped in mid-air and crashed to the concrete. Nestor yelled animatedly at Damien, who yelled back and held up his hands in confusion.

Nestor pulled Damien away from the panels and flipped a hidden lever. The lanterns flared up again, and the trolley slowly rose back into the air and toward the dock.

Natalie felt a twinge of sadness, suddenly realizing that the only people she knew in the station had just left.

Her shoulders rose and fell with a sigh.

She *knew* that she knew a lot of people here on Arcadia, but she would have trouble sifting through the names and faces.

Natalie was about to indulge in a pity party for herself when she saw a tide of travelers moving toward a doorway marked IMMIGRATION.

She decided to follow along.

*

Immigration was a dark, cavernous room that housed a maze of lines. Spherical honeycombs hung from the ceiling, and fireflies darted in and out of the spheres, lighting the room. Enormous ceiling fans filled the space with a cool breeze.

Natalie stood at the back of the longest line, which wound across the entire room and in and out of other lines. Various signs were posted at the front of the lines:

ARCADIANS

AEON RESIDENTS

FOREIGNERS, AEON VISA PLUS

FOREIGNERS, INCORPOREAL BEINGS

FOREIGNERS, MISCELLANEOUS

Natalie wasn't sure, but it looked like the word "UNLUCKY" had been scratched out in front of "MISCELLANEOUS."

She had joined the Arcadian line. Natalie stared at the queue of incorporeal beings, which passed through her own line. Most of the spirits had a humanoid shape. Some of them had a more substantial appearance than others, who were barely visible at all.

One translucent man had a trench coat and a solid-looking briefcase. As Natalie stared at the spectral man, the hand holding the briefcase dissipated like a cloud. The briefcase dropped to the floor with a clunk. The businessman swore under his breath and picked the briefcase up with his remaining hand while the other slowly reappeared.

Natalie watched him as their two lines converged at the same spot. When he was about to pass in front of Natalie, a ceiling fan suddenly blew harder and faster, dispersing the gloomy, floating travelers into the other lines. Natalie moved out of the way as the breeze swept the businessman across the room, light as a feather. The frustrated groans of the businessman and his scattered companions echoed faintly across the room.

A few immigration officials herded the spirits back into their queue with miniature handheld fans. Another angel fixed the troublesome ceiling fan. His wings stuck out from his long-sleeved white shirt, flapping irritably as he adjusted the fan with a screwdriver.

Natalie turned away from the scene to examine the white booths at the front. Some very intimidating angels were solemnly examining each traveler's documents. Their tall wings were folded behind their backs, twitching now and again while the officials inspected each passport.

Natalie felt a sudden thrill of panic.

Did she have her passport?

She had burned up into ashes, and yet she had resurrected with her yellow raincoat, blue jeans, pink shirt, golden watch, and white rain boots. She had been wearing the clothes when she died, so their ashes had been preserved in her journal along with her body.

But...all of those clothes were part of who Natalie *was*. They defined her—Natalie *came* with a yellow raincoat. It just made sense.

But a passport?

Natalie didn't know if the passport had resurrected with her. On Mithris, her pockets had carried her journal, her passport, bubblegum, coloring pencils, tissues, a ball of yarn, rubber bands, balloons, and a few toothpicks. She searched the inside of her pockets, amazed that she could remember particular possessions while forgetting so many other things. Memory was a tricky thing.

She sighed in frustration. None of those items had resurrected with her. The only thing in her pocket was her journal, and that's because she had put it there after she came back to life.

What was she going to do without her passport?

As if sensing Natalie's fear and panic from afar, the immigration angel at the front of her line locked eyes on Natalie. The angel's blue eyes were ice cold. Her blonde hair was held up in a sharp cone above her head, and two loose strands framed her thin, symmetrical features.

Natalie gulped. She could wait a little longer before coming face to face with *that* angel.

She opened her journal, wondering if a past incarnation had left any help for her. She examined the inside cover, and to her surprise there was a small pocket with a little book.

It was a passport.

Trembling with relief, Natalie opened the passport at the centerfold. A kaleidoscope of color made her eyes water. She closed the passport immediately, her mind whirling from the psychedelic chaos. She blinked to clear the burning image from her eyes, almost tripping when she moved ahead with the line.

She cautiously reopened the passport, squinting to protect herself. The page looked like a tie-dye explosion of every color in the visible spectrum—and a few colors from other spectrums. Eyes watering, she tried to make sense of the multicolored mosaic.

She finally realized that they were stamps.

Many stamps.

She gasped—and stopped in line.

Someone hit her in the small of her back.

Natalie turned around to see a gnome holding his forehead.

"Sorry!" she apologized.

She hurried to catch up with the person ahead—and she had to duck under a floating spirit who was finding his way back to the Incorporeal Beings queue.

A strange sensation swept through Natalie's chest. She had been to a *lot* of places. She knew that—after all, she had been there. But it was a bit overwhelming when the full facts hit you with a seizure-inducing menagerie of color. Natalie had traveled a lot...and for a long, long time.

She got back in line and stared at the little book. The balding elf in front looked over his shoulder and noticed Natalie's anxious examination of her passport. He turned around, pulling out his own passport and self-consciously checking to see if he had everything in order. Natalie stood on tip-toes to sneak a peek over his shoulder. She wanted to see if his stamp page was as psychedelic as hers.

It wasn't even close.

"Passport, please." The stern angel extended a white-gloved hand and deftly took the passport from Natalie. "How old are you, young lady?"

"Just a month or so, ma'am."

The angel glanced sharply at Natalie, who couldn't resist noticing that the angel's eyes *glowed*.

"Species?"

"Phoenix."

"Ah." The angel's mouth was a line, thin and flat. "You are a phoenix?"

"Yes, ma'am."

The angel scanned the passport pages. "Phoenix Guardian?"

"Yes, ma'am."

"And where have you been, Miss Bliss?"

"Mithris."

"Business or pleasure?"

"Business, ma'am."

"And how long do you plan to stay here?"

"I'm not sure." Natalie cleared her throat nervously. She looked at a large security troll who was watching their conversation carefully. "But I do live here, ma'am."

The immigration officer raised an eyebrow. Her silence made Natalie doubt herself. Natalie glanced at the security troll's heavy jaw—and the two brick-sized teeth that protruded from his lower lip. A heavy, three-horned helmet sloped over his eyes. He swung a spiked club in his left hand, back and forth...back and forth.

Natalie gulped. She played with a strand of red hair to give her shaking hands something to do.

The immigration official narrowed her eyes at Natalie, sensing weakness. Natalie stopped playing with her hair and froze. Sweat trickled down her brow.

She *did* live here, right?

The angel stared at Natalie for a long minute. Then she handed the passport back as if she never wanted to see it again.

"Welcome back to Arcadia, Miss Bliss. Next!"

Natalie held her breath as she walked past the security troll. One of the troll's eyes focused on the immigration booth, and the other roved to follow Natalie until she rounded the corner.

A shiver of relief ran down Natalie's spine when the security troll passed out of view. She had survived immigration.

Imagine what it would have been like if I had something to hide.

She wiped the sweat from her brow.

After reaching the end of a long corridor, she walked through a pair of security doors and found herself in a sea of people that began sweeping her along to who-knew-where.

She was about to go with the flow, harboring ambitions of finding a lady's room, when she heard the most unexpected noise in the crowded trolley station.

Someone shouted her name.

CHAPTER 3:
THE CHASM AND THE CATACOMBS

"After this tunnel, there's a large chamber that leads to a bridge," Jerome whispered. The sound was amplified in the cold, dark catacombs. He pointed his flashlight at the tattered map in his hands. "The Colossus Pit is on the other side. The Army Chamber and the Valkyrie Gate are beyond that."

He glanced back at the dozen elves standing nearby. They were huddled together for warmth in the dreary underground. Their fair-skinned features and pointy ears looked unnaturally pale under black hoods. Were it not for their bright faces, the elves would have been invisible in their black cloaks.

The shortest of the group was a teenage boy with olive skin. Black hair fell across his forehead and down to his hazel eyes. The faint blue glow from the flashlight revealed round ears under his hood, distinguishing him from the elves.

"Stay close to me, Bellamy." Jerome beckoned the boy to his side. "All right. Let's move."

They started down the underground tunnel, drawing their cloaks closer to ward off the cold. No one spoke.

Jerome was fine with silence. Since they had entered the tunnels, the elves had walked through the dark passages without incident. But Jerome's heart skipped a bit every time he shone his flashlight around a corner.

Anything could be lurking on the other side.

He and his elves moved quickly and quietly, taking care not to broadcast their presence to the denizens of the deep.

Even so, the tunnel amplified the elves' boots louder than Jerome would have liked. Their footfalls reverberated through the passage and betrayed their cautious steps. After a particularly heavy echo, Jerome grabbed a passing elf.

He stared at the offender, Anton. The elf's face glistened with sweat, from the curls of his blonde hair to the tip of his chin. Jerome held a reproachful finger to his lips. Anton swallowed and nodded. He tried walking slower. It didn't help.

19

Fog swirled around their waists as they entered a large cavern. Their boots sloshed through unseen puddles beneath the mist.

Jerome stepped around a stalagmite that protruded ten yards from the ground. He ran his hand along its slimy surface and swung his flashlight around the cavern. Shadows danced against the walls as the soft beam caught the strange limestone formations.

He raised his flashlight to the ceiling and illuminated a forest of stalactites. They were harder to distinguish because the ceiling was so high, but they were thicker than the stalagmites. Some of them looked loose.

Drip...

Droplets of water fell from the stalactites and splashed into the puddles at their feet. The dark rocks seemed to twitch when he shone his light over them.

Drip...

Jerome lowered his flashlight and signaled to the group.

"Come on." He jerked a thumb at the ceiling. "Those things look like they could fall at any moment."

Drip...

They jogged toward the far side of the cavern, carving a path through the mist. Jerome kept glancing up. He hoped that they weren't making too much noise.

Someone swore behind him.

Jerome swung his light around.

Anton was picking himself up from the mist and favoring his right leg.

"Quiet!" Jerome hissed.

"Slipped, sir. Caught my foot in a deep puddle," Anton muttered, feeling his damp pant leg. "Almost broke my ankle."

Jerome shook his head. "Watch your step."

Scraping noises from above caught Jerome's attention. He raised his flashlight at the ceiling, where the forest of limestone was stirring violently.

"Anton!" one of the elves hissed. "You've loosened the stalactites!"

"Run!" Jerome took off at a sprint. The others followed close behind.

They sprinted on the wet, rocky floor. Heavy objects hit the ground behind them.

Jerome strained his ears to listen. He couldn't hear the rock breaking on the floor.

The falling noises stopped abruptly. The only remaining sounds were the elves' heavy footfalls and a strange rustling, which was getting louder.

Jerome slowed to a halt about twenty yards from the exit. He wiped his brow and sniffed, shining his flashlight on the ceiling. Shapes were definitely moving, but it wasn't the—

"It's not the stalactites," Bellamy whispered.

Jerome turned around to face the boy.

"What do you mean?"

Bellamy pointed. "We woke something up."

Jerome jumped back as a reptilian shape detached itself from the stalactites. It crashed to the ground beside Anton, who was catching his breath at the back of the group.

Jerome's heart beat faster.

Standing behind Anton was a skeletal, lizard-like creature, about six feet tall.

"Drake," Bellamy whispered. "Cave-dwelling dragon."

The drake's lengthy arms scraped the ground with foot-long claws. Glistening black scales covered the dragon's emaciated body. Spiked ridges protruded from its back. Two red slits glowed between reptilian eyelids.

The drake flicked its scarlet tongue at Anton, who was standing perfectly still. Then the creature's throat swelled with a low, undulating gurgle. Similar cries echoed from the shadows.

Jerome drew a sleek hand-crossbow from his robes. The sounds of rustling cloth and clinking metal confirmed that his elves had done the same. Only Anton remained motionless, afraid to make the wrong move.

"Anton," Jerome hissed. "Get over here."

Skeletal black shapes stalked through the mist toward the elves. There had to be at least three dozen.

Anton took a tentative step back and reached for the crossbow at his side. The drake tilted its head, watching him.

"He's too close," Anton whispered out of the corner of his mouth. "You'll have to run."

"Anton—"

In a movement of practiced expertise, Anton drew his crossbow and shot the drake in the eye. The glowing blue bolt trailed a streak of light as it flew through the creature's skull.

Anton was already running after the other elves when he waved frantically. "Run!"

The elves broke for the tunnel mouth in front of them, but Jerome withdrew slowly. He fired two quick shots to Anton's left and right, killing the dragon frontrunners.

But then a third drake jumped onto Anton's back.

"Jerome, go—" Anton was cut off as the creature shoved a claw into the back of his neck.

Blood spurted into the air, and Anton collapsed under the dragon's weight. He disappeared in the mist and was covered by three more drakes.

Jerome turned and ran for the cave mouth, his ears ringing with Anton's screams and the dragons' screeches.

The drakes were in hot pursuit, whipping their long black tails and slicing patterns in the fog.

Bellamy was at the back of the group, having been outrun by the elves. Jerome grabbed the boy and sprinted into the tunnel. Their boots pounded against rocky ground. Jerome's flashlight bounced in its belt holster, shining haphazardly on the low ceiling.

"Bellamy!" Jerome turned off the light and glanced at the boy, who could barely keep up with him. "There are too many drakes for crossbows. Can you use one of your spells?"

"Yes." Bellamy's words came in ragged breaths. "If you can give me a moment."

Jerome grunted.

The tunnel sloped upward. An eerie green glow marked the mouth of another chamber.

"Through there." Jerome spat a trail of saliva from his dry mouth. "If the bridge is where the map said it would be, we can lose them at the chasm."

Bellamy glanced over his shoulder. The horde of drakes should have been able to overtake the elves, but the creatures were all struggling for first pick at the prey. Jerome could hear them snarling and fighting in the narrow tunnel. Heavy bodies slammed against the walls—and each other—as too many drakes tried to get through at once.

The passage before Jerome widened to reveal a floor of stalagmites. A treacherous pile of rocks lay at the far end, rising to the cave mouth. Jerome sprinted through the maze of stalactites to reach the pile. He jumped onto a boulder, following the elves that were already climbing. He turned around to grab

Bellamy's wrist and pull the boy up. They scaled the rocks, fueled by fear and adrenaline.

The drakes were just below them. Bony claws scraped against stony debris as the creatures scrambled up the pile.

Jerome nodded to Bellamy when they reached a rocky ledge.

"Here's your chance."

"Hold up your flashlight." Bellamy was trying to remain calm, but his voice hovered close to frantic. Jerome didn't blame the boy. This chamber had stalactites too.

Jerome raised his crossbow and fired a quarrel at the closest drake. The streaking blue bolt tore through the drake's forehead and into the neck of another.

Bellamy pulled a piece of paper from a satchel at his side. Fingers trembling, he raised the sheet to his lips and whispered something that Jerome couldn't hear. Faint scribbles appeared on the paper, which Bellamy folded into a plane. He took a breath and threw it at the writhing mob of drakes.

Jerome watched the paper plane float through air—a small white shape in the darkness.

"Come on!" Bellamy grabbed the elf's shoulder, urging him to climb higher.

A drake climbed the top of a boulder and jumped at the paper. As soon as the drake's claw touched it, the airplane exploded.

The blast splattered the dragon's remains into the faces of his pack. A few stalactites fell to the ground from the force of the explosion. Falling limestone impaled two drakes before the rest of the creatures scurried backwards.

One unfortunate drake slipped and gashed his thigh against a sharp rock. The dragon croaked pitifully. It stumbled down the pile and into the ranks of its fellows, who surrounded it. They kicked the wounded creature to the ground and sank their teeth into its flesh.

Jerome and Bellamy climbed to the top of the pile and listened to the dying drake's squeals.

The elf curled his lip in disgust. "Devouring their own kind." He spat as they hurried through the cave mouth and rejoined the other elves. "Like the Pantheon."

Jerome waved to the group, which had congregated a dozen yards from the tunnel exit. "That's stalled them, but it won't hold them for long. We need to get to the bridge."

He shone his blue light at the cavern floor. It was an enormous stretch of rock that emptied into an abyss. Down below, a rope bridge stretched from a ledge to a tall crevice in the wall on the far side. The chasm yawned beneath, ready to swallow them forever.

One of the elves swore. "All of this for some golems that might not even be there?"

Jerome pushed through the group and stood in front of the elf. "All of this for the Golem Army of Calypso, Hayden." He wiped his nose with the black of his glove. "Aren't you a Forerunner?"

Hayden clenched his jaw. "Of course I am."

Jerome glared meaningfully at him.

"Of course I am, *sir*," Hayden corrected himself.

"Do you hate the injustices of the Pantheon?"

"Of course I do, sir!"

"Do you long to rescue the Titans from the Abyss? To help them restore righteousness and order to the universe?"

"Of course I—"

"Do you trust the Elders?" Jerome interrupted him, pointing a stern finger at the elf.

Hayden narrowed his eyes. "Of course I do. Sir."

"Well." Jerome stepped forward so that his face was inches away. Hayden was taller than Jerome, but he shrank under the fury of his commander. "The Elders ordered us to get the Golem Army of Calypso. The Elders wouldn't have sent us if they didn't *know* the golems were here. So do you know what we're going to do?"

"What are we going to do, sir?"

"We *will* get the Golem Army of Calypso. If they don't exist, we will *make* them exist, because the Elders are going to attack the capital in a few days. Do you understand?"

"Yes, sir."

"Good." Jerome stepped back from Hayden, who slunk into the group of elves.

Jerome turned and surveyed the group. He put his hand to his heart in a salute.

"Righteousness is our sword and our shield."

"The Titans will rise again," they chorused.

"The Titans will rise again," Jerome repeated.

The distant cries of the drakes echoed from the tunnel behind them.

"Now move. The drakes are going to find their way through that rubble, and I want to be across the bridge when they do."

CHAPTER 4:
SPIRIT OF THE AIR

"Natalie! Natalie Bliss, it's you!"

The voice was feminine, and it could be described as "glittery," "glossy," and every other word that sparkled and shone.

Natalie turned around, confused, trying to see where the voice was coming from. All she could see were the many other travelers milling around her. They looked tired, and not at all bubbly or bright.

The voice called out again.

"Natalie Bliss! I'm coming for you! Just stay where you are!"

That was the easy part. Natalie was hemmed in from all sides by the multitudes.

Then Natalie saw her. Or she noticed that *someone* was forcing a path toward her from the way the crowd was parting.

A blonde-haired girl with a green dress and green ribbons in her hair emerged from the sea of travelers, breaking from the crowd and jumping at Natalie with an excited squeal.

"Oh my freaking gods!" The girl hugged Natalie tightly. "I'm so glad you're back! I've missed you so much!"

She pulled away from Natalie for a moment, holding her shoulders and drinking in her appearance. Travelers still surrounded them, but the blonde-haired girl only had eyes for Natalie.

"Oh I missed you!" The girl beamed. "Did you miss me?"

"I..." Natalie hesitated. She couldn't remember who this girl was.

The other travelers made frustrated noises at the girls standing in the middle of the hallway. A dwarf with an overcoat and a briefcase bumped into the blonde, nearly upsetting her balance.

"Do you mind?" The girl's eyes flashed like emeralds. The dwarf backed away, waving his hands and muttering apologies.

"Honestly, how hard is it to watch where you're going?" The girl clenched her fists, glaring daggers at his diminished, retreating figure.

25

People started giving them space.

The girl cleared her throat. She brushed a wayward strand of hair behind her ear and composed herself. Then she smiled at Natalie, whose mouth hung open in surprise.

"Gosh, Natalie, you look so young and your red hair is so beautiful!" Before Natalie could stop her, the girl was feeling Natalie's hair. "I mean your hair has always been so beautiful. But how do you manage to look so young? I mean you always look young—but you look even younger than when you left!"

"Er...do I?"

"Oh, you're so modest. But you're just as cute as ever!" The girl winked knowingly. "I can think of somebody who will be more than happy to see you."

Natalie's face drew a blank. "You can?"

The girl put her hand on her hips in mock-frustration. "Of course I can! And you can too." She punched Natalie's arm playfully. "A certain young phoenix..." She raised an eyebrow, leaning in close and grinning.

She was obviously waiting for a reaction.

Natalie reacted by leaning back to get some personal space.

"What's your name?" Natalie asked. The girl's face was only inches away from hers.

"That's a silly question, Natalie. Of course you know my name. Not that I ever get tired of saying it! Quincy!" Quincy fluttered her eyelashes happily. "The boys never get tired of saying it either." She sighed dreamily. "Mmm...*boys.*"

Quincy suddenly jumped and clapped her hands, making Natalie blink in self-defense.

"And oh my *gods*, Natalie! You did such a good job at Mithris! Abbess Persephone told us about it and I read about it in some of the universal publications. Well, *a-hem*" she cleared her throat daintily, "some of the more illustrated publications with not as many words—but I *did* read about it. *Faerie Interest* ran a short blurb about it next to the feature on Io. He's *such* a dreamy athlete. I can't wait to see him in the Arcadian Games. And they start this weekend!" She sighed again, filling the air with heartfelt longing. "But anyway—you did so well, Natalie! I'm so proud of you!"

Quincy hugged Natalie and squeezed her tightly.

Natalie managed to respond with an "Erk" and a "Thanks" and a muffled "Those-are-my-lungs-you're-squeezing."

"There aren't as many gods around Mithris anymore, are there?" Quincy asked. She didn't wait for Natalie to respond. "Mithris isn't such a vacation spot now that Julius is cleaning up the place and putting those gods to work."

She wiped her hands theatrically. She was obviously proud of Natalie—and, by association, herself.

"Yes ma'am, good money was on Julius being removed as the God of Gods, but he sure turned things around. You'll have to tell me all about it in de-*tail*." She made a point of emphasizing the last syllable.

Natalie opened her mouth to speak.

Quincy cut her off. "Come on. We need to get out of here. There too many people. We have to get to the train station."

"The train station?"

"Yes, the train station!" Quincy sang. She grabbed Natalie's hand and forced her way through the crowd with an authority and power that defied her slender appearance. "We always take the train to get back to Radcliffe, or don't you remember?"

"Not really—"

"Yes, you do, silly!" Quincy smiled sweetly, rolling her eyes. "You love the trains because they're steam trains, and the one time that we had to take a diesel train you practically threw a fit because you said it wasn't a proper train and you made me sit there on the platform with you until we could wait for a steam engine."

"I did?" Natalie blinked.

Quincy talked very fast.

"Yes, you did, and that was the same day we got that wonderful strawberry milk drink—the 'Yeehaw' or something exciting like that. It was so delicious you said it brought us into an entirely new world of flavor. Do you remember?"

"No..." Natalie answered, but Quincy had ignored her and was already talking about something else.

Natalie noticed that the station walls were plastered with advertisements for THE ARCADIAN GAMES and THE DIVINE WEDDING OF THE GODDESS APHRODAINTE AND THE GOD OLI—TO BE BROADCAST LIVE FROM PARLEMAGNE, ¡THE CITY OF LOVE!

Natalie stopped to look at the slender blonde whose image smiled dreamily from dozens of posters. "Who's Aphrodainte?"

"Who's Aphrodainte?" Quincy looked offended. "Honestly, Natalie, don't you read *anything*? Were you cut off from all civilization on Mithris? She's only the most gorgeous goddess in Calypso! In the whole universe! Oh, her *wardrobe...*" She sighed with so much passion that Natalie blushed. "I was watching a special on one of her summer homes..."

They started walking again, and Quincy chattered along happily. They made their way up a flight of stairs and across a walkway over a busy street. The crowd thinned on the walkway, and Natalie was able to get a good look at Quincy's back for the first time. Wisps of cloud protruded from beneath her shoulder blades.

As the light from the passing windows reflected on these curious clouds, Natalie realized that they must be wings. But the wings disappeared once they entered the crowded trolley station lobby.

"Quincy, are you an angel?"

Quincy laughed, her green eyes sparkling. "Oh, you're so sweet." Then she frowned. "What kind of angel? You know, some angels are really stupid. Even the really beautiful ones can be really stupid—which is surprising, isn't it? That a beautiful person could be stupid, I mean. It takes a sylph to truly exemplify both beauty and intelligence—and pretty much any other virtues that are worth having."

Natalie blinked. "A sylph?"

"Remember? That's what I am, sweetie." Quincy glanced back at Natalie as they exited the station through a revolving door.

"A slyph," Natalie repeated, following Quincy down the steps to the street. She looked up at the sky and noticed the thick, heavy clouds casting shadows across the city.

"Yes, it even sounds beautiful, doesn't it? Sylph! A nymph of the air." Quincy reached the bottom of the stairs and performed a pirouette. The green ribbons in her hair caught the light as her dress twirled. The sight was mesmerizing. A young elf boy stopped in the middle of the street to watch Quincy—and almost got run over by a chariot.

Quincy finished the movement and closed her eyes dreamily.

"Some people call us fairies, you know, but that's too general. It's always better to be specific. And *sylph* is such a beautiful word. Why would you want to say anything else?"

"I like beautiful words." Natalie crossed the street with Quincy. They stopped at an island in the middle, where the lucky elf boy had sat down to recover from his near-death experience.

28

"Of course you like beautiful words—oh my *gods*! I forgot!" Quincy clapped her hands over her mouth. The alarm in her voice almost made Natalie jump.

"Do you have any luggage?" Quincy asked.

Natalie felt a surge of panic—had she left any luggage behind on the trolley?

No, of course not. She didn't have any luggage. She just had her raincoat and her rain boots.

Natalie felt inside a pocket for her journal. It was still there, and the passport was inside.

"No, I'm fine. I don't have any luggage."

"Oh, right." Quincy laughed. "Natalie Bliss. You always travel light. Nothing but your umbrella and whatever you can fit in your pockets."

The girls crossed the street, and then Quincy shrieked in alarm. Natalie actually jumped this time.

"Stop doing that!"

"Oh my gods! Where's your umbrella?" Quincy held Natalie's shoulders.

"I don't know." Natalie blinked, feeling a mixture of frustration and fear. Quincy seemed to know a lot more about her than she did.

"You don't know..." Quincy said breathlessly. She grabbed Natalie's wrist and looked at her golden watch. "Oh my gods. *That's* why you look so young." Her eyes widened. "You totally died!"

CHAPTER 5:
CALYPSO

Natalie swallowed. As a phoenix, she had died and resurrected many times. Integrating back into society after resurrection was always an uncomfortable experience.

And it was never nice to be reminded that you had died.

"Oh my gods." Quincy blushed. "That was so rude of me. I totally said that I was never going to freak out like that again. Especially after the last time." She played with a ring on her finger, looking embarrassed. "And the time before."

After an awkward silence, the girls started up a steep hill that led away from the trolley station.

"Those are thick clouds." Natalie pointed up at the sky, casting about for a different subject. "Is it going to rain?"

"Oh, those aren't clouds. Those are air-buildings and air-terra."

"What?"

"Skybergs, skytowers—they're just airborne sections of the city. Look, you can see the tops of the buildings on that one." Quincy pointed to a skyberg as a real cloud moved away. Domes and spires peeked over the edge of the floating landscape.

Now that Natalie knew what to look for, it did look like a floating piece of earth—a chunk of city plucked from the ground and set in the sky.

"The skytowers are the individual buildings." Quincy pointed to a slender, cylindrical one drifting up out of a cloud. "And the huge landmasses are skylands. There's only one in Calypso, and it's right there, over the bay."

Natalie followed Quincy's gaze and found herself looking at an enormous body of water. Below them was the trolley station, built on the coastline of an ocean. An enormous golden bridge stretched over the water, linking their part of the city with another landmass. Open water stretched far off to Natalie's right. A vast shape dominated the horizon, casting a shadow over the Calypso Bay.

"That's the Pantheon Palatium." Quincy smiled at the look of awe on Natalie's face. "It's where the Pantheon assembles. They rule the universe from there, and that's where all of the important gods live. At least," she snorted, "they have homes there, for when the Pantheon is in session. A lot of them have other homes on the skybergs closer to shore, or in other parts of the planet." She frowned. "Or on other planets even."

The girls started walking up the hill again. A newspaper blew against Quincy's high heels. The top of the paper read *The Calypso Times* in large black letters. An article about the Arcadian Games was on the front page.

Quincy kicked the newspaper aside. "So how much do you remember?"

Natalie frowned. The cry of seagulls from the shore awakened something in her memory. She was starting to recall more details.

"I remember some things. You're Quincy."

Quincy made a face. "I just told you that."

"And you work for the Phoenix Guardian Department."

Quincy clapped. "Very good!"

"And this is Calypso."

"And Calypso is the...?"

"Capital of Arcadia, Home of the Pantheon."

"Yes! So Radcliffe is...?"

Natalie hesitated. "Where we live?"

"Who's 'we'?"

"The Phoenix Guardians. We live in Radcliffe at...Resurgam Abbey!"

"Wonderful!" Quincy gave her a hug. "So you're remembering things now?"

"Bits and pieces." Natalie managed a small smile.

They paused at an intersection. Natalie watched a mixture of horse-drawn buggies, chariots, flying bicycles, and automobiles go by. A blue man with red hair and orange eyes gave Natalie a strange look as he passed in his golden chariot. He slowed down, apparently fixated by her white rain boots. Natalie stared at the fluffy buffalo pulling the man's chariot.

"Those boots are fabulous," the man squeaked. "Where did you purchase them? On High Street?"

Natalie put a hand over her mouth to keep from laughing at his high voice. Quincy kicked her in the back of the leg, and Natalie cleared her throat.

"Er, no, not High Street!" Natalie shouted as the man drifted away. "On...another street!"

He continued staring at Natalie's boots until he reached an intersection, where the chariot turned by itself. He never blinked. It was unnerving. Natalie was suddenly reminded of the blue-haired banshee.

Those two had to meet.

Natalie looked back at Quincy. She had a reproachful look on her face.

"Natalie, you know it's rude to make fun of the Azulri!" She crossed her arms. "They're very sensitive about their voices."

"Sorry. I guess I forgot myself."

"They're dreamy singers though." Quincy sighed wistfully. "Alto sopranos, most of the males. All right, let's cross the street."

She grabbed Natalie's hand to cross. Natalie glanced over her shoulder to see the Calypso Bay and the Pantheon Palatium one more time.

"Make way for a god! Out of the way, created beings!"

Natalie heard Quincy scream, and she turned around to see an emerald chariot hurtling toward them. Four radiant white horses pulled the vehicle. A tan god with flowing black hair stood tall in the chariot. Wearing a stunning rainbow robe, he stood next to a short angel, who was clad in a simple white toga. Natalie grabbed Quincy and pulled her out of the way. The horses' enormous hooves stomped on the ground where the girls had stood a moment before.

A gnome carrying a pot of flowers barely avoided the chariot. He tripped in his desperation to get out of the horses' path. His head smacked against the sidewalk, and his earthenware pot shattered on the ground. The emerald chariot continued without stopping, but the herald angel who stood beside the god continued to shout, "Make way for a god! Move aside, created beings!"

A small crowd gathered around the injured gnome, who was bleeding from the forehead.

Natalie helped Quincy to her feet. "Are you okay?"

"I'm all right." Quincy brushed herself off, looking flustered. "That stupid god. He almost killed us—and that poor gnome!"

She hurried to the unlucky pedestrian, and Natalie followed.

A couple of dwarves helped the gnome to his feet. His blue jean overalls were dirty and stained with blood where he had wiped his hands on them. Another gnome with curly hair and an apron chattered anxiously while he nodded wearily. She helped him toward a flower shop while more gnomes poured onto the street to lend a hand. A crowd of curious onlookers gathered outside. Some of them cast dark looks at the chariot as it turned a corner and drove out of sight.

"Is anyone going to do anything about that?" Natalie's mouth hung open in shock. "That chariot could have killed us! It wasn't going to stop!"

"No, it wasn't." Quincy scowled. "But that's how the gods act in Calypso—most of them, anyway. When they condescend to walk the streets of the 'created beings.'"

"When they condescend to walk here? Where else would they be?"

"Up in the skybergs." Quincy pointed up. "The gods like to have distance between themselves and us. They hate having to walk the same ground that we do. Some of them just come down here to remind us of their *superiority.*"

She glared at a skyberg until it disappeared into the clouds.

"But not all of the gods are like that, surely." Natalie's heart sank. She hadn't remembered this at all.

"No, not all of them, I guess." Quincy shrugged. "But there are enough to make things difficult. Oh, well." She sniffed. "We're not going to let them ruin our day, are we?"

They walked in silence for a few minutes, but the city's beauty quickly pulled the sylph out of her sulk. Soon she was reveling in the sights around them. Nothing seemed to get Quincy down for long, especially if her surroundings were bright and shiny.

Bulbs of light stretched across the streets on white strings, illuminating the parts of the city cast into shadow by the skybergs. The road rose higher and higher, away from the ocean, and a gentle breeze blew at their backs. People walked in and out of shops under wide awnings that stretched over the sidewalks. Thin houses were stacked next to each other—the only feature that distinguished one house from another was the change in color.

"How much farther to the train station?" Natalie asked, interrupting Quincy as she lamented the lack of cute fairy artists who were interested in dating.

Quincy shot an annoyed look at Natalie. "Were you listening to anything I was saying?"

"Of course I was. You were talking about fairies and how they don't like girls. Or something like that."

Quincy pursed her lips in frustration. "Well, maybe I was and maybe I wasn't. Even if you weren't listening to me, *I* was listening to *you*, because I'm a good friend and good friends listen. And the train station is just a few blocks away."

They walked through a small tunnel alongside the road. When they emerged, Natalie could see a huge building rising up against the sunny sky. Massive columns crowned the stairs surrounding the station entrance.

"Calypso Central Station," Natalie read the huge words above the columns. "I think I remember that."

"Probably not. That lettering is new because someone vandalized the old sign. You wouldn't believe how inventive and crude some people can be. But come on—we need to hurry or we'll miss our train."

Natalie followed Quincy across a city square that lay below the train station. A huge statue of a god riding an enormous dragon dominated the middle of the square. Natalie followed Quincy up the steps and between the huge columns of Calypso Central Station.

Through the crowds and the series of glass doors separating them from the tracks, Natalie could see the steam engines coming and going. Smoke curled from a beautiful black engine in front of them, and Natalie felt a thrill of excitement.

She was going home.

CHAPTER 6:
THE BRIDGE

Jerome and his elves walked cautiously down the slope to the rope bridge. The commander moved to the front and motioned for three elves to guard the rear. They fixed their crossbows on the tunnel mouth behind them. The drakes' guttural cries echoed from the passage.

"Hurry!" Jerome quickened his descent to the bridge. He could hear the drakes spilling out of the tunnel.

His heart pounded in his ears. As he neared the bottom, a loose slab of rock slipped out from under his feet. He fell hard on his back and slid forward. His feet slipped over the edge and he was falling—

—something jerked him backwards.

Jerome held his breath and watched the thin slab plummet into the abyss.

"That could have been you." Hayden pulled Jerome from the cliff and hoisted him to his feet. "Be careful, sir."

He slapped Jerome on the back. Jerome nodded his thanks, but the sounds of drakes meant there was no time to lose. He and Hayden hurried to the bridge, where Jerome was compelled to swear.

Before him stretched a thin, rickety contraption made of boards, rope, and sheer stupidity. The bridge had obviously been a temporary construction of the worst kind: it had served its purpose once, so the builders had decided it would work a second time. And a third. Predictably, no one had ever bothered to build a decent one.

But then, how many people ever came this way?

The drakes were sliding down the slope. Jerome looked up to see his rear guards shooting crossbow bolts at the dragons. Wounded drakes stumbled down the slope and hurtled over the precipice. But still the dragons came. The rear guards retreated slowly to the bridge.

Jerome stepped onto the bridge behind four elves who had started crossing before him. A sudden fear gripped him, and he looked around to find Bellamy—but the boy was already standing alone on the other side. Jerome shook his head, wishing that he had the boy's power.

Jerome grabbed hold of the ropes. He stepped on the first board and accidentally kicked it out from under him.

He swore, swaying precariously in the air.

"Be more careful, sir," Hayden said from behind him.

"You try this," Jerome growled.

"I will in a moment, sir, as soon as you move along. And if you don't move quickly, we'll all be dead."

Jerome glanced at the hundred or so planks before him. He carefully lowered his foot onto the second board. It held his weight.

He pulled himself along by the ropes, trying not to place too much weight on the wood. The cries of the drakes grew louder.

"Hurry up, sir!" Hayden urged.

Jerome quickened his steps. Hayden was close behind, stepping lightly along the planks. Soon, all of the elves were on the bridge.

Jerome heard a scream and turned around. Out of the corner of his eye, he saw an elf fall off the bridge. He had missed a step on the treacherous planks. In that moment of distraction, Jerome's foot reached for a hold but found empty space instead. He fell forward. His forehead hit the edge of a board, and his eyes looked down into nothingness.

His stomach lurched.

"Sir, get up! The drakes are at the bridge!"

Jerome struggled to his feet, grabbing at the rope on his right and trying to gain a foothold. The bridge lurched to the side.

"No, sir!" Hayden shouted. "Both ropes at once!"

Jerome wiped the sweat from his brow. He grabbed both ropes and looked over his shoulder. Hayden was holding desperately onto the edge. It looked like he had almost fallen over when Jerome had shifted their weight to the right.

Behind them, the drakes were congregating at the ledge. The two elves at the rear were firing as many bolts as possible. Drakes piled upon their dead and pushed them over. Some of the living drakes slipped on their fallen and plunged over the cliff with high-pitched screeches.

"Move, sir!" Hayden screamed, spit flying from his mouth. "Move!"

Jerome pulled himself forward, clumsily saving his elves the trouble of loose boards by kicking them out himself. He almost fell again, but he managed to catch both ropes before slipping off.

Finally, he reached the other side.

Hayden joined him, and they stood at the cliff, unslinging their crossbows and urging their comrades forward.

The elves at the back were still shooting at the drakes. They had to move slowly to avoid falling, which allowed the creatures to gain on them.

And the drakes had no sense of how much weight the bridge could take.

Three drakes fought for position at the far end. Jerome cringed as the bridge lurched to the left. Two of the dragons fell over the side. Another got his tail twisted in the rope and nearly flipped the entire bridge.

An elf had been holding the rope in one hand and his crossbow in the other. The wild movement of the bridge loosened the elf's hold on the rope and sent him falling to his death.

His screams echoed in Jerome's ears while the taut ropes righted the bridge with a snap. Four elves held desperately onto ropes and boards, trying not to slip off. They scrambled to their feet, hurrying toward the other side before more drakes got on.

Jerome pulled one of his comrades to safety—and then another. The elves lined up on the edge, shooting at the drakes on the bridge and far side. Streaks of light traced the bolts through the air, lingering for a moment in the darkness. Some of the drakes backed away, dissuaded by the crossbows. They hissed angrily and flicked their long, scarlet tongues.

Two elves remained on the bridge, pursued by the drakes. Jerome shot the closest dragon between the eyes. The drake snarled in pain, and then it fell through a gap in the boards.

A few more drakes jumped onto the bridge, taking no care for its pitiful condition. They ran forward with alarming speed, their light skeletal bodies bouncing from board to board.

One of the drakes stepped too hard, and it fell through the bridge, breaking at least three boards in a brief, desperate scrabble for safety.

Jerome swore. They wouldn't be able to use the bridge to get back.

An elf on the bridge shot another drake and hit the creature in the throat. It staggered back into the others, who pushed it over the side without hesitation. A particularly large drake scurried forward on all fours, bouncing the bridge with reckless speed.

"Cain!" Jerome shouted. "Run!"

Cain took a few steps toward safety before turning to fire at his pursuer. But, in his haste, he failed to find good footing. His foot slipped on the edge of a plank, and his shot went wide. For a moment he teetered on the bridge, grabbing the rope with one hand. Then the drake reached him and slashed at his throat. Cain leaned back to avoid the dragon's claws—and lost his grip completely.

His arms flailed in desperation before darkness swallowed him.

Jerome fired at the large drake, trying to save the last elf on the bridge. The shot sailed over his shoulder and toward the dragon's head—but the creature ducked just in time.

The elf stumbled over the boards. Hands reached out to pull him to safety—but the drake was too fast. The dragon lunged forward and sank his teeth into the elf's neck. He screamed.

Hayden shot the drake in the head, but it held onto its victim. The dragon thrashed about wildly, trying to break the elf's neck. Two more bolts hit the dragon in the neck and shoulder. The drake jerked backwards, claws flailing—and slashed the rope in its throes.

The bridge swung down. Dragon and elf were thrown into the abyss.

Hayden screamed. He took another shot at the drakes gathered at the far edge. His aim was wild. The bolt hit the rock below the dragons, who screeched at him.

Jerome pulled Hayden from the edge. Hayden's shoulders were shaking, and he was swearing under his breath. He started to move toward the edge again, but Jerome grabbed him by the shoulders.

They stared at each other for a long moment. Finally, Hayden let out a deep, shuddering breath. He nodded at his commander, who released him.

Jerome turned to face his remaining elves. They stared back with stunned expressions. Bellamy's hands were clasped in front of his face. His eyes were closed.

Jerome took slow, heavy breaths, clenching his jaw until his teeth hurt.

It was going to be worth it. It had to be. The Golem Army of Calypso would be there, and it would be magnificent. The Elders wouldn't have sent them if they didn't think—Jerome shook his head sharply—if they didn't *know* that the golems were powerful.

The golems would be worth it, and the Pantheon would suffer for their evil.

"Keep moving," Jerome said in a low voice, fighting to keep his voice steady. "The Colossus Pit is up ahead."

CHAPTER 7:
RESURGAM ABBEY

"You there, young ladies!" shouted an old, grumpy voice. "What do you think you are doing?"

Natalie and Quincy looked at the statues above the gates of Resurgam Abbey. Two stone men stood watch. They wore dignified gowns and tall, pointed hats that reminded Natalie vaguely of fish heads. The statues looked down upon the girls from their ornate alcoves.

"Bartholomew, it's me: Quincy." The sylph put her hands on her hips and glared at the statue on the left. "You see me every day."

"Quincy, eh? What does that name mean to us? Who knows how many wily young females are named Quincy?" Bartholomew stroked his long beard, leaning out from his alcove to look at her, twisting his upper body while his feet remained rooted to the stone.

"Plenty of girls, perhaps. But none so beautiful as Quincy, the sylph of Resurgam Abbey." Quincy flapped her wings and batted her eyelashes.

"Cease your flirtation, young lady! There will be none of that behavior while I am on watch." The statue on the right, whose face boasted bushy stone sideburns, wagged a finger at Quincy. "And you will notice that Good Bartholomew did not ask *who* you were. He asked *what* you were doing!"

"In point of fact, Good Matthias, I asked the young lady what she *thought* she was doing."

"So you did, Good Bartholomew. So you did."

"I'm going inside, *Bartholomew*." Quincy pronounced the statue's name with as much condescension as she could muster.

"So you say, so you say..." Bartholomew stroked his rocky beard. "What do you think of that, lads?"

He looked down at the row of grotesques over the gate.

"It could be a trick! Don't trust them!" shouted a stone head with bulging eyes. He had a pair of hands pressed against his cheeks, which gave him a look of permanent alarm.

"They're women! Don't trust them!" An angry-looking head with a unibrow glared accusingly at Natalie. His unibrow bobbed up and down aggressively, causing Natalie to step back in alarm. Her boots almost slipped on the cobblestones.

"Shut your mouth, Throckmorton!" A lady's head with curly stone ringlets glared at Throckmorton and his unibrow. "See how you've frightened Miss Natalie Bliss?"

"Wendel!" The wrinkled head of an old man hissed at his neighbor. "That's against the rules! You're supposed to challenge strangers and make them identify themselves!"

"But she *lives* here, Cecil."

"It's the rules, Wendel."

"The rules! The rules!" Many of the grotesques began to shout at once. A cow head joined with a mournful "Mooooo!"

"Wait!" Throckmorton's voice rose above the others. "If they live here, let them administer...the *Test*!"

"They can't *administer* the Test, you silly old fool." Wendel scowled at Throckmorton. "They have to *pass* the Test, or *take* the Test, or *undergo* the Test. Stop using words you don't understand!"

"Well, you should stop—"

But Throckmorton was drowned out by another chorus from the grotesques.

"The Test! The Test!"

"The Sacred Test!"

"Mooooo!"

Natalie blinked. "The Test?"

The sylph rolled her eyes. "He means this." She pulled a small, thin wooden horse from her pocket. The horse's varnished wood reflected the fading sunlight.

"What's that?"

"It's a Pokket. You have one too, but you left it in the porter's lodge."

"I left my pocket in the...what?" Natalie looked inside her raincoat.

"Not that kind of pocket. Just watch." Quincy took her Pokket and placed it in a small bowl on the gate wall. The keyhole glowed green, and Natalie heard a metallic clink. Quincy pulled on the door handle, and the heavy gate swung open.

"They have passed the Test! Their hearts are true!" the head with bulging eyes shouted.

The other grotesques joined in.

"Rejoice! Rejoice!"

"Their hearts are true!"

"Mooooo!"

"Hmmph." Throckmorton glared at the girls, still suspicious.

Wendel rolled her eyes. "I'm sorry you have to go through this every time, girls."

"Don't worry about it, Wendel." Quincy pulled her Pokket out of the bowl and put it in her pocket. "Every day, I tell myself that I'm going to ignore the peanut gallery, but every time I come home *Bartholomew challenges me like I'm an imposter!*" She stamped her foot and glared at the statue, who grinned back at her.

"Maybe not *every* time." Bartholomew folded his hands innocently. "But we are simply doing our jobs, are we not, Good Matthias?"

"You speak the truth, Good Bartholomew." Matthias winked at Quincy. "We could do nothing less."

She waved her hand dismissively. "You couldn't do any more, either."

Matthias frowned. "Whatever do you mean?"

"I mean you're stuck to the stone. You can't move."

He crossed his arms. "The young lady has affronted us, Good Bartholomew!"

"Indeed she has, Good Matthias."

"I hear they are recruiting guard statues at the University of Calypso."

"That would be more than acceptable. There are lots of pretty girls there!"

"Indeed there are, Good Bartholomew. And sometimes the pretty girls wear sandals...and show their ankles!"

"Oh *my*! But do not speak of such things now, Good Bartholomew. There may be children listening!"

"MoooOOO!"

"And cows. I am sorry you had to hear that, Noble Maurice."

Quincy made an irritated noise, grabbed Natalie's hand, and pulled her through the gate. She slammed it shut behind them.

"I wish the weather would erode their mouths." Quincy glared back at the door. "Then I wouldn't have to hear them every single day."

Natalie shrugged. "I thought they were kind of funny."

Then her attention was drawn to the huge archway of the porter's lodge and the cloisters beyond it.

It was late at night—almost ten according to a clock inside the lodge. Outside, the setting sun illuminated the tan brick abbey walls. No one else was around except the porter, a tall man dressed in a dark blue suit.

Upon closer inspection, Natalie noticed that the man seemed to be shedding straw.

As if sensing her stare, the man immediately looked up at her.

Natalie cleared her throat, embarrassed. She looked away and played with a strand of hair.

"On to my room then?"

"You have to say hello to George first!"

Natalie heard a door open and close, and then the porter, presumably George, was standing next to her.

"Miss Bliss?"

Natalie examined George's face. His features had been distorted through the window, but now she saw that his skin wasn't skin at all, but a light brown fabric with a rough texture. His eyes were blue beads. They gleamed with intelligence. His mouth was a thin line in the fabric.

"Miss Bliss?" When George spoke, his mouth opened to reveal a dark interior lined with the same fabric.

Natalie blinked and came out of her reverie, ashamed that she had been so distracted by his appearance. "Miss Bliss? Yes, that's me."

"Of course it is." George smiled, and his blue eyes shone with surprising friendliness. He grasped Natalie's hand and shook it. His touch was very light. She could feel the straw underneath his glove-like fingers.

When their hands parted, a bit of straw floated slowly to the ground. Natalie didn't know whether to snatch it and hand it back to George, but he didn't seem bothered.

"Do you remember me?" He raised a string eyebrow. "We are friends."

Natalie felt a mixture of embarrassment and guilt. Why couldn't she have memorized her journal so she would remember who all of these people were?

"I'm also a—"

"Shay!" Natalie snapped her fingers in excitement, informed by a sudden burst of memory. "You're a shay."

"Yes. And I have your Pokket."

George reached inside his coat and pulled out a small wooden phoenix. He pressed it gently into Natalie's hand.

46

"You left this with me for safe-keeping before you went away."

"Thank you, George." Natalie examined the beautiful phoenix. Finely-carved flames curled around the bird's intricate wings.

"Hi, George!" Quincy waved, restoring some of the attention back to herself. Natalie was surprised that Quincy had kept quiet for so long.

"Hello, Quincy. Are you well?"

"Well and ready to go to sleep. Let's go up to your room, Natalie."

"Okay—bye, George! Thank you." Natalie waved as Quincy dragged her out of the archway.

"Goodnight, Natalie," he said quietly.

The red-haired girl followed Quincy along the stone tiled ground. In front of her was a square green lawn enclosed by square walls three stories high. Pointed roofs lined the buildings, and sets of arched windows filled the first two floors.

Natalie felt a rush of happiness. She knew this place. She sighed happily, stepping toward the lawn.

"Natalie!" Quincy grabbed her shoulder. "Don't step on the grass!"

CHAPTER 8:
THE COLOSSUS PIT

The enormous stone door loomed over Jerome. The top of the entrance was lost to the shadows in the high ceiling.

The door was dominated by a huge ring carved into the rock. A dozen green holes glowed at intervals around the inside of the ring. A blank rectangular block protruded from the center.

"Must have taken a lot of work." Hayden examined his gloved hand in the door's green glow. "All of this, just to bury an army."

"Someone in the Pantheon had a sense of style," Jerome said. "They certainly took more care with the chamber than the bridge."

"How are we getting out if the bridge is gone?" one of the elves asked.

"Don't you listen to anything I say, Mimas?" Jerome sighed. "After the Colossus Pit and the Army Chamber, there's a big archway. It's called the Valkyrie Gate. We'll take the colossus and the army through the Valkyrie Gate, and that will take us right under the heart of Calypso."

"But what if we can't get through this?" Mimas pointed at the forbidding door in front of them. "Sir?" he added.

"We *will* get through, Mimas. We'll get through because I'm smarter than you. I had a plan before we came. I didn't want to stay down here forever. You don't want to be stuck down here, do you?"

The elf shook his head. "No, sir."

"Neither do I. So I figured it all out. We're going to leave through the Valkyrie Gate. Now, that labyrinth that we came through," Jerome pointed over Mimas' shoulder at the rough-hewn tunnel, "that leads back to the surface. Eventually. But there are a lot of drake nests in that labyrinth. You don't want to take that route, do you?"

"No, sir."

"No. You don't. So we'll take the Valkyrie Gate, because I know what I'm doing. Don't I?"

"Yes, sir."

"Thank you for the vote of confidence, Mimas. Now, Bellamy." Jerome gestured to the boy. "Get us in."

Bellamy pulled a book out of his satchel. He opened it, selected a page, and held it up to the center block. Letters on the pages ignited and disappeared, flowing into a green mist that trailed from the book. The mist coiled and rose into the air to form a nebulous cloud above their heads. The cloud crackled with lightning, and then the particles dispersed and shot into the door's dozen holes.

Moments later, a thunderclap boomed, shaking the floor and reverberating in their chests.

The holes filled up and turned from green to white. Their glow intensified, forcing the elves to turn away from the brightness. A huge weight shifted behind the door. The ground trembled again.

The dozen lights went out, and the block withdrew into the door. The entrance slid back to reveal a cavernous chamber with a green granite floor and broad columns. The far end of the chamber was shrouded in darkness. The elves filtered into the room slowly.

Jerome patted Bellamy on the shoulder. "Good work."

He had just taken a few steps up the wide center aisle when a pair of luminous green tubes ignited with a resounding crack. The lights stretched from floor to ceiling on either side.

A bead of sweat slid down Jerome's brow. He walked further up the walkway.

Crack!

Another pair lit up.

When he reached a circle at the center of the room, pairs of lights lit the path all the way to the end. The sudden illumination revealed a titanic shape staring down at them.

The golem colossus must have been over two hundred feet tall.

Gigantic plate armor covered the golem from head to foot. The golem's eyes were shrouded in darkness beneath a visored helmet. Enormous spikes protruded from its shoulders and back. The colossus's lumbering arms reached to the floor.

"It's magnificent," Jerome breathed.

Hayden's mouth gaped. For once, he seemed to be at a loss for words.

Jerome walked around the colossus to admire the tough armor on its back and shoulders. On the wall behind the colossus, massive metal rungs had been set into the rock. They were the right size for the colossus's hands. Jerome craned back his neck to follow the trail of rungs until it disappeared into the darkness far above. The ladder led to an exit.

But that would mean...

Jerome felt a sinking feeling in his stomach. He turned around, looking for a doorway to the Army Chamber. He glanced back at the ladder.

Was *that* the way to the chamber and the Valkyrie Gate?

Jerome's thoughts were interrupted by Bellamy's desperate voice.

"No—don't touch it!" Bellamy shouted. "The Script isn't right!"

Jerome started running to the front of the colossus—but then the colossus stirred.

Dust fell from the golem's ancient armor. The colossus's head creaked. Gigantic hands clenched and unclenched. Metal scraped against metal.

Hayden swore.

"Out of the chamber," Jerome said in a low voice. "Now!"

The elves sprinted down the long walkway toward the entrance, but Bellamy stayed behind. He hid behind a pillar, mouth gaping, eyes fixed on the awakening colossus.

"Bellamy!" Jerome hissed. "You change the Script right now, understand?"

Bellamy pulled the book out of his satchel again. The colossus let out a deep groan that sent shivers down Jerome's spine. Bellamy bit his lip and froze with the book halfway out of his bag. Then he pulled it completely out and closed his eyes.

A shadow passed from under Bellamy and shot toward the colossus. The silhouette ran up the golem's body and settled on its head.

Bellamy's lips moved silently—and then the boy disappeared.

*

A thought floated to the surface of Wrath's mind.

He had been touched. He had been awakened.

He had not thought since...

...since Many Days.

Bleary eyes struggled to focus. Sore body parts shivered. He heard Words.

Deah-leh...Tah-bahk...

Who was saying the words?

...Spey Es. Deah-leh...

He had heard those Words before. Many Days and Many Days ago.

Tah-bahk...Speh Es...

Wrath shook his head. Who was saying these Words? Confusion and anger stirred inside his massive frame. He felt a strange tingling in his mind. The Words were doing something to him.

He didn't like what they were doing.

You will destroy the city of Calypso!

Calypso?

A deep growl started in his throat and echoed in his helmet. The colossus took a ponderous step forward, and he heard a distant, muffled cry from below.

Calypso was part of his Purpose. His Purpose was to *protect* Calypso.

You will destroy the city of Calypso!

Who would tell him to betray his Purpose? Who had woken him?

His eyes narrowed.

It was the Enemy!

His roar boomed through the long chamber. He tossed his head in fury—and saw a tiny shape fall off before disappearing in midair.

He stepped forward heavily. Down on the floor, two small figures sprinted away from him.

The colossus clenched and unclenched his fists. The Enemy was here. He had to protect Calypso. He would kill the Enemy.

He took two massive steps toward the intruders below and swung a monstrous fist.

*

Bellamy winced. He had shadowcast himself in mid-fall, but the momentum had thrown him against a pillar. He hadn't expected the colossus to toss him like that.

His neck and shoulders throbbed in pain.

Overhead, the colossus stomped toward the elves and took a fearsome swing.

"Run!" Bellamy yelled. But the elves didn't need any encouragement. Their leather boots slapped on the hard granite floor.

The golem twisted to face Bellamy, who realized too late that he had given away his position.

He sprinted away from the pillar just before the colossus stomped his foot down. The impact threw Bellamy to the floor. He hit his knee and rolled on the hard granite.

The golem roared, and Bellamy's stomach turned. They had unleashed the colossus and made it their enemy.

Nothing had gone according to plan.

He struggled back to his feet. The colossus stood above him, red golem eyes fixed on his own. It took a terrifying step toward him, encompassing him in its shadow.

The sound of footsteps caught Bellamy's attention, and he glanced back to see Jerome running toward him.

"Take it and go!" Bellamy yelled, throwing the spell-book at him. The book hit the floor and slid across the granite toward the elf.

"Bellamy—" Jerome began.

The colossus raised a massive fist.

The boy rolled on the floor, trying to avoid the coming blow. He couldn't outrun the colossus. Its stride was too long. But he could shadowcast himself out of danger.

He focused on his shadow, willing it into awareness.

He felt it.

Go, Bellamy commanded. A patch of darkness shot out from beneath him.

Overhead, the colossus slammed his fist toward the ground.

Bellamy's eyes registered the blur of darkness.

Take me!

He disappeared—and the colossus pummeled the granite where he had been a moment before.

Bellamy opened his eyes behind a pillar and stumbled to the ground. He recovered his feet and held onto the column for support. Peering around it, he saw Jerome slowly back away from the colossus.

"Jerome! *Run!*" Bellamy screamed. Jerome's head jerked toward the sound of his voice. "Close the door! Page one hundred eighty-two! I'll shadowcast myself out!"

Jerome nodded and sprinted toward the open doorway. The colossus lumbered after him. It was almost on top of him—

"Hey! Hey!" Bellamy screamed at the top of his lungs, running out from behind the column. He shouted so loud it felt like someone was rubbing sandpaper down his throat. The colossus stopped in mid-stride and looked around for the source of the noise.

"Hey!" Bellamy waved his hands and ran the other way. The colossus turned with booming footsteps and let loose a deafening roar.

Bellamy glanced at the far wall.

Go.

Still running, he sent his shadow and watched it glide on the surface of the granite tile floor. Then he closed his eyes to shadowcast himself again.

Take me.

A moment later, he bounced against the wall and rolled onto the ground. He grabbed his knee and grimaced. Once again, his momentum had carried into the shadowcast. Bellamy bit his lip and tried not to think about the pain in his knee.

Meanwhile, the colossus was searching the chamber for him.

Bellamy glanced at the tall green tubes on either side of him, wishing that they didn't expose his position. He scooted between the two, trying to hide in the darkest spot.

He wondered if the lights would go out when Jerome closed the door.

The colossus looked in his direction and Bellamy's heart skipped a beat. Maybe it wouldn't see him.

The red eyes flashed. The colossus growled and got down on all fours, crawling on its ape-like arms.

It had seen him.

A thunderclap boomed through the chamber, and the colossus stopped. Its head turned toward the entrance.

Bellamy breathed a sigh of relief. Jerome had closed the door.

There was a crack at the back of the chamber, and the two green lights at the end went out. Then the next pair, and the next—and then the whole line running down to the entrance.

The chamber fell into total darkness, except for a red dot shining through the gloom—and then two red dots as the colossus turned his head toward Bellamy. It started crawling toward him again.

The boy gulped, looking through the line of columns at the entrance. He closed his eyes and sent his shadow, getting ready to shadowcast himself again.

He heard the terrifying footsteps of the colossus coming toward him. Fear shot through his veins.

Take me.

Bellamy opened his eyes to darkness in a wide space. Off in the distance, he could see a dark, titanic shape moving between two columns. Then he heard the colossus's roar of anger when it failed to find him against the wall.

The boy turned around carefully, trying to keep track of where the walls were. He walked quickly in the direction of the door, arms outstretched, until the hard stone scraped against his fingers.

He pressed his ear against the door, listening for sounds on the other side. He couldn't hear a thing.

A bead of sweat trickled down his brow. He had no idea if Jerome and the other elves were still waiting for him outside. They might already be making their way to the surface through the labyrinth.

Bellamy would have to get out, join them, and figure out why he had failed to rewrite the colossus's Script. His spell-book had been missing something. He needed a better codex, and he knew where to get it.

He didn't want to go back there. But he would have to.

Bellamy stared at the dark stone in front of him, imagining the task that lay ahead in navigating the labyrinth. He had studied the map before the mission. He could probably make his way through the tunnels and the drake nests by shadowcasting...and getting lucky.

But Drakes could be waiting outside the door right now.

He bit his lip. He couldn't just stay here.

The colossus roared again. It was moving toward the entrance.

Bellamy would have to take his chances. He took a deep breath, hoping that the doors weren't enchanted to guard against shadowcasting.

If they were, his shadow could be destroyed when he sent it through. Or he could die when he tried to reunite with it.

But he was guaranteed to die with the colossus.

Go.

He sent his shadow through the crack in the door—and felt it emerge on the other side.

Breathing a sigh of relief, he closed his eyes to see from his shadow's perspective. The green glow from the door illuminated the empty antechamber. There were no drakes, and the elves had moved on.

But who knew what waited beyond the light?

Another bellow from the colossus sent a shiver down his spine. Heavy footsteps shook the ground.

Bellamy's hands trembled. He thought of the girl with long black hair—his girl. He would make it through this for her. She was his strength, and he would be hers.

He was going to make everything all right again. He was going to survive and make it all better. No one was going to stop him from saving her—not a colossus, and not a pair of doors.

Bellamy took a deep breath.

Take me.

CHAPTER 9:
STAIRCASE V, ROOM V

"Don't step on the grass!"

"What?" Natalie paused, her foot hanging in the air over the lawn.

"It's the rules, remember? You're not supposed to step on the grass."

Natalie looked at Quincy and then at the beautiful green lawn. "But it looks so nice. Why would there be a lawn if I wasn't allowed to walk on it?"

"It's nice *because* you're not allowed to walk on it. That's how it stays nice."

"So nobody walks on it?"

"You're only allowed to walk on it if you don't have to ask."

"But I wasn't about to ask."

"I know. That's why I had to warn you."

"But—"

"Come on, Natalie. It's late and you're tired." Quincy grabbed Natalie's arm firmly and steered her off to the wall on the north side of the lawn. They stopped at the first door.

Natalie looked at the arched stone frame. The door had three tall windows in it, and the middle window had a "V" on the glass.

"What does the 'V' stand for?" Natalie peered closely at it. "Victory?"

"No, 'V' stands for five." Quincy pointed above the door. "See?"

A small, stylish metal "5" hung above the doorway.

"Why didn't they just put five on the window?"

"Because 'V' means the same thing."

"It does?"

"Yes. It's just five in a different language."

"Numbers come in different languages?" Natalie shot the numeral a perplexed look. "I definitely don't remember that."

Quincy pulled open the door and steered Natalie inside, walking her up a flight of creaky wooden stairs. They reached a landing and climbed a winding staircase covered with purple carpet.

"It's a good thing we're not carrying any luggage." Natalie carefully navigated a sharp bend in the staircase where the steps shortened and curved dramatically. At the top of the stairs, she found a doorway with another "V."

"Ha! Staircase five, room five." Natalie put her hands on her hips, pleased with herself.

"Actually, the 'V' here does stand for 'Victory,'" Quincy answered absentmindedly, pulling a key out of her pocket. "It's the Victory Suite, named after Abbess Victoria Morning, who used to live here."

"Oh." Natalie frowned.

"Just kidding." Quincy punched Natalie playfully in the arm. Natalie shot a reproving look at her. "Oh, come on, Natalie. You're so serious. Honestly, I can't wait until you get some rest."

Natalie followed Quincy inside the room. It was a nice living space with a window seat, two armchairs, a swivel chair (which Natalie couldn't wait to spin on), a desk, and a floor with a noticeable depression in the middle.

"Well, what do you think?" Quincy squeezed her shoulders together happily. "This is one of the abbey's nicest suites. It's been yours for a while."

"It's nice," Natalie said. "I was hoping for a bed, though."

"Oh, Natalie." Quincy rolled her eyes. She pointed to another door that led into a little room. "There's your bedroom."

They walked in. Quincy tapped on the wooden frame. "I have to remind you that there's a closet just inside the doorway, and there's no way of opening the closet when the bedroom door is open."

Natalie looked around her room. The bed was against the wall opposite the window. There were two dressers, some shelves, and a round mirror.

She blinked, suddenly conscious that she had been noting every little detail from the room and the abbey grounds. Warmth spread through her chest. This was home. She *knew* this place.

"Your room has an excellent view of the quad, see? There's the dining hall just across from us, and next to it is the archway that leads to South Quad. We're in North Quad now. And over the rooftop there you can see the Sayornis Camera."

"The domed building? Why is it called a camera?"

"'Camera' is an old word for 'room.'"

"It looks bigger than a room. And why not just say 'room'?"

"Things sound more important when you say them in dead languages."

"Dead languages?" Natalie looked at the beautiful flowerboxes on the windows of the lower floors. "Who killed them?"

"Oh, you're a comedian, Natalie. But it's late." Quincy yawned dramatically. "Get some sleep. I'll see you for breakfast tomorrow at seven, all right?"

Natalie nodded, taking off her raincoat and hanging it up in the closet as Quincy walked out.

"If you need anything tonight," Quincy paused in the doorway, "let me know tomorrow, because I'm really tired and I won't answer if you knock on my door."

Natalie paused as she took her rain boots off. "I don't remember where your room is."

"I'm in Staircase Fourteen, room twelve. In South Quad—all the way at the other end."

"Oh."

"Don't worry, you'll be fine. I'll see you tomorrow at breakfast."

"Right, okay. See you tomorrow." Natalie nodded, walking Quincy out.

The slyph stopped again.

"I should probably mention that Florentina's been acting weird recently. Like, weirder than usual."

Natalie was taken aback. "Florentina?"

"One of the housekeepers. She hasn't done anything *dangerous* yet, but in her condition...well, let's just say it disturbs me that she can enter our rooms at any time." Quincy shrugged. "Oh, well. It's probably just a phase she's going through."

"Wait, so she's dangerous and she might enter my—"

"Natalie, you're not becoming a worrier, are you?" Quincy raised an eyebrow. "You'll be fine. I'll see you tomorrow, okay? Bye!"

Quincy waved goodbye, and Natalie listened to her friend bound down the stairs. She closed her door and noticed a sign posted inside:

Be warned that skilled thieves are present in Radcliffe. Lock your doors when you leave. Keep track of your possessions, money, and internal organs. Stay in groups and be careful when traveling out at night.

Natalie swallowed nervously. She turned the lock once, twice, three times before it finally clicked into place.

Skilled thieves.

A crazed housekeeper.

And this was her home?

She tried to turn the lock one more time, just to make sure it was secure.

Natalie walked back into her bedroom, drew the curtains shut, and checked her dresser for pajamas. She opened the top drawer, and there were no clothes at all.

Puzzled, Natalie checked the remaining drawers. Nothing.

When she maneuvered her closet door open, she found it empty as well.

In spite of the many things that Natalie couldn't remember, she *did* remember having clothes. She wore her yellow raincoat whenever she could, but she wore *different* pink shirts every day. Occasionally, she wore a shirt that wasn't pink. And Natalie definitely had pajamas, because pajamas were like a fuzzy hug. But there wasn't a single item of clothing anywhere in her room.

That was inconvenient. Jeans were uncomfortable when you wrapped yourself up in the covers.

Natalie sighed and got into bed anyway.

"The covers," as she soon discovered, were actually just "the cover": a single blanket that matched the exact dimensions of the bed. Wrapping-up wasn't possible.

Natalie lay under her cover, frowning in puzzlement. This was her room. Why weren't there clothes in the dresser? Had someone moved them out?

Maybe the housekeeper, Florentina, had washed all of her clothes. But they would have been washed before she arrived. Unless Florentina washed them every night?

Natalie shivered. No housekeeper could be *that* obsessive. Although Quincy did say that Florentina was acting weird.

Natalie noticed a yardstick leaning against the wall by her bed.

She had a yardstick in her room. But no clothes.

Oh, well.

At least she was home. With her room locked and her bedroom door closed, Natalie felt cozy and secure.

She leaned back on her small pillow, looking at the cube-shaped light illuminating her bedroom. It was a nice light. She sighed in contentment and stared at the cube-light for a minute before turning it off.

Click.

It was a very satisfying click. She turned the light back on.

Click.

She turned it off.

Click.

Natalie closed her eyes. Her breathing slowed, and she let the warmth of the cover wash over her.

She opened an eye. Maybe one more time.

It was, after all, very satisfying.

Click.

Light on.

Click.

And off to sleep...

*

When Natalie woke up in the middle of the night, she wished that she hadn't closed the curtains. Her room was pitch black.

She drew her legs up and pulled the cover over her shoulders. Total darkness was unhelpful for her nerves, but it was incredibly useful for her fears, which were feeling very imaginative.

Her fears were currently imagining that two white dots were staring at her. As Natalie's eyes adjusted to the darkness, her fears imagined that the dots were eyes belonging to someone standing over her bed.

Then, in Natalie's imagination, the white eyes leaned in close, so that the imaginary person was inches away from her face.

Click.

The cube-light revealed a very real person inches away from her face.

Natalie screamed.

CHAPTER 10:
VERY BAD NEWS

"Goodnight, Miss Bliss."

Natalie stopped screaming, stunned into silence by the intruder's greeting. She took a deep breath to calm herself.

"Florentina?"

"I am Florentina, Miss Bliss. You know who I am. Unless you have died again and forgotten who I am."

For the third time tonight, Natalie found herself facing someone not of flesh and blood. The lady standing before her was made of moon-colored porcelain. Curly brown ceramic hair was intricately fashioned above the fine features of her face. Her lips were painted light red. Natalie could see where they had been chipped and repainted.

Florentina's body was muscular and shapely. She seemed to have a very athletic build for a...statue lady. Her sculpted robes had been painted navy blue. There were rough patches on her belt and shoulders. It looked like something had been cut off or filed away.

There was no doubt about it—Florentina was a work of art.

Nevertheless, Natalie could tell that Florentina's glowing white eyes would take some getting used to.

The red-haired girl sat up in her bed and rested her chin on her knees. Florentina took a seat on the end of her bed. Natalie was surprised at the statue's ability to bend and sit.

Florentina tilted her head inquisitively. "Would you like to Make Conversation?"

Natalie pursed her lips. "Um...sure. What made you decide to drop by?"

"I came to see you, Miss Bliss. You have been gone."

"I know, and it's good to see you." Natalie rubbed her eyes. "But I was also sleeping. You startled me by coming into my room and standing inches away from my face."

"I am sorry for startling you. But you would not be awake if I had not startled you. I had to wake you up so we could Make Conversation."

"Maybe next time you could just tap—*lightly* tap—on the door?"

"You want me to lightly tap on the door?"

"Yes."

"I will remember that next time."

"That would be great, thanks." Natalie yawned. "Well, it's been good to see you. You get a goodnight's rest—er...have a good night."

Natalie raised her eyebrows expectantly to see if the housekeeper would leave. She didn't.

"My Purpose here is not only to see you." Florentina folded her smooth hands in her lap. "I could have waited until morning if seeing you were my Only Purpose."

Natalie nodded. "Okay."

"I did not wait until morning because I have Important News. And now that I have seen you and you have seen me and we have Made Conversation, I will tell you why I surprised you by visiting your bedroom in the night."

Natalie leaned forward to show interest. The sooner she could hear the reason, the sooner she could go to sleep.

"I came to tell you that someone is trying to steal an army of golems. This army includes a golem colossus."

Natalie blinked to keep her heavy eyelids from closing.

"That sounds bad."

Florentina frowned. "It is more than bad. It is Very Bad. Would you like some Context to understand the Situation?"

Natalie nodded encouragingly, stifling another yawn. "Sure."

"The golem colossuses were created long ago to fight the Titans in the War of Chaos."

"The War of Chaos?" Natalie jolted upright, stirred by resurging memories. "But the Titans lost the war—they were locked in the Abyss! Has someone brought them back?"

"No. But someone is trying to steal a golem colossus and a golem army."

"So they haven't stolen them yet?"

"No. They have not stolen them yet. But they found the colossus and tried to change his Script. They could not change his Script because they did not have the complete spell. But if they were cunning enough to find the golem colossus, they will find a better spell-book. They will change his Script and the Scripts of the golem army and destroy the city of Calypso."

Natalie felt a headache coming on. "How do you know about this?"

"The golems are my brothers and sisters. They are the Golem Army of Calypso. They are Clay of My Clay. I am one of them. The Clay speaks. I hear the voice of my brother, Wrath, through the Clay."

"Wrath?"

"Wrath is my brother. He is a colossus. I fought many battles alongside him." Florentina's white eyes flickered. "But now Wrath is frightened. He tells me that the Enemy wants to change his Script. They will turn him against us and make him destroy Calypso."

"And the rest of your brothers and sisters are afraid too?"

"I cannot hear their voices because they are still asleep. But Wrath tells me they are nearby. They will not want to betray their Purpose, but the Enemy will try to change their Scripts." Florentina touched Natalie's hand. "We must stop the Enemy from taking control of my brothers and sisters. We must go to my brothers and sisters and fight the Enemy."

"*We*?" Natalie gave a start. "Isn't there someone else who can stop the enemy? I mean, I would love to—but I just *died*." She pointed to herself, pulling at her pink shirt in a demonstration of her mortality. Or, sort-of-mortality.

"Yes. You died. And you are alive." Florentina raised a sculpted eyebrow. "Rebirth is a helpful trait in war."

Natalie bit her lip, staring hard at Florentina. Too many questions poured through her mind. One question, which raised its voice above the din of queries, asked how a golem could have such a strong connection with another golem if they were just...baked clay.

Florentina seemed to read the question in Natalie's eyes.

"Do you wonder at the Mystery of the Clay?"

Natalie blushed. "No, it's just—"

"Long ago, I lived among golems. I fought alongside my brothers and sisters. We won many victories. Then the gods decided that golems could fight no longer." Florentina scowled, and Natalie was shocked by how frightening the golem's face became. "The gods decided that golems were a Risk. 'If the Script can be rewritten,' they said, 'then what if the Enemy rewrites the Script? What if the golems are turned against us?'"

Florentina glared at the floor. "If friends had not intervened, the gods would have destroyed us all. Instead, friends hid my

65

brothers and sisters. Friends changed us so that we would be housekeepers and servants. They saved our lives, but we lost our True Purpose." Florentina pointed at the cuts on her shoulders. "Miss Bliss, the gods stole my Purpose. They stole my armor and my honor. They robbed me of my family. They left me empty inside."

Once again, a thought betrayed itself in Natalie's expression.

But aren't *you empty inside?*

Florentina stared at her.

"Now I am empty. I used to be full of Purpose. I used to be complete with my brothers and sisters. I used to burn with the undying fire that drives us to accomplish our Purpose and to live according to our True Script. But now my Script has been rewritten, and I am not a soldier but a housekeeper. Now the golems are scattered and asleep. Now they are gone."

Natalie glanced at the journal on her dresser. "But they're not gone inside of you."

Florentina lowered her head. "No. And the emptiness is deep."

"Yes. I know."

Florentina looked at Natalie, and a shiver ran down the girl's spine. "Do you see the faces that are not there? Do the voices echo inside of you?"

Natalie bit her lip.

"Do you hear them?" Florentina asked. "The voices from the past?"

A tear traced its way down Natalie's cheek.

"Yes, Florentina. I hear them."

"Then you must help us." Florentina placed her hand on Natalie's. "The world has forgotten us. But it will be in danger soon. We must save the Golem Army of Calypso from the Enemy. We must wake them up first. They must not suffer the dishonor of betraying their Purpose."

"How do you know they'll attack Calypso?"

"It is the Enemy. They will attack Calypso."

Natalie nodded. Florentina's conviction was infectious.

"You must sleep now." Florentina rose and walked to the door. "Tomorrow we will leave to wake up the Golem Army of Calypso."

"Oh—tomorrow?" Natalie held up a hand. "Let me...just check my schedule, actually. I just got back, so I have a few things to take care of..." Her voice trailed off under Florentina's somber gaze.

"By the way," Natalie cast about for a change in subject. "Where are my clothes?"

"They are being washed."

"Why didn't you wash them before I arrived?"

"I washed them before you arrived. I washed them yesterday. I also washed them the day before. And I also—"

"Florentina!"

"Yes?"

"You don't have to wash them every day."

Florentina dropped her head in disappointment.

"Very well. I hoped that you would change your mind about the washing. But I know that you never change no matter how many times you die."

There was an awkward pause.

"I'll take that as a compliment." Natalie turned off her light. "Oh—and Florentina."

"Not 'and-Florentina.' Just Florentina, Miss Bliss."

"Right. Florentina. Just so you know, 'Goodnight' is more of a farewell than a greeting."

Florentina stared at Natalie from the doorway. Her piercing white eyes were so unsettling.

"It's just that you said 'goodnight' when you woke me up. 'Hello' would have been more appropriate. Or even 'good evening.'"

"You wish me to say 'hello' or 'good evening' when it is night? Even if it is a good night?"

"Um…yes," Natalie answered, somewhat lamely.

"I understand now. Thank you, Miss Bliss."

"Goodnight, Florentina."

"Goodnight, Miss Bliss."

CHAPTER 11:
COOKED BREAKFAST

London choked on his orange juice. It dribbled down his face and onto his light gray hoodie.

He sat at one of the three long wooden tables in the dining hall.

Natalie was standing by the doorway. Her yellow raincoat stood out against the wooden paneling. Shay waiters in white shirts bustled past her with heavy-laden breakfast trays.

London grabbed a cloth napkin and wiped the juice off his face. He patted his brown hair with his hand to try and straighten it.

Natalie was standing *right there*.

The morning sunlight cascaded through the tall windows and illuminated Natalie's beautiful, flaming red hair. Her green eyes shone as she looked for a place to sit.

This was London's moment.

Invite her to sit next to you!

A funny sensation swept through his stomach. A bead of sweat slid from his armpit and trailed down the inside of his sleeve.

Natalie glanced at his table, which was nearest to the entrance.

London raised a hesitant hand and waved.

Natalie met his gaze for a moment.

London's heart skipped a beat.

Natalie turned away.

London's heart plummeted. She had seen him and looked away. That was a bad sign.

He became vaguely aware that his hand was still in the air. He salvaged the situation by scratching the inside of his ear. Then he put his hand back in his lap.

Other voices called after Natalie from the opposite end of the dining hall.

"Natalie! You're back!"

"Come sit with us!"

Maybe he would just let her sit somewhere else.

It wasn't a big deal.

Call after her!

Before London could stop himself, noise was coming out from between his lips.

"Natalie!"

The red-haired girl turned around and arched an eyebrow at him.

"Are you hungry, Natalie? There's good here. I mean food here." London stumbled over his words, pointing to the plates in front of him. "Good food here." He swallowed. "I mean, if you want to eat it. If you're hungry."

Natalie stared at him. She looked unimpressed.

London's throat was very, very dry.

A blonde gnome with a bad mustache and overalls was sitting next to London, who was on the end of the bench. London scooted the gnome aside and shifted both of their plates to clear a spot for Natalie.

"There's an empty spot here for you. You can sit down."

Natalie raised her eyebrow higher. She walked over to London's table—his heart beat madly—and then she sat across from him.

"There's a spot right there." London cleared his throat, pointing to the place where Natalie had already sat down. "How—how are you doing?"

Natalie pulled a plate of chocolate croissants toward her and grabbed two from the basket. "Do I know you?"

"Yes." London answered and took a gulp of orange juice at the same time. He choked, spraying orange juice onto his baked beans.

He grabbed his damp napkin and wiped his face. His cheeks burned with embarrassment.

"Excuse me, miss, would you like a cooked breakfast?" A shay, dressed in a white collared shirt and black slacks, held a plate in front of Natalie.

"Oh, yes, please." Natalie's eyes widened. "Thank you."

She eyed the plate hungrily. There were scalloped potatoes, ham, runny scrambled eggs, sausages, and baked beans.

Natalie picked up her fork and was about to eat when she spotted a piece of straw that had fallen from the shay's hand. She glanced at the shay's retreating back and then brushed the straw off the table.

London cleared his throat.

"You know me. I'm London." He answered the question that Natalie had asked a minute ago. "Or you knew me. I mean, we've known each other for a long time." He ended the sentence on a hopeful, pleading note.

Natalie was focused on her potatoes.

"Tea, Natalie?" London offered.

"Oh, no, thank you," Natalie answered without looking up. "I had some yesterday. All over me, in fact. Could you pass me a juice box?"

"Absolutely." London reached across the gnome's plate—almost unsettling the gnome's cup of tea. He grabbed a small green juice box and pointed at the straw. "Do you want me to—?"

"No, thank you." Natalie relieved him of the juice box with practiced finesse. She managed to take it from between his fingers without brushing his hand at all. London felt a twinge of disappointment.

He cast about for a topic of conversation.

"Are you excited about the Arcadian Games? They start this weekend!"

"The what?"

"The Arcadian Games! They're spectacular! They're held every seven years to commemorate the defeat of the Titans. Sayornis receives special honor with the lighting of the Undying Fire, so it's a great time for every Phoenix Guardian." London smiled and tried to catch Natalie's eye. Her attention was fixated on the chocolate croissant in her hand. "The athleticism of the gods is always phenomenal. Every planet sends their best athletes. Of course, Arcadia always does better than anyone else."

"Hmm." Natalie nodded and glanced at London. "That's interesting."

"Yeah, it is!" London spoke quickly, nervous with excitement. He was having a real conversation with Natalie! "How are you settling in after your mission to Mithris?"

"Could you pass the butter, please?" Natalie indicated the tray.

"Right, the butter. Of course." London set the tray down gently in front of her.

"Thanks."

London nodded encouragingly, waiting for Natalie to say more. She didn't.

He raised his glass to his lips and realized that all of the orange juice was gone. He put the cup back on the table. He wanted to ask Natalie more questions, but he waited quietly to see if she wanted anything else, fearful that he might interrupt her melodious voice.

She took advantage of the silence to eat her runny scrambled eggs without interruption.

London brought the glass to his lips again. It was still empty.

He tried not to stare at Natalie, but it was hard. A strand of red hair had fallen across her face so beautifully—

He might have been thinking too loud. Natalie suddenly brushed the strand of hair behind her ear.

Blushing, Natalie put down her fork with a clatter. London almost jumped in his seat.

"Are you staring at me?" She narrowed her eyes.

"No," London answered much too quickly. "Not at all. I'm...looking at the sundial over your shoulder. Out of the window. The sundial outside."

"The sundial." Natalie's voice dripped with skepticism.

"Yes."

"What time is it?"

London hesitated. "Uh, it's..."

"I thought so." Natalie pushed her plate away and made to leave.

"Wait, I haven't asked you—I mean," London stammered. "We haven't really even...did you get enough to eat?"

"Yes." Natalie indicated her empty plate. "But I have to go now. Thank you for inviting me to eat with you."

"Oh. You're welcome." Desperation sizzled down London's esophagus and plopped into his stomach. Natalie rose from the table in a movement of perfect grace.

London made a final bid for conversation.

"Are you off to see Abbess Persephone?"

Natalie stopped. "How did you know that?"

London cringed, wishing he had said something else.

"Oh. No reason. She just told me that you were going to talk today."

Natalie crossed her arms. "Why would she tell *you* that?"

"I asked her. I just wanted to know how you were doing...?" It was a statement, not a question, but it ended as a plea for permission.

Natalie's green eyes flashed.

London slouched on the bench and blushed.

"I see," she fumed. "Well, if you need to know how I'm doing, you can ask me personally."

"At lunch maybe?"

"Goodbye, London."

Natalie turned on her heel and walked out of the hall without a backward glance.

Someone cleared his or her throat. London looked down the table for the source of the noise.

Quincy peeked out from behind an enormous dwarf. She gave London a thumbs-up.

"I think that went really well!"

*

As Natalie rounded the corner and walked out of the dining hall, a broad smile spread across her face.

She had recognized London as soon as she walked into the dining hall. She remembered that he liked her a lot.

So naturally she had ignored him.

Her smile widened.

London was really cute. He had green eyes.

She had green eyes too.

Natalie skipped off toward Staircase VI to see Abbess Persephone. On the way, she even let her feet brush the lawn.

CHAPTER 12:
ABBESS PERSEPHONE

"Hello, Miss Bliss."

Natalie stood in the doorway of Staircase VI. She looked at the golem standing in front of her. He was wearing a blue apron and standing in a bathroom behind a half-closed door.

He pushed the door open, allowing a terrible smell to enter the hallway.

Natalie noted the fish and birds painted onto the golem's arms. They looked like tattoos. He moved his arm up in a practiced wave. The arm started through the air slowly, gained momentum, and finally snapped into place at a right angle to his shoulder. His open palm swayed in the air gently.

"Oh, hi." Natalie closed the door behind her. "What's your name?"

"My name is Florence. Florentina is my sister. She is your housekeeper."

"Nice to meet you, Florence."

"We have met before. It is nice to meet you again." He tilted his head. "Have you died since the last time we talked?"

Natalie cleared her throat. "Actually, yes."

"I am sorry to hear that. I am glad that you are no longer dead."

"Thank you."

"What are you doing in Staircase VI?"

"I'm here to see Abbess Persephone."

Florence looked up. "Abbess Persephone lives on the third floor."

"Thank you."

"The stairs will be the most convenient way to her room." Florence pointed at the steps in front of them.

"Thank you—what's that smell?"

"I do not know. I cannot smell. But inside the bathroom there is vomit all over the floor and the toilet seat and the shower stall."

Natalie pinched her nostrils. "Oh. That's disgusting."

"Yes. It is disgusting. It is also unusual and it may account for the bad smell. People do not normally mention a bad smell when they Make Conversation with me in this staircase."

"Well," Natalie walked up the stairs quickly to get away from the bathroom, "it was nice to meet you, Florence. Good luck cleaning the bathroom."

"It was nice to meet you again, Miss Bliss. Thank you for the good luck. But I do not think that luck will help me clean. I have a mop and that will be sufficient."

*

"Just a moment, please," Abbess Persephone called from behind the door.

"Okay." Natalie rocked back and forth in her white rain boots. While she waited, she enjoyed the view from the third floor of Staircase VI.

Down below, abbey residents were leaving the dining hall and walking back to their rooms. Over the east wall, Natalie could see the beautiful Sayornis Camera against a blue sky.

She drummed her fingers on the windowsill. Her fingernails found a loose scrap of peeling paint. She pulled on it absentmindedly—and suddenly she had ripped off a four-inch strip and exposed the wood beneath.

Natalie gaped. Her brain was processing ways to hide the gouge when Abbess Persephone opened her door.

Persephone was a short, stocky woman with blue eyes, a petite nose, and a halo of curly black hair. She wore a crimson bathrobe.

Persephone arched an eyebrow at Natalie's reddening face.

"Ah, Natalie." She looked at the windowsill and examined the source of Natalie's guilt. "You've been back less than a day and you're already destroying abbey property."

"I—"

"Don't think up an excuse. Just come in."

Persephone shunted the red-haired girl to a couch in the center of the room, across from the fireplace.

She filled a cup and poised the kettle over another. "Would you like some tea?"

"No, thank you." Natalie folded her hands in her lap.

"Odd." Persephone seated herself in an armchair by the couch. "You've always liked tea."

"Have I?"

"Well, not *always*." Persephone sipped her tea. "But in most incarnations you like tea."

Natalie nodded. Persephone looked the red-haired girl up and down. Natalie felt awkward. She focused on a painting above the mantelpiece. It was a stonewalled path running through a windswept meadow.

Persephone broke the silence.

"So, Natalie, tell me what's new in your life."

"My life." Natalie looked back at Persephone. It wasn't a joke, and the abbess didn't laugh.

"True." Persephone sipped her tea. "What else?"

Natalie traced the lines in her hands. "Florentina visited me last night."

"Did she? In the middle of the night?"

"Yes. I woke up and she was in my room—standing over my bed, actually." Natalie shivered at the memory. "It was unsettling."

"I can imagine. But she meant you no harm."

"No, of course not."

"I'm not too surprised to hear about that." The abbess sighed. "Florentina's been acting odd recently."

"It's because of a golem army."

Persephone paused in the middle of a sip. "A golem army?"

"Apparently, someone wants to attack the capital, and they're trying to steal the Golem Army—"

"—of Calypso," Persephone finished.

Natalie blinked in surprise. "You've heard of it?"

"Of course I have." She rested the cup on her plate. "Florentina has mentioned it before. It's the stuff of legend among her people."

"Yes. Well." Natalie stared at the floor. "Florentina wants me to go with her and stop bad people from stealing it."

She glanced at Persephone out of the corner of her eye, expecting a dramatic reaction. The abbess was impassive.

"That's very interesting." Persephone tilted her head. "Why you?"

Natalie shook her head. "I'm not really sure. She says that I understand the golems because I know what it's like to miss people. To feel emptiness inside."

Persephone stared at her interlaced fingers. "And what do you think about *that*?"

"Well, everyone loses loved ones. Everyone has feelings of emptiness."

The abbess nodded slowly. "I think that's the real problem here. Florentina is lonely. She misses her people."

"But her brother is here—Florence. I met him today."

"Oh, you met Florence again, did you? He's a wonderful housekeeper." Persephone smiled. "So is Florentina. But Florentina's never adjusted to being a housekeeper the way Florence has. Every golem is different. I have done my best to help Florentina, but some people find it hard to move into new seasons of life."

"You were the one who helped Florentina become a housekeeper?"

"I found homes for Florentina, Florence, and more. It was either that or let them be ground into powder like the rest of their people."

Natalie covered her mouth in horror. "No."

"The Pantheon doesn't think very much of golems. Not anymore. When the gods decided to disband the army, most of them believed that golems were tools. Tools can be discarded—and that's what they did with the golems. Most of the gods don't realize that golems can develop self-awareness over time. A few golems were rescued. Most were destroyed. I think the survivors invented the story about the army to help cope with the loss. They want to believe that they can all be reunited someday." Persephone sighed. "But sadly, the Golem Army of Calypso is no more."

Anger boiled in Natalie's stomach. *How could the gods treat golems like that?*

Persephone saw the frustration on her face. The abbess leaned forward.

"Natalie, Florentina has emotions just like you do. She's very unstable right now. What she says can't necessarily be trusted. If the golem army still existed, her worries might mean something. But there is no army."

"But Florentina says she knows where the army is. Can't someone just go and make sure it's not there?"

"And who should go?"

Natalie shrugged. "Someone from the Pantheon. Anyone. If there's a danger to Calypso, the Pantheon needs to know about it."

"But Natalie, I don't think there *is* a danger to Calypso, because the army does *not* exist. I am on the Pantheon Security Council, but I don't think it's wise to pass along a tip from an unstable golem housekeeper about the potential theft of the nonexistent Golem Army of Calypso." A look of great annoyance passed over Persephone's face. "I am already unpopular among many members of the Security Council. The Phoenix Guardians have no shortage of political enemies, and they would love to discredit me with a false alarm."

"But Florentina is sure that someone is trying to steal the golem army," Natalie insisted. "She said that her brother, a colossus, spoke to her."

"He spoke to her?" Persephone raised an eyebrow. "Through the Clay?"

"Yes! Florentina says that the Clay speaks to her."

"I'm sure she does." Persephone adjusted her glasses. "And I don't deny that the Clay is a powerful magic. But there is no golem army, Natalie. Don't worry anymore about it."

"I'd like to at least help her look and make sure that everything is okay." Natalie was getting hot, and it wasn't the room temperature that was rising.

Persephone stared into Natalie's eyes for a long moment. When she spoke, her voice was soothing.

"I know that you want to help." Persephone patted Natalie's knee. Natalie didn't know why, but she flinched. "You like helping people, Natalie. That's who you are. Your heart is overflowing with love for others. You hate to see them hurting. Your compassion is part of what makes you such a wonderful person."

Natalie stared at the leaf patterns in the carpet. She took a deep breath to calm herself.

"And who you are is an important part of this discussion. Even if there *was* a golem army—you are not the one to help Florentina."

"Why not?" Natalie's head shot up. Frustration boiled at the brim and threatened to spill over.

Persephone shook her head. "Natalie, think about it. You just admitted that your life itself is new. You're recently resurrected. You're not ready to go on any adventures." She gestured at Natalie. "Look at yourself, dear. Where's your umbrella?"

"I don't have one anymore." Natalie bit her lip. "It burned up."

"And that's not your fault. You completed your last mission—and did a phenomenal job. It's been hard for *me* not to get a big head about it." Persephone smiled broadly.

Natalie stared at her.

The abbess sighed.

"Natalie, you need time to heal and recover. The last thing you need is to chase after an imaginary golem army."

"But Florentina is convinced that someone's going to steal it." Natalie insisted angrily. "She says that the colossus could destroy the entire—"

"Natalie," Persephone interrupted. Her voice was stern. "I didn't want you getting emotionally invested in this. It is obvious that you already are. What you need right now is rest. I want you to stop thinking about it."

"You underestimate me!" Natalie shouted.

Persephone leaned back in surprise.

There was a long pause.

Natalie stared at her white boots.

"I'm sorry, Abbess." She blushed. "I shouldn't have shouted. That's not something I normally do."

Persephone sighed.

"That's what I'm trying to tell you, Natalie," she said quietly. Natalie, upset as she was, could not mistake the tenderness in her voice. "You're not ready for adventure. To be frank, right now *you* are unstable—emotionally, mentally, and physically. You haven't realized how unstable you really are. You need time to heal, time to get adjusted to your new life." She glanced at Natalie's watch. "What time is it, by the way?"

"I'm not sure. This watch doesn't tell time very well."

"Not well at all." Persephone nodded. "But that's not what it's made for, is it?"

Natalie waited to see if Persephone would say anything else. The abbess remained quiet. She just looked very carefully at Natalie.

The red-haired girl felt even more uncomfortable now. The memory of her outburst echoed in the room.

Natalie twisted a strand of hair and focused on the stone wall in the painting so she wouldn't have to look at Persephone.

"Well, I'm sure that you have things to catch up on," Persephone said, rising from her seat. Natalie got up too, understanding that she was being dismissed.

"Abbess, I'm sorry I yelled."

"Thank you for apologizing, Natalie. Don't worry about it—but remember what I said."

Natalie nodded and walked to the doorway.

"I know how you feel, Natalie. We've both gone through this before. I just want what's best for you."

The calm expression on Persephone's face made Natalie even more ashamed that she had yelled.

The abbess opened her arms, and Natalie gave her a hug.

"I'm just trying to help. Do you understand?"

"I understand," Natalie whispered.

Persephone let her go. She smiled, and the corners of her eyes shone a little. Natalie managed a smile of her own, and she walked out of the room and onto the landing.

She walked down the stairs. Her white boots made a satisfying *thunk* on each wooden step.

She knew that Persephone was just trying to help her.

But Natalie was just trying to help Florentina.

She had to help people.

And that couldn't be helped.

CHAPTER 13:
SHADOWCASTING

"Mooooo!"

"Who goes there?"

A rush of anxiety shot through Bellamy's chest. He dropped to a crouch in the shadows of the Sayornis Camera. His satchel bounced against his knee.

He winced. His whole body ached from the catacomb escape. Taking a deep breath, he drew his jacket close and told himself to ignore the pain.

Before him stood the stone arch that framed the heavy wooden gates of Resurgam Abbey. Two statues, and the row of grotesques at their feet, were looking around to see what the commotion was about.

"Noble Maurice, what did you see?" Bartholomew asked the cow grotesque.

"Moo-ooo."

"A woman in a cardigan, you say?"

Matthias shielded his eyes and scanned the cobblestones. "I do not see any women."

"Of course you can't see 'em! They're women—and not to be trusted!" Throckmorton arched his unibrow. His eyes darted back and forth, surveying the dark ground of Resurgam Square.

Wendel rolled her eyes. "Maurice didn't say anything about women or cardigans. He saw something in the shadows, that's all."

"Moo."

"Perhaps not, Good Wendel. But I wish he did," Bartholomew sighed wistfully. "Women in cardigans."

"Mooo!"

"Calm down, Maurice," Wendel said. "It was just a trick of the light."

"How do you know what he said or didn't say, Wendel?" Throckmorton glared at Wendel. "What are you, the Cow Whisperer?"

"I've learned a thing or two about the inflections in Maurice's voice," Wendel snapped. "I think I would know if Maurice said something about women in cardigans."

While the grotesques argued, Bellamy relaxed against the wide walls of the Sayornis Camera. Maurice must have spotted Bellamy when he shadowcast himself. The boy was fine for the moment, but the sooner he could get himself inside the abbey, the better.

Bellamy closed his eyes and focused on his shadow. At present, it was just another part of the darkness cast by the Sayornis Camera. But he concentrated and heightened his awareness of his shadow. Then his shadow became aware too.

Go, Bellamy commanded.

Bellamy's shadow ran out from the shade of the Sayornis Camera. It darted across the street and paused under the gate's archway.

Bellamy had shadowcast himself through the doors of the Colossus Pit, but he knew better than to force his shadow under the gates of Resurgam Abbey. The formidable enchantments protecting the abbey were effective against spirit, shadow, flesh, and thought. The protective spells could destroy his shadow. Bellamy didn't know how that worked, but he knew it could happen. The pain was said to be excruciating.

He had to get into the abbey the way everyone else did: by opening the gate. But he couldn't just walk up to it. Even though Bartholomew and Matthias were busy looking for women, and even though most of the grotesques were asleep or arguing, Maurice would still spot him.

Nothing got past the cow.

Granted, the others might not *understand* Maurice, but they were bound to notice something if the cow made enough noise.

Bellamy's gaze swept the left side of the gate, searching for the Pokket bowl. He found it, and his shadow walked over to it.

The heads continued to argue.

"And you're always so defensive!"

"I am not defensive!"

Bellamy closed his eyes tightly, his brow wet with perspiration.

Take me. He held his breath—and then he vanished from the Camera.

He reappeared next to the Pokket bowl, reunited with his shadow.

"Anyway, I don't know why everyone gets all excited when the cow moos."

Bellamy ignored Throckmorton's voice. He reached inside his black leather jacket, pulled out a fox-shaped Pokket, and placed it gingerly into the bowl.

The keyhole glowed green—and Bellamy winced as the gate unlocked with a loud metallic click. He had been afraid of that.

"Moooo!"

"What is that, Noble Maurice?" Bartholomew asked. "A kebab vender, you say?"

"No, I think he heard something," Wendel said.

"I heard it too," Lyle said.

Bellamy imagined Lyle's bulging eyes looking down on the entranceway. He opened the gate slowly, making as little noise as possible.

"Should we sound the alarm, Good Bartholomew?"

"It might have been nothing, Good Matthias. There are lots of nightly noises. After all, it is nighttime. That is what nightly noises are for."

"But I heard something like the gate opening."

"You are quite right, Good Matthias. Something *like* the gate opening. But the gate could not have opened because we have been watching it."

"We have been watching the ground in *front* of the gate, but we cannot watch the gate itself."

"Oh, speak not of our limitations. We would have seen anyone come in."

"Unless they were invisible."

"Fair point, Good Matthias. But you still must possess a Pokket to enter the gate."

"Yes! The Test!"

"The Sacred Test!"

"The invisible cardigan-clad women must pass the Test!"

"Mooooo!"

"Good friends and Noble Maurice, please!" Matthias hissed. "Not so loud! It is nighttime. People are trying to sleep."

"Sorry."

"My apologies."

"Moo."

Bartholomew sighed. "If there *is* an intruder, Good George will spot him."

"You are quite right, Good Bartholomew. The abbey is well protected."

Bellamy wiped sweat off his brow. He opened the gate a few inches to peer inside. He could see George in the porter's lodge, leaning back in a chair and reading *The Calypso Times*. The shay must not have seen the gate open.

Bellamy focused on a patch of darkness in front of the lawn.

Go.

His shadow slipped through the gate and glided along the wall, flowing underneath the lodge windows and into the quad.

Bellamy swallowed and closed his eyes. He knew that the door would shut loudly when he let go to reunite with his shadow. That couldn't be helped. He would have to be quick.

Bellamy held his breath and shadowcast himself.

He reappeared by the lawn away from the pools of lamplight. He glanced at the door, which was shutting—and then he looked at the archway that joined North Quad with South Quad.

Go.

His shadow darted toward a staircase inside the archway.

CLUNK!

The door shut—not too loudly, but loud enough to be heard at night.

Bellamy heard the springs of George's chair as the shay sat up.

"What was *that*?" Matthias's voice sounded muffled through the gate.

"Moo-o*OO*o."

"George noticed something," Wendel said. "Is everything all right in there, George?"

"I'm not sure."

Bellamy peered around a corner to see George stepping out of the lodge. The shay pulled on the massive chain stretching across the door. It was still locked. George turned around to see the quad. Bellamy pulled his head back just in time.

He heard the shay's footsteps coming his way.

Bellamy closed his eyes and saw from his shadow's perspective. It was crouching in the darkness by the staircase.

He held his breath and disappeared—just as George rounded the corner.

From the safety of the dark staircase, Bellamy exhaled softly. George was staring at the space he had occupied a moment ago.

The shay turned toward the shadowy archway, but Bellamy was already moving up the stairs.

*

Bellamy ascended the stairs carefully, taking care to avoid the creaky steps that he had learned as a resident of Resurgam Abbey. He listened attentively for the sounds of anyone wandering about at night.

All was quiet. His heart lightened. Things were going well. He had passed the most difficult defenses. The trouble would be getting out—but first he needed to get the spell-book.

He glanced down the stairs. George would come this way soon enough. The shay would secure every part of the abbey before returning to the porter's lodge. If Bellamy was lucky, George would be absent when it was time to exit through the gate.

He strained his ears for noise as he reached a landing and continued up another flight. He would have preferred to hide himself in a corner and send his shadow up to the library. There was almost no chance that a casual observer would notice his shadow at night, but Bellamy couldn't risk George finding his body hiding somewhere. George was a keen porter.

Bellamy swallowed. It had been...good to see George again.

But that's not why you're here. Stick to the mission. You're here to get the book.

Bellamy walked on.

He reached another landing and looked out at the abbey's Deer Park. It was smaller than the quad lawns and it had no deer—but the abbey's founder wanted to have a deer park like the University of Calypso, so they had decided this small garden would be called Deer Park.

At the memory, Bellamy started to smile—but it turned into a grimace.

You're not here to reminisce. Remember the mission.

His hand trailed along the ornate wooden railing to the library landing. Paintings and tapestries lined the walls, leading to a set of swinging doors. He approached them reverently and felt their red velvet surfaces.

He knew this place well.

Bellamy opened the doors carefully, checking to see that the coast was clear. Everything was still and quiet.

The Great Library Hall was a good two stories high. He walked along the main center aisle, checking each row to make sure that no one was there. Enormous stacks and huge ladders stretched off into darkness on either side. The hall looked empty.

He reached the end of the hall and entered a small antechamber with a few cushioned chairs, and then went through another set of doors to the enormous Sayornis Reading Room.

Moonlight spilled down from the fourteen tall windows in the far wall. Stacks of books lined the room. Two long rows of thirteen lamps hung from the ceiling, illuminating the rows of tables below.

A long booth stood next to the entrance. Ornate woodwork decorated the roof of the peculiar structure. Bellamy walked up to the small door, admiring the opaque, stained windows and their carved frames.

He closed his eyes.

Go.

His shadow slipped through a crack in the booth's doorframe.

Bellamy looked at the inside from his shadow's perspective. Dim moonlight filtered through the thin windows. In the center was a chest covered in ancient runes. *On Creatures Created* had to be inside.

Take me.

Bellamy reunited with his shadow inside the booth. He leaned down and ran his hand over the box, feeling for the lock. He pressed his palm against it and said, "*Unlocked.*"

Nothing happened.

He hadn't really expected anything. The abbey would have placed stronger enchantments on the chest, but it had been worth a try.

Bellamy pulled a vial of Abri Gel from inside his leather jacket. He opened the vial and an amber-colored gel squirmed out.

"Gotcha!" Bellamy caught it before it dropped onto the floor. The gel wriggled in his grasp, but he held it firmly. He placed it on the lock, where it squeezed inside and then expanded to fill the hole. He could hear the sound of moving gears as the Abri manipulated the lock.

Then the lock shuddered and the chains clattered to the floor. The Abri poked a gelatinous tendril out of the lock. Bellamy grabbed it and returned it to the vial before it could escape.

He opened the heavy chest lid. Bellamy could see the shapes of books inside, but it was too dark to identify them by the faint moonlight.

Whispers filled the room.

"Who is it?"

"Someone opened the chest."

Bellamy tried to block out the voices. They filled the air, making it thicker, pressing against his skin like a cold blanket.

He pulled a small granitic rock from his pocket and dropped it. The rock flipped once, ignited with a pale pink light, and floated lightly at his shoulder. With this illumination, Bellamy examined the dusty tomes in the chest.

The voices of the books grew louder.

"Who is it?"

"It is not the Abbess."

"It is a stranger."

Bellamy wiped dust off the cover of one volume. The thick layer stuck to his fingers.

"It touched me! Make it stop!"

Bellamy recoiled in surprise and almost dropped the book into the chest. He took a step back.

"Do not panic. He may be one of the wardens."

"He is not. He should not be here."

"He is afraid. Can you sense it?"

Bellamy summoned his nerves and picked up the book again. He read the title on the spine: *Olde Souls*.

He put the book down and picked up another. The cover was worn, and the title letters were peeling away, but he could distinguish the words "Night" and "Invictus."

A chill started in Bellamy's fingers, traveling up his arm and into his chest. His heart palpitated in his ears—louder and louder. Bellamy felt the heat leaving his body.

He put the book down quickly and shuddered. His hands were pale, and when he drew back his sleeve he saw that the ghostly pallor extended to his elbow. He took a deep breath to compose himself. After a minute, his chest warmed up and the chill disappeared through his fingertips.

Bellamy exhaled in relief. Whatever that was, he didn't want it to happen again.

The next book was the one he had been looking for. His heart beat fast—but with excitement this time, not fear. He read the full title, which stretched over the front cover: *On Creatures Created by the Gods Without Self-Awareness But Which Have Developed Self-Awareness and Other Communicable Divine Attributes Over Time.*

There was a reason modern readers shortened it to *On Creatures Created.*

"What are you doing? Put me down!"

Bellamy ignored the voice, checking the table of contents and looking for instructions on Golem Script. He finally found the passage that he was looking for.

Scanning the page with his finger, he looked for a clue that would tell him what he had done wrong in the Colossus Pit.

"In order to rewrite the Script," he read quietly to himself, "the new master...sacred instruction...invoke the golem's name?"

He swore under his breath. He had to invoke the golem's *name*? Why hadn't the other spell-book mentioned that? How was he going to learn the colossus's name?

Bellamy read the next lines in a whisper. "Number two: utter the First Sacred Chant of the Rewriting...I did that. Write or speak...new Script...I have to speak a second chant?"

He shook his head. This was the codex he should have stolen before going to the Colossus Pit. The Forerunners' spell-book couldn't compare.

But it was too late for that. The important thing was that he had the book now. He would return to the catacombs and convert the colossus.

"Put me down immediately!"

Bellamy closed his eyes and sent his shadow outside of the booth.

Go.

He held *On Creatures Created* tightly in his hand—and a moment later he had reunited with his shadow. When he opened his eyes, he was standing outside the booth in the moonlit Sayornis Reading Room.

THUMP!

Bellamy gasped. The sound had come from inside the booth.

His hands felt light—

"The fool dropped me!"

The book!

He looked down to see that his hands were empty. The book hadn't shadowcast with him.

BOOM.

A shiver ran down Bellamy's spine. That sound hadn't come from inside the booth. It had come from the Great Library Hall.

Someone was coming—probably George. The shay's incredible intuition must have led him to the library.

Bellamy felt a surge of panic. How was he going to get *On Creatures Created* out of the booth?

He shadowcast himself back inside. The codex was lying on the floor where it had fallen. Bellamy looked at the chamber's thin walls, wondering if he could break them open.

He shook his head at the stupidity of the thought. The damage would broadcast his intrusion. Bellamy didn't want anyone to know that someone had tried to steal *On Creatures Created*, let alone that someone had broken into Resurgam Abbey or its library. If the Phoenix Guardians knew that someone was after *On Creatures Created*, they might fear mischief about golems.

Very few people cared about the legendary Golem Army of Calypso. Even fewer people knew that the army still existed. The Forerunners wanted to keep it that way.

"Do not leave me here! Put me back where I belong!"

Bellamy looked at the book. There must be some way of getting it out, surely? He examined the booth's small door. His floating granitic rock still illuminated the inside of the chamber. He snatched it out of the air and put it back in his pocket—he didn't want George to see the light if he came into the room.

He ran his hand along the inside of the doorframe. There was no handle.

Fair enough—he could just open the door from the outside. There would probably be a lock, but Bellamy had his Abri Gel.

Go.

Bellamy sent his shadow out and saw a lock on the door. He held his breath and was about to shadowcast when he heard the room's heavy doors swing open. He swore under his breath.

It was George.

The shay walked in holding a lantern. To Bellamy's horror, he immediately turned toward the booth. Then he stopped.

Bellamy felt like something was stuck in his throat. Had George seen Bellamy's shadow?

It was doing its best to press against the booth, but there was no denying something strange about it. George lifted his lantern to see what effect that had on the shadow. The shadow was cast at a different angle than everything else—an anomaly in the light.

George looked at the shadow.

"He is in here! The intruder is in here!"

"Help us!"

Bellamy's heart jumped into his throat. The books were shouting beside him. He covered his ears and trembled.

It was over. George would find him and Bellamy would be arrested.

But to his shock, George didn't react to the screams.

"In here!"

"The intruder is in here! Save us!"

Bellamy almost gasped—but he covered his mouth and stopped himself in time.

The shay couldn't hear the books' voices.

Relief coursed through Bellamy's body—the shay was insensitive to this kind of magic.

But George could still see the shadow.

Bellamy waited, hoping desperately that the shay would look away. He licked his dry lips. His heart pounded with anxiety.

A noise caught George's attention.

Through his shadow, Bellamy saw the cause: an owl had flown against a window on the far side.

As soon as George turned, Bellamy withdrew his shadow. George looked back at the booth and blinked. For an agonizing minute, the shay stared at the spot Bellamy's shadow had occupied. He must have noticed that the shadows had changed.

"Please help us! The intruder is in here!"

"You must save us!"

The books continued to shout in vain.

Finally, George shrugged and walked away from the booth. What else could he do? They were shadows. It was a trick of the light.

A trick of the light indeed.

George continued his search, examining the two rows of tables. He looked under the cushioned chairs and scanned the bookshelves lining the walls.

Then George circled back to the booth. He looked at it curiously, still suspicious. Then, at last, he walked out of the reading room.

Bellamy held his breath until the shay's footsteps faded into the distance. Then he exhaled in relief and slid down the side of the booth.

After a moment to calm down, he shadowcast himself out. He examined the lock and opened the vial of Abri Gel. Once again, the Abri squeezed out of the vial and dropped onto the lock. A moment later, it opened with a satisfying click. He gathered the Abri back into the vial, his hands shaking with anxiety. He wanted to get out of here as soon as possible.

"What are you doing? Get away from here!"

"Do not open that door!"

Bellamy opened the booth, stepped inside, and picked up *On Creatures Created.*

"Intruder! Filth!"

Bellamy ignored the shouting books and closed the chest, silencing their voices. A haunting echo lingered in the air. Even *On Creatures Created* stopped shouting. Perhaps the book was resigned to its fate.

Bellamy locked the booth with the Abri Gel and hurried out of the Sayornis Reading Room. He rushed through the Great Library Hall and down the stairs before stopping at a landing. He could see George holding a lantern and walking past the Deer Park, away from North Quad and the gate.

Bellamy hurried his pace, moving as quickly as possible without slipping down the stairs. He paused under the archway between North and South Quad. Then he crept swiftly against the wall toward the entrance.

In the porter's lodge, Bellamy examined the enormous chain across the gate. He held his breath and waited for a moment, listening to see if George was coming this way. He couldn't hear anything.

Bellamy put his Pokket into the bowl. It glowed green. The door opened with a creak.

"Mooo!"

"Oh, dear. Not again," said Bartholomew.

Bellamy stepped out of the gate and slowly closed it.

"Is someone going inside?" asked Matthias.

"Someone is probably coming out."

"Who?"

"Why, Good Matthias, someone who went in earlier, of course."

"Well said, well said. Hello there! Who is coming out at this hour of the night?"

Bellamy bit his lip. How was he going to get away without being seen? He didn't want to risk shadowcasting with the book again. What if it dropped and George chose that moment to check outside the gate? The shay could be back at any moment.

Bellamy would just have to run for it...quietly.

He pressed himself against the wall, poised to sprint along the side of the abbey. If he was lucky, the statues and grotesques would all be looking the other way.

"Can anyone hear me? I have been stolen!"

"Mooo*OOOO!*"

"Maurice says that a library book has been stolen!" Wendel shouted.

"What? Where? By who?" asked Bartholomew.

"By whom!" Matthias corrected.

"Who?"

"Him!" Lyle screamed.

Bellamy had been seen. He didn't wait to find out what would happen next. He disappeared into the darkness, leaving the cries of statues and grotesques far behind.

CHAPTER 14:
INNOCENT QUESTIONS

Natalie heard the knock on her living room door.

"Housekeeping."

She set down her journal and walked across the room. When she opened her door, Florentina was standing in front of her, wearing an apron and holding a blue bucket.

"Good morning, Miss Bliss. Housekeeping." She wore a strange expression. It took Natalie a moment to realize that Florentina was smiling. It was pleasant, after a sort. Porcelain smiles weren't the most normal of smiles.

"Come on in." Natalie stepped aside to let Florentina by. "Thanks for dropping off my laundry earlier, by the way."

"You are welcome, Miss Bliss. I can come by tonight if you want me to wash your clothes again."

"Oh, no—thank you." Natalie forced a smile. "I think I'm good for now. I don't think they'll get dirty just hanging in my closet."

"Let me know if you change your mind." Florentina walked into the bathroom. She took some sponges out of her bucket and began scrubbing the tub.

"I haven't actually used the bathtub yet." Natalie held up a finger. "It's probably not dirty."

Florentina scrubbed vigorously at a spot that was clean enough to shine.

"I must clean every day to keep the dust and stains away."

"Oh. Right." Natalie's heart sank a little. She really didn't want to have every morning interrupted by Florentina coming in and cleaning the entire room. "Will you be cleaning the—"

"Entire room. Yes, Miss Bliss. I must maintain the condition of the suite and keep the dust and stains away."

Natalie cringed.

"Tell you what, if I promise to clean a bit on my own..." She trailed off at the look that Florentina gave her. It was amazing how expressive a porcelain golem could be with limited facial movement.

"If you what, miss?"

"If I clean a bit on my own...?"

"But I clean, Miss Bliss. Do you not want to see me every day?"

"Oh, no!" Natalie waved her hands. "It's not that at all. It's just that I don't want to wear anything away with scrubbing. You know? And I like to clean too. Sometimes. It helps me clear my mind."

Florentina nodded knowingly and began wiping the sparkling white sink. "Is your mind full of many things?"

"Right now it is."

Florentina slid a small rag back and forth over the faucet. "Have you thought any more about what I said the other night?"

"Oh. That." Natalie swallowed. She felt uncomfortable knowing that she was about to tell Florentina that Persephone had forbidden her from going after the golem army. Natalie walked back to the window seat and picked up her journal to give her hands something to do. "Yes, I've thought about it."

"And?" Florentina turned her head all the way around her neck to look at Natalie. Her body was still scrubbing away at the sink.

That was unsettling.

Natalie cleared her throat. "And...I talked to Abbess Persephone about it."

Florentina's white eyes flickered. She shook her head briefly to erase the betrayal of emotion, but Natalie had caught it. Florentina must have guessed what Persephone had said. The golem turned back to the sink.

"The abbess told you not to get involved."

Natalie hung her head. "Yes."

"She told you that I was unstable and unpredictable. She said that I was inventing stories about the golem army."

"Not *inventing* stories," Natalie began, but Florentina cut her off.

"I know what she said, Miss Bliss." Florentina's shoulders went up and down slowly. Natalie realized that was her version of a sigh. "She does not trust my ability to think clearly."

It was Natalie's turn to sigh. "Yes. That's about it."

"Do not worry. I am not offended. I know that she doubts me." Florentina got down on her knees. It looked like an effort to get those porcelain legs to bend, but the golem managed. She turned on the bathtub faucet and soaked a sponge in the flowing water.

"The abbess doubts you too," Florentina said casually while she scrubbed the stainless floor.

Natalie was taken aback. "What makes you say that?"

"I say that because she does. Did she not say that you need time to heal and that you are not ready to fight? She said that you cannot go on adventures because you are also unstable."

Natalie crossed her arms. She was starting to get angry.

"Florentina, if you were eavesdropping on my conversation—"

"I was not eavesdropping, Miss Bliss." Florentina met Natalie's stern gaze. "I am old. I know the Abbess Persephone. I know you. I have seen your deaths and resurrections." She turned her attention back to the floor. "I know the way of these things."

Natalie sat in silence while Florentina finished cleaning the bathroom. The golem squeezed the sponge out over the bath and placed it carefully in her blue bucket. Then she stepped into the living room and looked at Natalie with what seemed to be a kind expression.

"I did not mean to hurt your feelings, Miss Bliss. I should not speak with so much bluntness. I think this is a difficult time for both of us."

Natalie nodded.

"Abbess Persephone is wise." Florentina looked out the window. "She knows what is best for you."

Natalie felt a pang of irritation at the phrase, "what is best for you."

She had a pretty good idea of what was best for her. Or at least, what was *good* for her. She had been through a lot. And even if she forgot her past lives in death, she had her journal to remind her.

"I understand if you cannot help me."

Natalie bit her lip. "I'm sorry, Florentina. But I don't want to disobey Abbess Persephone. It's just...not me."

"This is true." Florentina nodded. "You cannot disobey your Script. It is what you live by. I know." She held up her hand and stared at her moon-colored fingers. "Your Script is a gift and a burden. My Script draws me to my people. But I cannot help them."

Her voice was weighed down with so much sorrow that Natalie caught her breath. She looked at the golem, whose gaze was fixed upon the window.

Rain droplets slid across the glass, creating watery trails that flowed down to the windowsill.

She pointed at Natalie's journal. "What are you reading?"

"Oh." Natalie held up the journal so Florentina could see the cover, which showed a bright young phoenix sitting in a funeral pyre. "I was just reading about my old friend, Marianne Edge. I'm hoping to see her today."

Florentina tilted her head. "This book is about your friend?"

"Not just about her—it's my journal. I write all of my experiences in it. It records the people that I've seen, the places that I've been, and the things that I've learned." She caressed the leather-bound book with her thumb. "It has everything, really."

"Then it is a powerful book." Florentina stared at the journal. "The memory of friends is strong magic."

"Yes. I don't want to forget them. It's my only connection to their names and faces, and so many of them are gone." She sighed. "It's not easy to be around for millennia...to go through so many lives."

"Many things change when you live a long time. But some things you must hold onto. You must fight to remember them."

Natalie took a deep breath. "Yes."

She contemplated her journal while Florentina stared out of the window again.

Then Florentina abruptly broke the silence.

"It is beginning to rain hard." She tilted her head and looked at Natalie. Her voice sounded more cheerful. "Do you not need to get a new umbrella, Miss Bliss?"

Natalie blinked at the change in subject.

"Yes, I do. Actually, I was just talking to Abbess Persephone about that." She stood and watched the rain pouring from the sky. "Oh, dear. It really is coming down."

"You should get an umbrella now."

Natalie made a face. "I don't know. That's quite a storm."

"Not as bad as it will be. I am sure. Radcliffe is a city of much rainfall. You have to go out sometime. You might as well get an umbrella now and prepare yourself for the coming days."

Natalie shrugged. "You're right. I should get one sooner rather than later. Besides, I'll need to start training with my new umbrella. I was just reading about how hard it was to break in the umbrella that I had two lives ago." She placed her journal on the table. "They're tricky things. But I love them. Umbrellas conduct magic better than anything else for me." She smiled. "I just understand them."

"Yes you do, Miss Bliss. Therefore, there is no sense in delaying the purchase of a new umbrella."

"I guess I'll go now then." Natalie walked into her bedroom and grabbed her raincoat out of the closet. "Are you going to be fine here all alone, Florentina?"

"Yes, Miss Bliss. I will be fine. I spend much time alone. I will finish cleaning your room. Then I will clean other rooms and keep the dust and stains away."

"Okay." Natalie tugged on her white rain boots. "Well, you're doing a really good job cleaning."

"Thank you, Miss Bliss."

Natalie walked to the door. "In fact, you're doing such a good job that you probably don't have to clean again tomorrow."

"Yes, Miss Bliss. Or the day after tomorrow. I understand. Have an enjoyable time while you shop for your new umbrella."

CHAPTER 15:
A NEW UMBRELLA

"Oh my gods, Natalie, we are going to have so much fun shopping!" Quincy squealed with excitement as they walked through the porter's lodge and out of Resurgam Abbey. She had caught Natalie just before she walked out of Staircase V. After a quick interrogation, Natalie had confessed that she was, in fact, going shopping.

There was no helping it after the truth had been revealed. Quincy was coming along.

"I'm just going to buy a new umbrella," Natalie held a tattered copy of *The Calypso Times* over her head to block the rain. "We're not going *shopping*-shopping."

"Oh, Natalie." Quincy made an impatient noise. "You're out with me and you're going to have a good time. We're not in a rush. Just relax and let's see where our feet take us. Don't try to put a limit on what you might buy."

Quincy was holding a ridiculous half-bubble umbrella over her head. She said that she liked the umbrella because it was transparent. ("That way, boys can still see my face even if the umbrella is covering me!")

Natalie rolled her eyes and splashed over the wet cobblestone ground. She loved wearing her rain boots. They made her feel invulnerable. Where slippers shied away from puddles and mud, rain boots said, "Come at me if you're game enough. I'll walk right over you."

They walked to Trout Street, one of the many shopping hot-spots in Radcliffe. Elves, dwarves, gnomes, and an assortment of other species filled the street, window-shopping and carrying bags.

Quincy tugged urgently on Natalie's arm and pointed to a shop. "Oh, look! It's Nickel's! They have such cute dresses there!"

"I'm not out to buy a dress!" Natalie hurried across the street after Quincy. The sylph was already at the door to Nickel's when Natalie called after her. "Quincy!"

The sylph paused in the act of opening the door. She put her hands on her hips and glared at Natalie. "Oh, Natalie, you're just no fun!"

"Quincy, I need a new *umbrella*." Natalie pointed at the saturated newspaper above her head. It was dripping water and ink. Soggy bits of the opinion column stuck to Natalie's hair.

Quincy rolled her eyes. "Fine. We'll put off going into Nickel's—but only because I love you."

"I appreciate the sacrifice. Now can you..." Natalie turned on the spot, looking at the plethora of stores. "Can you remind me where a good place to get an umbrella is?"

"For an ordinary umbrella you'd want Beatrice's Bountiful Beautiful Products—because their accessories are *so* cute. But you always buy *your* umbrellas at Oswald's." Quincy grabbed Natalie's hand and pulled her away again. Natalie sighed and bounded across the gray brick pavement of Trout Street.

Quincy's disappointment about Nickel's dissipated when they walked into Oswald's. From the outside, it was a modest shop with a blue sign that read, "OSWALD'S." Inside was a humongous, brightly-lit store. Natalie blinked at the white shelves covered from top to bottom with lotions, lipsticks, creams, shampoos, fake nails, rouge—all of the beauty products that Natalie would have expected (and a few more that she hadn't).

"Quincy." Natalie shook her head. "I said I wanted an *umbrella*, not—"

"I know, Natalie, I know! This is just one part of the store. Come on, we need to go upstairs."

"Upstairs? I thought this place was too small to have an upstairs."

"It just looks small from the outside."

"And the umbrellas are upstairs?"

"Sort of—just follow me."

Quincy pulled Natalie past a display stand of hair dye (black, blonde, brown, red, green, blue—and, Natalie was pleased to see—plaid and argyle) and up a set of rainbow-colored stairs. The steps went up and into the hitherto-unseen depths of the store before the girls finally reached the second floor.

This room had jackets, t-shirts, pants, socks, and underwear (for elves, dwarves, gnomes, and more!). There were racks upon racks of athletic wear for the Arcadian Games. Natalie noticed jerseys bearing the names "Io" and "Oli."

"Oli—isn't that the god who's marrying Aphro-what's-her-face?"

"Aphrodainte, and yes! That is Oli—ooh, look! An *Io* jersey!" Quincy picked up the red jersey and pressed the name against her lips. "Ooh, I want this. Should I buy it?" She glanced at the price tag. "Too expensive. Oh, well. My love for Io is greater than money can buy. Come along, Natalie. No umbrellas here."

In a swift motion, Quincy hung the jersey back on the rack and grabbed Natalie's hand.

"We have to go through this door." She walked past some skinny jeans through a small door that Natalie hadn't seen. This next room was filled with board games, decks of cards, more stuffed animals (including a beluga whale that filled a corner and talking llamas that sang the alphabet), toy planes that flew near the ceiling, and a model train set that ran along the walls.

"Oh! Trains!" Natalie ran toward the track. She watched a small red train go through a tunnel. It blew a long whistle blast. Natalie clapped her hands in delight.

"Come on, Natalie. We're not here to buy trains. You need to get an umbrella." Quincy tugged her away from the track.

"But, but—" Natalie watched the red train go through a small station. Model townspeople walked around on the platform. A miniature conductor waved at Natalie—but he disappeared out of sight when Quincy steered her past the beluga whale and down another staircase.

"I like trains," Natalie said resentfully. She gently but firmly extricated her arm from Quincy's grasp. "And I can walk by myself, thank you."

She surveyed the new room that Quincy had brought her to. These walls were covered with boxes of tea and all manner of souvenirs: cups, plates, forks, knives, spoons, ice trays, salt and pepper shakers, and shot glasses.

"Next room." Quincy walked through yet another door and Natalie followed.

This room faced the street—although Natalie had serious doubts as to whether it was the same street, or even city, that they had come in from.

"Ooh, I just love the kites in here!" Quincy pointed at one wall, which was covered in kites of all colors and sizes. Another wall was stacked with rows of bicycles.

"Umbrellas!" Natalie almost ran to the corner where a variety of umbrellas had been placed in a couple of stands. She immediately picked up the only red umbrella. She held it up and examined it with a smile. The umbrella was a good length, the end was pointed, and it had a crook handle. Natalie opened it to see how big the canopy was.

"Um, excuse me, miss—"

"Natalie, what are you doing?" Quincy covered her mouth and stared at Natalie in shock.

Natalie's eyes widened. Out of the corner of her eye, she saw a brunette elf behind the counter. The elf's face betrayed alarm, and she held a warning finger at Natalie.

"Laurel!" Natalie exclaimed in delight. She lowered the umbrella. "It's so good to see you!"

The elf looked confused. "Excuse me?"

"Don't you remember me, Laurel? It's Natalie!"

The elf squinted. Then a look of recognition crossed her face. "Oh—hello, Miss Bliss! Laurel is my mother. I'm Chloe."

"Oh." Natalie blushed. "How is Laurel—your mother?"

"She's getting along all right, thanks." Chloe nodded gratefully. "She doesn't leave the house much anymore, but she's in good spirits. I'll let her know you asked about her."

"Thank you." Natalie stared at the ground, feeling sober.

Chloe cleared her throat and pointed at the open umbrella in Natalie's hand. "I guess you're shopping for a new umbrella?"

"Yes, I am. I lost my last one on a mission."

"I'm sorry to hear that. But you've come at a good time. We recently restocked our umbrellas." Chloe smiled. "Mother always reminds me to keep a red umbrella with a crook handle. She knows you favor those."

Natalie smiled. "Yes, I do."

"It is, however, store policy that customers do not open umbrellas inside the store. It might knock over valuable merchandise." She pointed meaningfully next to Natalie.

The phoenix followed her gaze and saw that the edge of her umbrella canopy was inches away from a tenuous stack of collectible and very-breakable-looking cups. Natalie had no idea what they were doing in the flying object section—but that was department stores for you.

"I see." Natalie stepped away from the fragile merchandise and closed the umbrella. "Sorry about that, Laurel—um, Chloe."

The elf relaxed visibly and clasped her hands in front of her green dress. "It's quite all right, Miss Bliss. Do you like that one?"

Quincy interrupted before Natalie could respond.

"Natalie, I don't know what you were thinking when you opened that red umbrella."

Natalie gaped at her. "Excuse *me*, Quincy. I'm sorry—I just apologized to Chloe and closed the umbrella. What more do you want?" She brushed wet hair out of her face, feeling annoyed.

"I want you to try *this* umbrella." Quincy held out a small black umbrella. "It's so cute. It's absolutely *delicious*. Take a look!"

"I don't think—" Chloe held out another hand of warning, but Quincy had already opened the umbrella.

Fortunately, the sylph was standing in the middle of the floor, away from the breakables. Chloe sighed and rubbed the bridge of her nose.

"Look at it!" Quincy squeaked excitedly from behind the umbrella canopy. "It's beautiful!"

It was, in truth, a beautiful umbrella. A wonderful likeness of the Sayornis Camera had been printed on one side of the black canvas, and the walls of Resurgam Abbey wrapped around the other side.

"It's very pretty," Natalie agreed, stepping back to have a better look. "But don't you think it's a little small?"

"Oh, Natalie." Quincy clicked her tongue and closed the umbrella. "It's not as if you're a *big* girl, is it? It's perfect for you! It's cute, you're cute—and it's *so* your color!"

Natalie arched an eyebrow. "Black?"

Quincy nodded encouragingly. "Yes. It matches your hair."

Natalie held a strand of wet red hair between her fingertips. "Black and red? I don't know. It's not really me..."

"Na-ta-lie." Quincy rolled her eyes. "It's a new life! It's a new you! Come on, take a chance!"

Natalie frowned. She looked at the red umbrella in her hand, and then at the small black one in Quincy's hopeful arms.

Natalie hesitated. "Well..."

"You don't want to be stagnant, do you?"

"Stagnant? No..."

"You want to try new things, right?"

"Yeah..."

"And you love the Camera and Resurgam Abbey, right?"

"Yeah..."

"Then it's settled!" Quincy grasped the umbrella with both hands. She waved it at Chloe. "My friend would like this one."

"Oh, good," the elf said. "So you won't need to open any more umbrellas?"

"None at all—put away your money, Natalie. I'll get this one for you."

"Are you sure?" Natalie's coin-filled hand was poised at the edge of her coat pocket.

"I'm sure. You deserve it."

"All right. Well, thanks, Quincy."

"Don't mention it."

*

A few minutes later, Natalie had to mention it.

"Quincy?"

"Yes, darling?" Quincy bounced excitedly on the sidewalk, happily en route to Nickel's.

"About this umbrella..." Natalie frowned. *The Calypso Times*, while a respectable publication, had not kept her dry. In fact, her entire body had been *soaked*, save for her head, which had simply become *very damp*. Natalie's blue jeans had dried while the girls were in Oswald's.

But now they were soaked again.

"This umbrella really only covers my head." Natalie squinted at the umbrella, listening to the rain pound on the black canvas.

"But you have a rain coat, darling. You don't need it to cover anything else."

"Well, my blue jeans are really wet..."

"They'll get dry again. At least your feet are covered by your rain boots."

"But I'd really like an umbrella that covers *all* of me."

Quincy stopped in her tracks. She turned around and stared at Natalie. On Quincy's face, a wounded expression waged war with the angry realization that they were not going to Nickel's yet.

"*Fine*, Natalie. We'll go back and get a different umbrella. I was trying to be a good friend and give you a nice gift, but if you're determined to return this one—"

"It's not that, it's just—"

"—and get that plain, normal, red umbrella, same as you always get, then fine! We'll get that one!"

"Quincy, I just—"

"Say no more, darling. Come on."

*

A few minutes after that exchange, Natalie was bouncing excitedly along the sidewalk underneath a new red umbrella that covered her entire body. She felt happy and dry. Beside her, Quincy was more subdued.

"Want to stop by Nickel's?" Natalie asked.

"No, I'm fine. We can just go back to the abbey." Quincy stared determinedly ahead as she rounded a corner and headed down Hurl Street.

"I thought you wanted to go to Nickel's."

"No. I'm fine, Natalie. I don't need anything. I just want to go home and rest."

"Okay. You're not upset, are you?"

"No, Natalie. I am not upset."

"Okay. That's good."

Natalie and Quincy turned left from Hurl Street and walked down the long alley that ran under Natalie's window.

Natalie stopped to look at a small wooden signpost. "Oh! Resurgam Lane!"

Quincy raised an eyebrow at the sign. "What about it?"

"Oh, nothing. I was just reading in my journal that there's a famous book series about it: *Murder on Resurgam Lane*."

"Yes. It's written by Oswald Canteloupes. It's the one about the inspector in Radcliffe. A very popular series."

"That's fascinating." Natalie stared at the sign. "Wait!" She clasped her hands in front of her face, and then she began waving them excitedly. "Regina!"

Quincy hesitated. "What?"

"Regina!"

"What about her?"

"Regina loves *Murder on Resurgam Lane*."

"Oh, yeah." Quincy looked very somber. "She did."

"Where is Regina?" Natalie bounced back and forth on the balls of her feet. "Is she in Radcliffe? She should be at the abbey, right?" She looked up at the abbey walls, suddenly very excited.

"Not anymore. She lives south of High Street on Denver's Way."

"Well, let's go see her!"

"Do you really want to?" Quincy glanced at the sky. "It's still raining."

"I know! That's why we have umbrellas!"

"But...don't you have to get back to your room?"
"To do what? Read? I can read later. I want to see Regina!"
"Oh...all right." Quincy swallowed. "If you insist."

CHAPTER 16:
FORGOTTEN FRIENDS

Natalie and Quincy walked across Resurgam Square, sloshing through puddles on the cobblestones. As rain poured off their umbrellas, the girls passed little shops and negotiated the crowded streets of Radcliffe. They reached the busy intersection of High Street and Denver's Way, dodging the red double-decker buses when they crossed the street.

The girls came to a series of houses that reminded Natalie of the ones in Calypso. They could only be distinguished by the different colors of paint. Pastels seemed to be very popular: blue, teal, green, yellow, pink, burgundy—and then, to Natalie's great surprise, plaid.

Quincy stopped at a huge wooden gate with a decorative circle cut into the top. She opened the door for Natalie, who noticed that the sylph had grown more somber the farther they walked down Denver's Way. Quincy led them into a courtyard, and they passed a few doorways until they reached number nine. She ascended a short staircase and knocked on the door with a brass knocker shaped like a lion's head.

There was no answer. Quincy knocked one more time. Then she turned on her heel and walked back down the steps.

"I guess no one's there."

"Quincy!" Natalie clicked her tongue. "You give up so quickly." She walked past the sylph and knocked more strongly on the door—once, twice, three times.

On the third knock, the door opened with a heavy creak. It was dark inside. A short, wizened old elf with round spectacles peeked around the door. Pointed ears poked out from beneath her gray hair. She squinted up at Natalie.

"Can I help you young ladies?"

Natalie hesitated. "Er, is this the right place?"

"I don't know." The elf drew a white shawl around her shoulders. "What have you come for?"

"We're here to visit Regina," Natalie said. Out of the corner of her eye, she saw Quincy cringe.

"Oh." The elf raised her thin eyebrows in surprise. "Well, that's very nice of you. Come on in."

The lady ushered them inside and closed the door. Natalie and Quincy folded their umbrellas. Quincy left her umbrella by the door, but Natalie held onto hers. The sylph glanced reproachfully at Natalie's umbrella, which dripped onto the red tile floor.

Natalie ignored the look. She would wait until the elf *told* her to leave her umbrella by the door. And then she would, in all likelihood, invent an excuse to keep it with her.

But the elf paid no attention to either of their umbrellas. She had ambled through the dark hallway and out of sight.

"Regina, we have visitors," she said softly.

There was no answer—at least none that Natalie heard. The elf returned to the hallway and gestured for them to enter the living room. "In here. I'm Malinda, by the way."

"I remember you. I saw you a few months ago. My name is Quincy."

"Oh, yes. The fairy."

"Sylph, actually."

"Of course. And you are...?"

"Natalie Bliss."

"Welcome, Quincy and Natalie. Come on in."

She led them into a sitting room lit by a fireplace. A pale-skinned girl sat in a rocking chair, staring at the flames. She had a plain white nightgown. Black hair fell in curtains over her face.

Malinda indicated the girls. "Regina, you have visitors."

Natalie waved hesitantly.

Regina turned her wide, blue eyes toward Quincy and Natalie. Her face betrayed no recognition. She rose to her feet slowly, and Malinda rushed forward to help her.

"Oh, dear, you don't need to get up."

Regina's back was hunched and her shoulders were tense.

Malinda nodded at the girls. "Regina, do you remember Natalie and Quincy?"

Regina stared at the girls for a long moment. She tilted her head but said nothing. Then she squeezed Malinda's hand, and the old elf helped her back into her chair.

Natalie blinked rapidly and wiped something from the corner of her eye. A hot feeling of anxiety burned in her chest. She didn't remember Regina like this.

Malinda put a crocheted blanket over Regina's lap. Natalie heard the girl whisper something under her breath.

"People are outside the window. They're trying to come in."

Malinda looked at the window opposite the rocking chair. Long green curtains were drawn over it. She opened them to reveal a sealed window. It was still raining. She checked the locks to make sure that it was closed.

"There's no one outside, darling. And the window is closed."

Regina shook her head slowly. "Someone has been trying to get in."

Malinda sighed. "There's no one out there, Regina. Just rest."

Regina fidgeted with her blanket for a moment. Then she gazed into the fire once more.

Malinda glanced at Natalie and Quincy.

"I'm sorry about that. Have a seat, please." She pointed to a couch by the rocking chair and settled herself into a chair opposite the couch. "So, how do you know Regina?"

Quincy sat down and crossed her legs. "Resurgam Abbey."

Natalie nodded silently. She felt too stunned to say anything.

"Oh, that's right," Malinda continued. "You told me before. You are Phoenix Guardians?"

"Yes, ma'am. Or, Natalie is. But I live there too."

"Ah..." Malinda nodded. She looked sadly at Regina. "Regina was a Phoenix Guardian once. Isn't that right, Regina?"

Regina played with a strand of black hair.

Malinda and the girls sat silently for a minute, waiting for an answer that didn't come.

"Are you hungry, Regina? It's time for your lunch." The elf got up and walked past the fireplace into the kitchen.

Natalie looked at Quincy, who met her gaze with a sad expression, as if to say, *I tried to warn you.*

Malinda came out a moment later with a tray of soup and a mug of something hot. She set the tray on a table by Regina's chair.

"Lunch time."

Regina shook her head.

"Come on, Regina."

The girl glanced at Natalie out of the corner of her eye. She leaned close to Malinda and whispered loudly, "I don't want to."

"But you're hungry, aren't you?"

"I don't want to eat with them watching me."

Malinda sighed and looked helplessly at the girls.

111

"Not them," Regina hissed. "The ones outside."

"There's no one outside."

Regina shook her head. "You didn't lock it." She looked at Natalie and held a finger to her lips. "Shh."

"What?" Natalie blinked.

Regina shook her head again.

Malinda made an irritated noise in her throat. She stood. "Regina, do you want your food now?"

The girl shook her head and drew her blanket tighter around herself.

"Do you want it later?"

When Regina didn't respond, Malinda sighed and took the tray back into the kitchen. Regina watched the elf disappear around the corner. Then the girl beckoned Natalie to come close.

Natalie knelt beside the rocking chair. "Yes?"

Regina shot furtive glances at the kitchen. "She never feeds me."

"Malinda?"

"Never."

Natalie bit her lip, fighting back tears. She looked for a hint of understanding in Regina's eyes. She saw confusion.

"But she just brought some food out for you."

"It's not for me. She never brings me food. And she leaves the window unlocked so they can come in and watch me." She grabbed Natalie's hand. Tears glistened at the corner of Regina's eyes. "I'm so hungry. And I don't like it when they watch me."

"There's no one out there." Natalie massaged Regina's hand gently. "And Malinda has food for you."

Regina shook her head and stared into her lap, tears sliding down her nose.

"Want me to get the food for you?" Natalie asked. "I think there was soup."

"You don't believe me!" Regina screamed at Natalie. "You don't believe me!"

She stood and flailed her blanket out like a whip. It burst into a sheet of flame. Natalie tumbled backward as the flaming blanket fell to the floor. Quincy screamed. Something crashed in the kitchen.

Regina's eyes widened in terror. She grabbed the blanket and shook it, trying to put the fire out. Her hands wrenched back from the pain. She fell into her rocking chair with the fiery blanket on top of her.

"Regina!" Malinda stumbled into the living room and shrieked at the sight. "Oh *gods*! What have you done?"

Natalie stumbled to her feet and pointed her umbrella at Regina, who was screaming underneath the burning sheet. The fire flared to greater intensity, licking the ceiling.

"Natalie!" Quincy screamed.

Malinda clutched her head in horror. "What are you doing?"

"No—that's not what I meant to do!" Natalie yelled over the shrieks and the crackling heat.

Natalie closed her eyes in concentration and squeezed her umbrella.

Consume the heat. Draw it in.

There was a great rushing noise, and the flames funneled into her umbrella.

She opened her eyes. The handle was warming up underneath her fingers. She twisted the umbrella, siphoning the fire into the tip until the flames were extinguished.

The damaged rocking chair collapsed to the tile floor under Regina, who was sobbing in her burnt nightgown. Natalie and Malinda knelt beside her. Quincy stood behind them, hands covering her mouth.

Natalie hugged Regina around the girl's frail, trembling shoulders. She raised her umbrella tip to Regina's ashen arms.

"What are you doing now, girl?" Malinda asked sharply.

Natalie was trembling too. "Just healing the burns, ma'am."

She cleared her throat—now was not the time to cry.

"I'll take care of her," Malinda said firmly.

Natalie flinched. Perhaps the elf thought she had come off too harshly, because she gave Natalie's arm a quick pat. But the message was still clear. The red-haired girl removed her umbrella and scooted back.

Malinda began to massage Regina's shoulders and back. The pale girl's breathing slowed to a steady rhythm, and she closed her eyes. The elf rubbed Regina's earlobes and stroked the back of her neck. Soon, Regina's blackened skin had healed to a dark red color, and the lesser-burned areas adopted a ruddy complexion.

In a few minutes, the girl was fast asleep in Malinda's arms.

She nodded to the hallway. "Help me take her to bed."

The three of them carried Regina, who was frightfully light, into the main hallway and through another before entering a small bedroom. A bed, a dresser, and a standing closet occupied the simple room. They laid Regina on the green bedspread. She looked peaceful.

"She'll be better in a few days," Malinda said, before ushering them into the hallway.

They stood in awkward silence for a minute, and the girls understood it was time to leave. The elf walked them to the front door.

Quincy and Natalie paused at the threshold to open their umbrellas before venturing into the rain.

Malinda grabbed Natalie's hand as the girl walked out.

"Thank you for your quick thinking. I'm sorry I panicked. Regina could have been hurt very badly if you hadn't put out the fire."

Natalie nodded and wiped her eyes.

Malinda gave a curt nod and closed the door.

The girls went out of the courtyard and through the tall door with the circular cut. They walked along Denver's Way in silence.

Quincy was the first to speak. "That was terrifying. I was so scared."

"I was scared too."

"You almost made the fire—you—"

Natalie's jaw stiffened. "It was a mistake. I'm not used to this umbrella yet."

"But the flames! If you hadn't fixed—" Quincy spoke fast and waved her hand animatedly.

"But I did fix it!" Natalie snapped. "I stopped the fire, okay? She's going to be all right!"

Quincy bit her lip and nodded.

Natalie's breathing was short and frustrated. "I have more control than you think. I just need time to get familiar with the umbrella. That's all."

Quincy nodded again. She wiped the tears sliding down her face.

Natalie sighed. They started walking, and after a few minutes she asked the question that had been weighing on her mind.

"What happened to Regina?"

"I don't know all of the details." Quincy sniffed. "Abbess Persephone said that Regina died on a mission."

"But lots of phoenixes die on missions. I just died on a mission, and I'm not like Regina."

"You still have your journal. And that's been your Anchor for a long time."

"Yes—of course it has."

"Well, the abbess said that Regina lost her Anchor before she died. She had to store her ashes in a new Anchor—one that didn't have her memories. When she died, she lost herself." Quincy took a shuddering breath. "She has no connection to her past lives."

Natalie clapped a hand over her mouth. "She lost her memories?"

"Her new Anchor didn't have any of her identity in it. It was just an object to store her ashes and save her from perishing."

A shiver ran down Natalie's spine. "Perishing?"

"Persephone said you can still resurrect without your memories, but if your ashes are scattered and lost, there is no resurrection. You perish."

Natalie bit her lip. "But Regina is still alive..." She was starting to cry again.

"Of course she is. Her ashes were preserved in a new Anchor," Quincy said softly. "She's just not herself anymore."

"And never will be again." Natalie blinked rapidly, trying to see through a film of tears and the sheets of rain beyond.

"I think something else must have happened to Regina too." Quincy pulled out a handkerchief and wiped her eyes. "Something that damaged Regina even after she resurrected. I've visited her a lot. She never remembers me. I don't know if she can remember at all anymore."

Natalie stopped and stared at the puddles beneath her feet. Her head felt weighed down with sorrow.

Quincy put her hand on Natalie's shoulder to give her a hug. "I'm sorry."

But Natalie pulled away from her grasp. She hurried down the sidewalk and into the street—almost getting hit by a double-decker bus.

"Natalie! Where are you going?" Quincy yelled.

Natalie called back over her shoulder, her voice shaky. "I need some time alone!"

"Are you sure you don't want me to come with you?"

"I'm sure!"

CHAPTER 17:
VOICES IN THE GRAVEYARD

Enormous wheels rolled a few feet from Natalie's face. A sharp horn blast made her jump.

She stepped away from the curb and watched the cars, chariots, wagons, and double-decker buses go by from a safe distance.

Natalie had walked for a long time without knowing where she was going. She had a vague sense that it was north. Confronted by heavy traffic, she debated whether to go on or try to find her way back.

She decided to go around the traffic circle before choosing a street that took her further north.

Heavy branches covered Natalie and protected her from the thinning rain. The street went through a residential area with brick houses and well-kept gardens. Beautiful sprays of roses leaned over wooden fences. Water dripped from the pink and red petals.

Farther down the street, the neighborhood gave way to a vast graveyard. Natalie entered through a small wooden gate and began wandering through the aisles of tombstones.

There was a small white mausoleum at the center of the graveyard. A large house stood at the main entrance. Natalie walked through a long stretch of graves to a gravel road. She meandered along the path for a while, kicking loose stones.

When the rain stopped, she sat underneath a tree in a row of gravestones. She picked at the wet grass and flicked the broken blades into the air.

As she tore tufts of grass from the ground, she began to remember times she had spent with Regina—riding on the train, reading books in the library, eating chocolate chip cookies, visiting the river. Once, Regina had almost been bitten by a duck because she tried to pet it.

Her laugh had been so beautiful. She loved to sing.

But now Regina was empty. She had lost her self...all because she had died without her Anchor.

117

A terrible shiver ran down Natalie's spine. That would have been her fate at Mithris if Serena hadn't kept her journal. That was why relationships and connection were so important. They were what made life worth living, and they were the tethers that tied a phoenix to life.

Natalie picked up a stone and tossed it down the aisle of graves. Death and perishing were always risks when you went on a mission. But the Phoenix Guardians knew the risks. They also knew how powerful they were, and they were more than a match for most enemies. Natalie had been particularly concerned about the Mithris mission because of her watch. But she knew that she would find someone in time.

At least, she had *hoped* she would find someone in time. And she had.

But if my Anchor doesn't hold my memories, my identity dies with me. And if I don't find someone who can preserve my Anchor and keep my ashes safe...

Natalie felt a lump in her throat.

...I perish.

She shuddered.

Mortals never had to worry about such things. They lived once and died once. They had their problems, namely the brevity of their existence. But to live across the ages was its own burden. You had to fight to maintain your self-identity. It was tragic to live countless lives with loved ones and then, suddenly, forget who they were. It was heartbreaking to span countless ages while the brief lives of mortals flickered like candles through the long night of your undying fire.

Natalie took a deep breath and glanced at the gravestone she had sat next to, wondering what kind of life this mortal soul had led. She read the name—

"No! It can't be!"

She dropped to her knees, brushing aside the weeds that had grown across the name:

M RIAN E E GE

Natalie pulled off a tangled green clump to reveal the entire name. She covered her mouth and fell back.

It was Marianne Edge.

Natalie screamed. Marianne was her friend—the one she had been reading about in her journal when Florentina walked into her room. Natalie stretched a hand toward the tombstone.

"How?"

She had planned to see Marianne this afternoon. She would have asked Quincy to go with her...and Quincy would have been forced to deliver more bad news.

"Oh gods!" Natalie cried. "When?"

She looked at the date—and gasped.

Marianne had died over seventy years ago.

Natalie ran a hand through her hair, feeling hot with confusion. Her breathing was short and quick.

Why didn't she know that Marianne was dead? Had Natalie misread the entry in her journal? Was it simply undated?

She looked inside her raincoat to find her journal, but it wasn't there. She had left it in her room.

Natalie pressed her hands against the marker, as if she could feel an echo of Marianne through the cold stone.

Marianne had been dead before Natalie went to Mithris—long before. Natalie had cried these tears before. And now she had to live the grief again?

A deep, incoherent scream tore from Natalie's throat. She snatched her umbrella from the damp grass and swung wildly into the air. A spurt of flame escaped from the tip. It blossomed into a fireball before bursting through the canopy of branches. The misfire sailed high into the air before exploding like a firework.

Limbs crackled and groaned as flames spread through the tree before Natalie's horrified eyes. Half-blinded by her tears, she stumbled against a tombstone behind her.

"Goodness! You're going to put that out, aren't you?"

Natalie did a double-take at the unfamiliar voice in her head—but she had more important things to worry about.

She pointed her umbrella at the tree.

FOOMP!

The flames circled around the point Natalie was aiming at. The umbrella siphoned the fire, which funneled into the tip like a burning whirlpool. In a few moments, it was all over.

Charred leaves floated to the ground. Natalie collapsed to the damp grass in exhaustion. It was the second time in a day that she had to put out a fire. Once had been too many.

"That was close. It wouldn't have happened if you had controlled your temper, but I must credit your recovery."

Natalie hiccupped. "Who's there?"

"Behind you, young lady."

Natalie turned around to see the tombstone she had fallen against. The gravestone read, OSWALD CANTELOUPES.

"You're the author! Oswald Canteloupes!"

"Can-te-LO-pez, actually. Not the fruit."

Natalie blinked. "But you're dead!"

"Well spotted. And your name is...?"

"Natalie Bliss."

"Pleased to meet you, Miss Bliss. I would kiss your hand, but my lips have decayed."

"Oh. I see."

"For your sake, I sincerely hope you do not. What remains of my lips is not a pleasant sight."

Natalie pursed her own lips self-consciously.

"Now, what is the fuss all about? Why are you setting the trees on fire?"

"I'm really sorry about that." Natalie waved at the tree. "But I'm having a...a rough time right now."

"I can see that. But what's—"

"How do you *see* anything?"

There was a long pause.

"The afterlife is a very complicated place. I don't presume to understand it."

Natalie glanced at Marianne's grave. "Do the other tombstones talk?"

"Eh, most of them do not. I am, of course, an author, so my wisdom and writings survive me. Therefore, it makes sense that I can speak beyond the grave."

"It does?"

There was another pause.

"Do you have a more plausible explanation?"

Natalie shrugged.

"Exactly. Now, what's troubling you?"

"My friends are dying or dead."

"I can relate. Particularly to the 'dead' category. I am sorry. That, as they say, is 'life,' although 'they' missed the fact that death is the primary problem here."

Wind blew through the wet grass and shook the ashen boughs above Natalie. She gave the tree an apologetic pat on the bark.

"Aren't you a very young girl to be surrounded by so much death? Are these elderly relatives who are passing away?"

Natalie kicked at a charred leaf. "I'm a phoenix."

"Ah. I see...that would do it."

The wind blew stronger, and Natalie pulled her jacket close. Quincy would be wondering where she was.

"What are you going to do now?"

Natalie looked at Oswald's grave. "About what?"

"Your friends dying."

"There's not much I can do, is there? Except remember them."

"Well, remembering them is certainly important. But don't you have friends left?"

"I do."

"And they sympathize with you?"

"They do...sort of. But mostly they don't understand."

"Even your phoenix friends?"

"I guess they might."

"Perhaps they will."

"Maybe." Natalie blinked as a leaf brushed against her cheek. "I should be heading home now."

"Very well. Go home to your friends and treasure the time you have with them. You have a lot to live for."

"How do you know that?"

"Well, let's just think about this for a minute, shall we? You are a phoenix, you are young, and you are healthy. You strike me as a bright, thoughtful girl, and—provided you keep your temper in check—I think you'll do all right. But the main reason I say you have much to live for is that you are alive. That means you have hope. The dead have no hope, no worries, and no opportunities. Hope is for the living. You can still influence the world for good."

Natalie fastened the top button on her raincoat. "A sermon from beyond the grave?"

"Don't ignore wisdom when you hear it."

"I'm not ignoring you." Natalie stood. "I understand what you're saying."

"Maybe not, but at least you heard what I said. Now run along and enjoy yourself."

Natalie turned to leave.

"Before you go, Miss Bliss, could you wipe some of this foliage off my tombstone?"

"Sure." She cuffed her jacket sleeve and wiped the grass and twigs off the stone.

"Thank you. Cleanliness is next to godliness."

"Goodbye, Mr. Canteloupes."

"Can-te-LO-pez."

"Sorry, Canteloupes," Natalie pronounced carefully.

121

"Thank you. Goodbye, Miss Bliss. Come by and see me again sometime. I'm not going anywhere."

*

Back at the abbey, an exhausted Natalie Bliss staggered into Staircase V. She thumped up wooden steps and ascended the purple, carpeted, spiral staircase, wondering if Florentina had finished the last details of her immaculate cleaning session.

Natalie entered the bathroom and opened her umbrella to let it dry in the tub. Then she went into the living room to make a new entry in her journal.

It had been an emotional day.

She needed time alone to write, and read, and think. Maybe she could find something in her journal that would trigger Regina's memory.

Natalie froze. Her journal wasn't on the table.

In its place was a piece of paper. A horrible feeling churned in Natalie's stomach. She picked up the paper hesitantly. On it was a short note, written in a large, tidy script.

> DEAR MISS BLISS,
> I AM SORRY THAT THE ABBESS PERSEPHONE DOUBTS YOUR ABILITIES. I DO NOT. I HOPE THAT YOU HAVE BOUGHT A GOOD UMBRELLA. YOU WILL NEED IT. I HAVE GONE TO MY BROTHERS AND SISTERS. I KNOW THEY ARE WAITING FOR ME. MY BROTHER WRATH WILL LEAD ME TO THEM. YOU WILL DISCOVER THAT I WAS RIGHT.
> YOUR PEOPLE ARE IMPORTANT TO YOU. MY PEOPLE ARE IMPORTANT TO ME. YOU UNDERSTAND ME. I DID NOT WANT TO HURT YOUR FEELINGS, BUT I KNEW YOU WOULD NOT DISOBEY ABBESS PERSEPHONE BY COMING WITH ME. NOW I HOPE YOU WILL COME AFTER ME.

Natalie clutched her forehead as she read the last line.

> I HAVE YOUR JOURNAL. TAKE THE TRAIN TO ALBAKIRK. BRING YOUR UMBRELLA AND SOMEONE YOU TRUST. THERE IS DANGER AHEAD. BUT SOME THINGS ARE WORTH FIGHTING FOR.
> YOU ARE A BRAVE GIRL AND A KIND GIRL, MISS BLISS. I HOPE YOU WILL FORGIVE ME FOR STEALING YOUR JOURNAL. BUT THE WORLD WILL NOT FORGIVE US IF WE DO NOT STOP THE ENEMY

FROM FORCING MY BROTHER WRATH TO ATTACK CALYPSO. HE
MUST BE SAVED. THE CITY MUST BE PROTECTED.
    YOU CAN HELP. YOU MUST.

    I AM CLAY OF YOUR CLAY,
    FLORENTINA

Natalie couldn't breathe. Her knees felt weak. She needed to
sit down...to take a moment and process all of this.
    Instead, she fainted.

CHAPTER 18:
FOLLOWING FLORENTINA

Quincy paced back and forth in Natalie's room. "I can't believe Florentina would just run off like that!"

Natalie sat on the ground, hands folded, a blank expression on her face.

"She stole my journal." Natalie said, picking at the carpet with her fingernail.

Quincy threw her arms up in the air. "She's just as unstable as Persephone said she was!"

"She tricked me."

"I can't imagine what she was thinking—running away like that. She could get lost."

"We need to get my journal back."

"She could be stolen!" Quincy clapped a hand over her mouth.

Natalie looked up in alarm. "Stolen?"

Quincy wrung her hands nervously. "Most people view golems as property."

"Then we have to go now!" Natalie sat up. "We could lose my journal forever!"

Quincy held up a hand. "We need to tell Abbess Persephone first."

"Quincy, we can't waste any time! We need to go now!"

"We can afford five minutes to tell Abbess Persephone!"

"But what if she doesn't let us go after her?" Natalie ran into the bathroom to get her umbrella, which she had left in the tub to dry.

"Then Persephone will send someone who's capable of bringing her back. The abbess cares about Florentina too, you know. That's why she brought her to Resurgam Abbey."

"Quincy." Natalie shook her umbrella and closed it. "I need to get my journal."

"I know your journal is important," Quincy said hesitantly, "but don't you need to think about Florentina too?"

"I need to think about *me*!" Natalie shook her umbrella at Quincy. "If I lose my journal, I'll perish, remember? All of my memories will be lost forever!"

Quincy bit her lip.

"Don't you understand? If I lose my journal, everything that makes me who I am will be gone!"

"I understand, Natalie. We'll get your journal back. Florentina can't have gone far." Quincy crossed her arms. "But you know, some people live *once*, and they die *once*, and that's it. They don't get a chance to come back and work out who they were. They're just dead."

"And some people have to live for eternity like broken shells!" Natalie's voice rose to a scream, and Quincy stepped back. "Didn't you see Regina? She was my friend, and now she's lost her self! She might as well be dead!"

"Don't you dare say that!" Quincy pointed a finger at Natalie. "You don't know what the future holds for her! How dare you judge whether someone should live or die just because they're— just because they're not completely there!" Quincy's wings twitched animatedly. "And she was my friend too, remember? She still is!"

Quincy glared at Natalie, who glared back.

The sylph sighed. "Besides, Natalie, what happened to Regina isn't going to happen to you. We'll get your journal back—"

"You don't know that! How can you know that?" Natalie gestured wildly. "And by the way, don't talk to me about people who only live once! Don't you understand that I've known hundreds and thousands of people who are gone forever? Whose names mean the world to me? People who I always outlive because I'm a phoenix? People like Marianne? I didn't even remember that she was dead, and I had to lose her all over again! My friends are here for a moment—and then they're gone! And I'm left alone!"

Quincy flinched. "You're not alone, Natalie."

"I'm not alone as long as I have their memories! They're still alive in the journal."

Quincy shook her head and sighed. "You can't keep them alive."

"I can try!" Natalie sat down on the window bench and buried her face in her hands. She closed her eyes and sat there, taking deep breaths.

The hot emotion flowing through her veins began to cool. She felt a headache coming on.

Extra weight on the cushion informed Natalie that Quincy had sat down next to her, but Natalie didn't open her eyes.

There was a knock at the door. Neither girl moved to answer it.

"Are you okay, Natalie?"

It was London.

"I'm fine!" Natalie tried to yell, but her voice cracked.

There was a pause, and then London spoke again, this time more hesitantly.

"Oh. Okay. It's just that I heard yelling. Is anyone else with you?"

Natalie was about to say, "No," but Quincy interrupted.

"Yes, London. I'm here."

"Oh, Quincy! Hi. That's good that you're here too."

Natalie glowered at the door. "Is it?"

"Yeah, it is. Can I come in?"

"No."

"Yes, I'll let you in." Quincy got up and opened the door.

The brown-haired boy walked in cautiously, head lowered and shoulders hunched, even though he was in no danger of hitting the ceiling. His long, skinny arms were stuck firmly in his jean pockets. He must have been embarrassed to step inside a girl's room.

His eyes found Natalie on the bench. He tilted his head in concern.

"You don't look like you're okay, Natalie. Are you crying?"

Natalie sniffed and wiped her red eyes. "No. I'm not crying."

"Oh. It looks like you're crying. And I heard shouting. Are you upset?"

"No."

"Yes, she is. And she was crying." Quincy stroked her blonde hair thoughtfully. "Actually, London, go back outside."

"What? But you just—"

"I know, darling, but give us a minute, okay?" Quincy shunted London outside the room and closed the door behind him.

She turned to face Natalie.

"Look, I'm really sorry."

Natalie wiped her eyes. "For letting him in? Or for what you said?"

"For yelling at you." Quincy sat next to her. "And for being insensitive about your journal. I know it's very important to get it back. And we will. I was just thinking about Florentina, and I thought you were being selfish."

Natalie frowned. "And you're sorry for thinking that I'm selfish?"

"I'm sorry that what you said made me think you were selfish."

Natalie sniffed and wiped her nose with the back of her hand. "That still doesn't sound like a complete apology."

"Wiping your nose with your hand isn't ladylike." Quincy handed Natalie a tissue. "Do I need to give a complete apology?"

"Well—yes!" Natalie blew her nose.

"Can I come in now?" London asked from behind the door.

"*NO!*" Quincy and Natalie shouted together.

"Sorry," London mumbled.

"Look, I'm sorry, okay? Totally sorry." Quincy put her hand on Natalie's knee. "But you need to remember that you're not alone."

Natalie stared at her feet and nodded.

"Don't forget that I'm here for you. Appreciate the people you're with."

Natalie grasped Quincy's hand. "I appreciate you."

"I know." Quincy smiled. She brought her arm over Natalie's shoulders, and the red-haired girl responded with a hug.

"Now we need to get Florentina and your journal back."

"Yeah." Natalie swallowed. "And I'm sorry too."

"It's all right."

The girls sat on the bench for a quiet minute.

London interrupted the silence. "Can I come in now?"

"No. We're coming out." Quincy let Natalie go, and they rose from the bench. "We need to see Persephone."

*

Quincy knocked on Abbess Persephone's door for the fourth time.

"She's not there." Natalie sighed.

Quincy kicked the door. "What a terrible time to go out. Where is she, book-shopping? She has plenty of books. And the gods know she isn't going to buy a new dress." She stuck out her tongue in disgust. "That hasn't happened in ages."

"I guess we'll just have to go without telling her." Natalie balanced a foot over the stairs, showing her eagerness to leave.

"Go where?" London asked.

Quincy arched an eyebrow at Natalie. "You just want to go because you're not supposed to."

"I just want to bring back Florentina and my journal. And maybe find out if there's a golem army."

Quincy crossed her arms. "Abbess Persephone said there wasn't a golem army."

"The abbess might have been wrong about that." Natalie twirled her umbrella. "And she might be wrong about other things."

"Like you being ready to fight?"

"Maybe."

"Fighting? Golem army?" London threw his hands up in the air. "I don't understand what's going on!"

"Nobody said you needed to." Natalie narrowed her eyes at London. The boy flinched at her tone.

Quincy glanced at Natalie and mouthed, "*Vicious.*"

Natalie almost rolled her eyes, but then she stopped. "I'm sorry, London." She pressed her tongue against her cheek. "I shouldn't have said that."

London waved her away. "No, it's not a problem, I shouldn't have interfered." He took a step toward the stairs. "I'll go back to my room—"

"No, London." Natalie sighed in exasperation. "It *is* a problem that I was being rude, and you don't have to leave. In fact..." She bit her lip. "You can come along."

A huge smile broke across Quincy's face before she could do anything about it. She tried to cover it with her hand, but the grin was too wide. She looked meaningfully between Natalie and London.

A smile trembled at the corners of London's mouth.

"Really? Come along with you? Sure—absolutely! But...where are we going?"

"Albakirk."

"Why?"

"Because Florentina ran away with my journal and she's looking for the Golem Army of Calypso."

London frowned. "Is the army in Albakirk?"

"I don't know." Natalie shrugged. "That's just where Florentina told me to go."

"London, I'm impressed that you question the army's location more than its existence," Quincy said.

"Oh, it's a myth by all accounts," London said. "But I'm surprised that Florentina would send us to Albakirk."

"Where else would she send us?" Quincy asked.

London shrugged. "Calypso."

"Because...?"

"It's the Golem Army of Calypso."

Quincy blushed. "Oh. Right."

"Albakirk is a start at any rate." Natalie turned and walked down the stairs.

London watched Quincy and Natalie leave. "So you're going right now?"

"Yes." Natalie had already disappeared around the corner.

"But we don't know how long we'll be gone," London protested. "And it might be dangerous."

"*Will* be dangerous," Natalie corrected him, her voice echoing up the stairwell.

"So we need to be prepared!"

"I am. I have my umbrella and we'll get some food before we go."

"But—"

Quincy stuck her head around the corner. "London! Are you coming or not?"

She nodded knowingly in the direction that Natalie had gone.

London hesitated for a moment at the top of the stairs, and then he sighed.

"I'll grab my jacket."

CHAPTER 19:
VARIABLE TRAIN TRAVEL

Natalie looked at the ticket prices board in the Radcliffe Train Station. One column was labeled, "Normal Train," and the other was labeled, "Variable Train." The Variable tickets were half as expensive as the Normal ones.

"Which train is faster?" Natalie asked the bald, bespectacled gnome clerk behind the small arched window.

The clerk pointed at the column to the right. "Variable can be much faster."

"Really? But it's half as much."

"That's right." The clerk smiled, enlarging a double chin. "It's a special deal. Variable Trains can be very fast."

"That's excellent," Natalie said. "Then I'll take three tickets to Albakirk by Variable Train."

"Coming right up." The clerk pushed his glasses up his nose and spun around on his swivel chair. He punched some keys on an boxed contraption against the wall.

A tiny voice squeaked, "Three Chancers for Albakirk!"

The tickets came out from a bottom slot.

"Here you go." The clerk placed the tickets under the glass as his spectacles slid down his nose again.

"Thank you very much." Natalie put the tickets in her pocket. "We have to get to Albakirk very quickly, so the Variable Train will be a huge help."

The clerk chuckled. "Could be, could be. Good luck, miss."

"Thanks."

Natalie walked back to the wooden bench where Quincy was eyeing her warily.

"What kind of tickets did you get? He didn't talk you into riding Variable, did he?"

"What do you mean, 'talk me into'?" Natalie asked indignantly. "And as a matter of fact, I did buy Variable Train tickets."

Quincy sighed. "Oh, Natalie."

"What? They're fine!" Natalie showed the orange tickets to Quincy. "To Albakirk, see? That's where we're going! And the clerk said that the Variable Train is faster than the Normal Train."

"He probably said the Variable Train *can* be faster."

Natalie paused.

Quincy narrowed her eyes. "Didn't he?"

"He might have." Natalie held a finger to her lip in thought. "But that's basically the same thing, right?"

"No, Natalie, it's not the same. The railroad is required by law to say that Variable Train Travel *can* go faster. It can also be much, much slower. But you said that you wanted to order the tickets, so we'll live with the consequences."

Quincy started toward the platforms. A few heads turned to follow as she walked past, her blonde hair flowing and wings fluttering.

"What do you mean 'live with the consequences'?" Natalie sputtered. "I wasn't trying to mess everything up. I just wanted to order the tickets by myself. I need to relearn how do to simple things like this."

"I didn't say you were messing everything up. I just thought you could have used some help." Quincy flashed a smile at an elf in a tracksuit. The elf winked. Her smile widened, and then she returned her attention to Natalie. "You know, I'm noticing a stubborn streak in you. You're acting like you don't need people to help you."

"That's not true, and I'm not stubborn." Natalie sniffed. She glared at the elf in the tracksuit, unfazed and unbothered by the fact that no athletic males had winked at *her*. "Where's London, by the way?"

"I sent him to get food while you were in line." Quincy stopped by a round information desk. She leaned against the side and examined her nails. "There's a little shop over there. He should be out any moment."

On cue, London emerged from the train store with a big brown paper bag.

"I got us some sandwiches. They were out of everything but salmon and chili and something called convocation chicken."

"Convocation?" Natalie asked. "Shouldn't that be 'coronation'?"

"Er..." London opened the bag and examined the triangular sandwich box. "No, it says 'convocation.' It's green," he added helpfully, as the trio got in line for the platform.

132

"Sounds interesting," Natalie said, utilizing the vague, dismissive power of the word *interesting*. "I'll take the salmon."

"And chili?" London showed his ticket to a small gray imp in a kiosk. The blue-eyed, scaly creature checked the ticket and punched a button to swing the gate open.

"Just the salmon." Natalie answered, giving the imp her ticket.

"It comes with chili." London sounded apologetic.

"Oh."

"But I did get that strawberry drink you like." London handed Natalie a small milk bottle. "The 'Yeehaw.' Do you remember them?"

"Oh, thank you!" Natalie examined the label. "They're delicious! Quincy reminded me about them when she picked me up at the trolley station." She gave London a quizzical look. "How did you know that I liked them?"

London blushed, pleased with her attention. "I just remember you saying that you liked them one time when we—uh..." He cleared his throat and looked away. "One time when we ate food."

"Oh. Well, thanks."

London stood under the sign for Platform One, but Quincy called him away.

"No, London. We're over on Platform Four."

London made a face. "Variable?"

"What's the big deal about Variable?" Natalie glared at London—but she was standing behind him, so he missed the look.

"It's totally unreliable. You never know when you'll get anywhere." London sighed. "Quincy, why did you get Variable? Is it because they're cheaper? I could have bought the tickets."

"I didn't *order* the tickets." Quincy glanced meaningfully at Natalie.

"Oh!" London's face glowed red with embarrassment. Natalie's face was red too, but for a different reason.

London looked around desperately for a way of escape. He found one in the arrivals and departures board.

"Look at that! The train leaves in six minutes. We better get on board!"

*

Natalie soon discovered why there was a Big Deal about Variable Train Travel.

She sat in a window seat next to Quincy. At the front of the car, the conductor gave an estimate for when they would arrive in Albakirk.

"Ladies and gentlemen, thank you for choosing to travel with us today. We should arrive at Albakirk in seven hours."

The horn sounded, and the train started out of the station. It was raining. Droplets splashed against the windows and streaked across the glass. Natalie traced the patterns with her finger, feeling the cold glass against her skin.

Then the train began to rise. Natalie looked at the ground in mild alarm as the streets fell away. There was a railroad crossing overhead that spanned two stationary skybergs. Airborne traffic, including flying cars and bicycles, stopped behind the barriers to let the train pass.

The train went up through a cloud, drenching the entire window in water. When it emerged, the train was soaring over plains of clouds. Skybergs and skytowers peeked through the clouds, drifting in and out of view.

Natalie pressed her face against the window. A little girl walking her dog on one of the skybergs waved at Natalie as the train passed over a house. Natalie waved back.

The train had just established a steady course when a skytower began to descend through the clouds in front of them. Natalie gave a small scream as the train ducked below the skytower and dipped through a cloud.

"That was...close." Natalie blushed when she realized that none of the other passengers had been alarmed by the near-collision. Quincy was reading an edition of *Faerie Interest*.

"Hmm?" She turned a page absentmindedly.

"There was a—oh my!" The train accelerated toward the ground and Natalie braced herself against the seat in front of her. "Shouldn't we slow down when we go down?"

"We're going down?" Quincy glanced over the top of her magazine. "Oh, look. It's raining. How pretty. And the grass is so green!"

Natalie looked at the trees and fields rising up to meet them. Just before the train plowed into the earth, it pulled up and leveled out.

Natalie took a deep breath—and jumped in her seat when a voice came over the loudspeaker.

"This is the conductor again. We have an adjustment to make. The train will be arriving at Albakirk in fifteen minutes."

Natalie was forced back into her chair by an invisible hand. She slammed into the cushions with a WHOOMP.

Tears streamed out of Natalie's eyes. She looked outside, where colors blurred in an indiscernible cacophony of scenery. The train was shooting along the countryside at speeds unknown.

Ten minutes later, the conductor's voice, modified by the speed of the train, came over the PA again.

"Ladiesandgentlemen,Iamsorrytoinformyouofaslightdelay:itwill nowtakeusapproximatelynineteenhourstogettoAlbakirk.Pleasesettl einandenjoytheride."

The train began to slow, but Natalie still couldn't distinguish the ground from the sky.

With a great effort, Natalie forced her head away from the window so she could see Quincy on the aisle seat.

"What is he saying?" Natalie shouted.

"He said 'settle in,' because it will take about nineteen hours to get to Albakirk."

"What? Nineteen hours?" Natalie gasped—and then she *really* gasped. The train decelerated so quickly she felt her teeth might fly out. She clamped her hands over her mouth just to be safe.

They hadn't stopped, but after the previous speed, it felt like a stop. Natalie's brain sloshed like soup inside her head.

She looked out of the window again. A brown cow stared at the train as it trundled slowly past. It was chewing its cud and watching the train with mild interest. The cow stayed in Natalie's window for a good five seconds.

"You said it's going to take nineteen hours now?" Natalie blinked. She peeled her yellow raincoat from the seat, where it had been pressed against the chair. The raincoat came free with a loud *thyuuuuck!*

"That's the problem with Variable Travel." Quincy sat up in her chair to watch the cow disappear from sight. "There's the possibility that you could get somewhere instantly. There's also a chance that it could take a week to go three miles."

Natalie's eyes widened with horror.

"Why didn't you tell me to get the other tickets then?"

"You said you could do it on your own." Quincy shrugged. "But don't worry. Chances are we can just hold out for the next adjustment."

Natalie looked across the aisle to see London, who was looking in her direction. They made eye contact and he immediately turned away. Natalie managed to appear annoyed when they saw each other, but she smiled after he looked away.

"Ladies and gentlemen, I'm pleased to announce that our trip to Albakirk will not take nineteen hours as anticipated. We will be pulling into Albakirk Station in twenty minutes. Please prepare all of your belongings and make sure that you don't leave anything on the train." The clerk paused. "Oh, and you may want to brace yourse—"

Once again, Natalie was thrown back into her seat. The outside world became a watercolor painting pouring off a canvas.

Twenty-nine minutes later (a minor adjustment had been necessary), Natalie's eyes were stained with tears and her knuckles were white from a death grip on her armrests.

"We're here!" Quincy smiled, prying Natalie's frozen hands from the armrests. "Maybe you made a good choice after all. That wasn't too bad."

Quincy stood, getting a good grip on Natalie's arms before pulling the red-haired girl from the seat. Once again, the yellow raincoat gave a loud *thyuuuuck!*

Natalie rubbed her hands in an effort to revive feeling in her fingers. "No. That wasn't bad at all."

CHAPTER 20:
CREAM, MELLOW, AND FLAKE

Some cities provide a very distinct impression when you see them for the first time. When Natalie stepped off the train at Albakirk, she was grateful for her umbrella. The city's first impression was *very wet.*

In that respect, Albakirk was similar to Radcliffe, but Albakirk's "raining" made Radcliffe's storms look like "spitting."

"Wow. It's raining hard." London huddled inside the train door and watched water pour onto the platform. He looked like he was being polite by allowing the other passengers to leave before him. Natalie had the suspicion that he was just delaying stepping out into the rain.

Quincy joined Natalie under the cover of the platform while the last of the passengers exited the train. Finally, London jumped off and hurried to the shelter of the platform.

In front of Natalie, a hill sloped down to the sea. Tall trees and patches of bright green grass covered the ground between houses and winding stone streets. Gray storm clouds spread to the horizon, and ships rode the rolling sea waves.

A main road stretched along the coast, running parallel to a sea wall. Waves swept the white sand beach and crashed against the high stones.

Buses, carts, and cars drove along a road to a high cliff that stretched out into the water. An enormous stone building, possibly a ruined castle, rested on top of the cliff.

"I like the view of the sea," Natalie said. "It's very pretty."

London pulled his brown leather jacket close. "And very wet."

Natalie followed a line of other travelers down the platform and into the station. "How far up north are we?"

"Pretty far." Quincy pointed at the water. "That's the North Gael Sea."

They walked up a flight of stairs to the station exit.

London looked at the girls. "So where are we looking first?"

"The first coffee shop we can find." Quincy opened her bubble umbrella as they went outside again. "That will eliminate one of

137

the possible locations. And if she's not there, then at least we'll be out of the rain while we figure out where else she might be."

*

The streets of Albakirk were narrow, and so were the sidewalks. The trio pressed themselves against a stone wall to avoid getting hit by oncoming traffic. Quincy kept her eye out for a coffeehouse, and London kept his eye on Natalie. He was walking behind her, so there was nothing Natalie could do about it. However, she did her best to emanate an aura of aloofness.

Natalie listened to the rain pelting her umbrella. One of the peculiar things about walking around with an umbrella in a crowded area was the Protocol. It was easy enough to walk with an umbrella when no one else had one. You just kept the umbrella above the tallest person and no one got their eye poked out.

However, in Albakirk and Radcliffe, everyone had an umbrella. When Natalie came across someone walking the other way, she would raise her umbrella to be polite. But many other umbrella-carriers were also polite—so they raised *their* umbrellas to avoid poking *her* in the eye.

What resulted was a strange situation in which both parties held their umbrellas very high and ended up whacking them against each other. This was inconvenient, but not disastrous (like eye-poking). Whenever this happened, Natalie and her counterpart simply apologized for the collision and went about their way (with both pairs of eyeballs safe).

Enormous tree branches with bountiful supplies of wet leaves reached down to wave in Natalie's face. They scraped against the top of her umbrella, sending drops of water pouring over the edge.

London walked in silence.

Out of the corner of her eye, Natalie could see him cast longing looks at her umbrella. Quincy had invited London to squeeze under her bubble-umbrella, but he had politely declined.

Natalie had made no such offer. She walked in the rain, perfectly dry under the enormous canopy, while London trod resolutely through the deluge. He didn't complain, but she knew that he would love to be under the umbrella with her. And not just because it was dry.

Quincy pointed to a white stone shop on the side of the road. "This place looks promising."

London hurried under the entrance and held the wooden door for the girls, grateful to get out of the rain.

"Hello, dears!" A white-haired fairy with a blue skirt and yellow apron waved at them from behind a counter. Her translucent wings sparkled faintly in the candlelight.

"Hello, ma'am." Natalie nodded, descending a set of stairs from the doorway.

"Come in and dry yourselves off. You can hang your coats by the bookshelves."

"Thank you, ma'am." Natalie took advantage of a rack to put up her raincoat. She adjusted the sleeves of her long pink shirt, noting that the coffeehouse was pleasantly warm.

London's jacket made a sloshing noise when he hung it on the rack. His brown hair was plastered against his face.

After they had taken a window seat, the fairy glided over to the table, her feet barely touching the floor.

"What would you like, dears?"

Quincy took a quick look at the menu. "We'd like three scones, please." She glanced at London, who was looking embarrassed while his clothes saturated the carpet. "And my friend here would like a mop."

"Oh, nothing to fuss about." The fairy smiled pleasantly at London. "There are paper towels in the water closet. You can dry off a bit."

London gratefully accepted her offer and slid out of his seat for the toilet. The fairy turned back to the girls.

"Anything to drink then? Coffee? Tea?"

Quincy was about to answer when Natalie interrupted. "What else do you have?"

"Well, there's Albakirk apple cider, rhubarb malt, and hot chocolate."

"Oh! What's in the hot chocolate?"

"It comes with cream, mellow, and flake."

"Mellow and flake!" Natalie's eyes lit up with excitement.

"What's mellow and flake?" Quincy asked.

"Delicious!" Natalie beamed at the fairy. "We'll take three, please."

"Of course," the fairy said. Specks of glitter twinkled beneath her fairy eyes. She half-skipped, half-flew back behind the white countertop to make the drinks.

Quincy made a face at Natalie. "What's cream, mellow, and flake?"

"I don't remember. But they taste delicious."

*

"You look drier than you did," Natalie said to London when he came out of the water closet.

It was true. He had progressed from Soaked to Unpleasantly Damp.

"It's a little better." He sat down.

"Come to think of it, I should probably wash my hands." Natalie rose to her feet.

"They're out of paper towels."

"How did you dry off then?" Natalie paused in the act of pushing her chair away. Then she frowned. "Oh."

"Here you are, dears." The fairy placed a white tray in front of them. The scones were round and fluffy with cranberries baked in. Natalie took a bite of hers before Quincy could even pick up a knife to scrape butter on.

"Natalie!" Quincy chided. "Take some time to enjoy it."

"I am enjoying it." Natalie grabbed her mug of hot chocolate.

"Cream" was, predictably, whipped cream. "Mellow" had been another easy guess. Natalie made a point of swallowing all of the marshmallows in her first gulp.

Natalie was particularly excited about the flake: a twisted stick of soft chocolate that you could melt in your drink or your mouth. It depended on whether you had the self-control to eat it slowly.

Natalie dipped the flake into the hot chocolate and took small bites while the delicious sweet disintegrated on her tongue. Filling up with warmth and good food, she settled into her padded chair and watched the rain pour down outside. Through the window, she saw the ruined castle that she had noticed from the station.

"I wonder what that is."

London put down his hot chocolate. "I've been wondering that too."

"That's Albakirk Castle," the fairy said, suddenly reappearing at the table.

Quincy gave a small jump and almost upset Natalie's hot chocolate—which would have upset Natalie because the cup was perched over her lap. The red-haired girl carefully pushed the mug away.

140

"Albakirk Castle?" Natalie repeated, noting the reverent tone in the fairy's voice.

"Yes. It's said the Golem Army of Calypso lies beneath it. Have you heard the story?"

The trio looked at each other, excitement spreading across their faces.

"No, we haven't." Natalie scooted her chair closer to the table.

The fairy smiled broadly, the wrinkles creasing around her bright eyes. She was clearly pleased to have an audience.

"Well," she took a breath, as if preparing to plunge into great depths, "the golems were created by the First Gods long ago, even before the humans were made. The golems were the greatest warriors for the First Gods in the War of Chaos—until the Titans learned how to change their Script. You know, the writing that gives a golem its instruction? Golems don't have souls, but if they did, the Script would be something like a conscience, I think. The Titans learned how to change the golems' Script to turn them against the First Gods. That's when Sol created terrible creatures like the Dark Angels to take the golems' place. To try and win the war."

A shiver crept down Natalie's spine. "Sol created the Dark Angels?"

"Of course," the fairy nodded conspiratorially, dropping her voice. "He made Dark Angels, giants, and other terrifying beasts that couldn't be turned against the First Gods so easily. The golems were hardly used after that. Eventually, the Pantheon decided to destroy the golems to make sure that no one else could ever use them. But there's a legend among the golems that the Golem Army of Calypso, the greatest of the golem armies, was sent to Albakirk so that it could be called upon in the Pantheon's most desperate hour of need."

"Why Albakirk?" London asked.

"Who knows?" The fairy shrugged. "Far enough and close enough, I guess."

"How did you find out about the legend?" Quincy finished off her last piece of scone.

"Well, it is a local legend, isn't it? And I had a golem who used to work here." The fairy sighed. "She could work like nobody else, of course. It's unnatural how focused they can be. But, like most of the survivors, she wasn't quite right in the head."

Natalie felt a knot in her stomach. "What happened to her?"

The fairy looked out the window, sadness filling her eyes. "Oh, well, you know...she went off searching for the Army of Calypso herself. She just couldn't live without her kin, I suppose."

Quincy, Natalie, and London held their breath, waiting to hear the rest of the story. The fairy wiped the corners of her eyes with a white handkerchief.

"And she never came back. It's strange and dangerous up at that castle. High on the cliff and all that. Some people say there are hidden tunnels under the castle, but I snuck around there when I was a girl and never found any tunnels. But my Glenda disappeared..." The fairy's lip trembled. "I try not to think about it too much. She was a good golem." She blew her nose loudly on the handkerchief. "Almost like a real person, if you'll excuse my saying so."

Quincy patted the fairy's hand sympathetically. "I'm sorry to hear that."

"Oh, thanks, love. You're a dear." The fairy gave her a watery smile.

"Thank you for telling us about the castle." Natalie rose to leave. "And the hot chocolate was excellent."

"Oh, you're very sweet." The fairy sniffed and wiped at her eyes. Thunder boomed overhead. "Now be careful out there. It's getting worse. A big storm is coming."

CHAPTER 21:
VISITORS IN THE DARK

Bellamy stood in the middle of a maze at the Radcliffe Gardens. Tall hedges surrounded him. It was past midnight, and thick clouds covered the stars.

Stalks of roses poked out of the hedges, billowing in the breeze. No one would see or hear him in the gardens. He needed privacy to contact the Brethren and tell them that he had stolen the abbey's spell-book. It would have been safer to leave Radcliffe before contacting the Brethren, but Bellamy had another errand after he informed the Forerunners of his success.

The wind blew through a willow tree on the edge of the maze, making the branches wave like tendrils. Bellamy pulled a small crystal pyramid from his satchel and set it on the grass. He tapped it on the peak and a thick wave of purple light rippled out from the crystal, creating a circle of energy that rotated in place.

A hooded figure rose out of the circle.

Bellamy nodded. "Galerius."

Galerius nodded in return. He had a long nose and a clean-shaven face. It was impossible to discern his skin tone or eye color from the image because his entire body was a pale blue light. His outline blurred at the edges.

"I have the spell-book." Bellamy pulled the hefty tome out of his satchel. "*On Creatures Created.* I outwitted the enchantments of Resurgam Abbey to get it."

"Well done, brother." A thin smile spread across Galerius's face. "I knew that you would succeed, even if some of the Brethren doubted you."

"Many people have doubted me in the past." Bellamy's tone radiated defiance. "I have always proved them wrong."

"So you have. And this book will help us where the other failed?"

"Yes. It has the full spell to rewrite the Scripts for the entire Golem Army of Calypso."

"Well done, Bellamy. Take the spell-book to Albakirk tonight. Convert the Golem Army of Calypso to our cause and bring it to

Calypso. We will attack at the opening ceremony of the Arcadian Games."

Bellamy's chest tightened with anxiety at the deadline. The games were almost upon them. "What of Jerome and the others? Will they come with me? I still haven't heard from them."

Galerius hesitated. "You will be on your own this time."

Bellamy froze, *On Creatures Created* sticking halfway out of his satchel. "They made it out alive, didn't they?"

"Jerome and Hayden were the only ones who survived the catacombs."

Bellamy's heart sank. "No..."

"The rest were lost to the drakes." Galerius shook his head sadly. "They were not as fortunate as you are...with your gifts of stealth."

Bellamy shuddered at the memory of the tunnels. He stared at the ground, trying not to imagine the elves' deaths. He had a few narrow escapes on his way out of the catacombs, but luck and his shadow had seen him through. Now he would have to go back, alone, and do it all again...

He pushed the thought from his mind.

"And how will we attack once we have the golems?"

"The colossus will begin the attack at the Arcadian Stadium. After you unleash the colossus, get to the *Marcion*. It will be hidden in the fog by one of the docks."

"How will the rest of the army join the battle?"

"The Valkyrie Gate leads to a network of tunnels underneath Calypso. The golems will emerge at various points outside the stadium. While they cause chaos on the ground, Captain Barias will provide air support with the *Marcion*."

Bellamy arched an eyebrow in surprise. "How will a frigate get into the capital undetected?"

Galerius's smile widened. "The Pantheon is overconfident about the security of Calypso. It has been so long since the city suffered any attack. I know the god who commands the fleet." Galerius snorted. "He is a fool. But more than that—the wedding between Aphrodainte and Oli will take place the night of the opening ceremony."

"You're kidding!" The exclamation sounded juvenile, but Bellamy couldn't help himself.

Galerius allowed himself a laugh. "Do you not read the news, Bellamy? Aphrodainte's demanded schedule-change is all they have been talking about for a month."

"But isn't Oli competing in the games?"

"He is scheduled to, of course. But he will not."

"Why not?" Bellamy asked in surprise.

"Because there will be no games," Galerius said impatiently.

The boy cleared his throat. "No, of course not."

"The wedding will be in Parlemagne. It is a high-profile event capable of competing with the games. Many of the gods and their security attachments will be gone. Senator Aphrollo will ensure that nothing goes wrong at his daughter's wedding. Trust me, he will redirect some of Calypso's finest to protect Aphrodainte's big day."

"But it's just Parlemagne," Bellamy snorted.

"Indeed. Such a dangerous place." Galerius laughed again. "Someone might light a flare."

"I still can't believe that the gods would allow any event to interfere with the Arcadian Games." Bellamy shook his head in disgust. "They don't even respect their own traditions."

"Yes." Galerius arched an eyebrow. "It is most telling how people respect certain traditions."

Bellamy swallowed.

"Your Phoenix Guardians value the games very much, do they not? After all, the Undying Fire honors Sayornis."

Bellamy clenched his jaw. "They're not my Phoenix Guardians anymore."

"No," Galerius agreed. "They are not."

They were silent for a long, uncomfortable minute before Galerius spoke again.

"You have done very well, Bellamy. Bring us the Golem Army of Calypso, and our agents in the city will take care of the rest. We do not have the strength to defeat the Pantheon now, but we will make a statement against their evil. One day, we will put out the candle of the wicked."

Bellamy nodded. "I won't fail you."

"I know. Oh—I almost forgot: give Captain Barias the spell-book when you reach the *Marcion*. Your work will be finished by then."

Bellamy's brow wrinkled in confusion. He was about to ask "Why?" but he stopped himself.

Galerius saw the question on his face. "We just want the spell-book in the captain's hands after we have the army. That is all."

Bellamy hesitated. "You don't trust me with it?"

Galerius sighed. "Oh, brother." He held out his hands. "Of course we trust you with it. That is why we are sending you into the catacombs to get the army at this late hour. But after you get the army, you will not need the book anymore, will you?"

Bellamy shook his head, fighting to keep the resentment from his face.

"No, you will not," Galerius finished. "You will give Captain Barias the book and worry no more about the matter. Now go." He put a hand to his heart in a salute. "Righteousness is our sword and our shield."

"The Titans will rise again," Bellamy answered. He reached down to tap the pyramid peak, and Galerius disappeared with a shimmer.

Bellamy glared at the crystal for a long moment before putting it in his satchel. Then he ran off into the shadows.

*

Bellamy walked along the dark, quiet streets of Radcliffe until he reached a wooden gate with double-doors and a circular cut overhead. Checking to see that no one was watching, he opened one of the doors and slipped into the courtyard. He crept along the houses, avoiding the pool of light pouring from a solitary lamp post. When he reached number nine, he walked past the front door and went through a thin alleyway to the back.

He stood on tiptoe to look through a window. Inside, the curtains were drawn. Bellamy stood back on his heels and closed his eyes.

Go.

He watched his shadow slide through the window. A moment later, Bellamy shadowcast himself into the house.

When he opened his eyes, he was in a small bedroom next to a mahogany standing closet. In front of him, a girl lay under a green bedspread.

"Regina..." A bittersweet feeling swelled up in Bellamy's chest. He took a hesitant step toward her. Then he stopped and turned to the closed bedroom door. He traced a glowing "X" in the air. He waved at it and pushed it against the door, where the "X" dissipated with a muffling sound. Now he could talk to Regina without being overheard.

146

Bellamy leaned over the girl and stroked her hair. He felt her forehead and was surprised to find that it was warm and sweaty. Was she feverish?

He drew back the curtains to let the moon shine on her face. She didn't seem to notice the pale light illuminating her sickly skin. Bellamy sat on the side of her bed and gently held Regina's hand. Her skin felt raw.

"Regina!" Bellamy gasped. "What happened? Were you burned?"

Regina made no response. She slept on, oblivious to the world. Her chest rose and fell gently.

Bellamy rolled back the sleeve of her nightgown and saw a ruddy skin tone running up to her elbow. Tears glistened at the corners of his eyes.

He pulled the sleeve back down and clasped Regina's hand. "Did you burn yourself again?"

He leaned over and kissed her on the cheek. He felt her soft, steady breathing against his face.

"I brought your music box." Bellamy sat upright and pulled a small wooden box from his satchel. He placed it on the bed and opened the top, revealing a tiny, carved songbird above a fountain. Bellamy wound the key, and the box began to play.

He placed Regina's fingers against the wooden cube so she could feel the vibrations.

A soft, slow melody played against broken chords, punctuated now and again by a sweet embellishment.

"Do you remember this piece, Regina? This was your favorite." He stroked Regina's long black hair. "It's 'Nocturne for the Caged Bird' by Frederick Francis."

Bellamy closed his eyes. He swayed gently to the music, waving his hand, playing invisible arpeggios in the air. The soft rhythm of unfulfilled desire resonated in his chest. It was a prayer and a lament from a beauty longing to break free.

When the music was over, Bellamy wiped his eyes with the back of his hand. He took Regina's hand from the music box and laid it across her chest.

After carefully returning the music box to his satchel, he kissed Regina on the cheek again.

"I promise to find a way to bring you back," he whispered in her ear. "The gods can't do anything for you. They're weak. But the Titans are strong. They can restore you." He bit his lip, clenching and unclenching his fist. His voice trembled. "And they'll help me take vengeance on whoever hurt you."

He kissed Regina once more on the forehead.

"Goodbye, my love."

Then he closed his eyes and shadowcast himself out of the room.

CHAPTER 22:
A LITTLE ADJECTIVE MAGIC

Quincy splashed through a puddle on the road leading to Albakirk Castle. "Lucky thing I wanted to stop for a drink, isn't it?"

"Lucky you did. I was about to drown." London shielded his eyes against the sheets of rain.

"I think the rain's let up some," Natalie said. "It's not pounding as hard on my umbrella."

"Oh, yes." London snorted. "It's loads better."

The sea wall rose hundreds of feet above the water, commanding an excellent view of the North Gael Sea. To Natalie's right, white-foamed waves crashed against the dark rocks jutting up from the water. The walk would have been more enjoyable with clear skies. As it was, Natalie kept a firm grip on her umbrella to keep it from blowing over—or blowing away and taking her with it.

When they finally reached the castle, London put into words what the rest of them were thinking.

"It's not so much a ruined castle as the ruined ruins of a castle."

It was a fair assessment. Little was left of the ancient stone keep. A few walls rose to their original height and boasted formidable ramparts. Most of the structure had lost everything but the first level. The interior structure of the castle was a maze of walls and archways. Patches of broken stone interrupted the green grass covering the ground.

Natalie looked at the hill above them. Some old houses had been constructed with stones that looked suspiciously like the ones from the castle. The people of Albakirk might have had respect for their history, but they were also practical.

Natalie pointed at the crumbling remnant of a tower. "The fairy said the secret passage was in the east wall, by the sea."

"Yeah, by the cliff. Where curious people fall to their deaths."

"Thank you, London." Quincy fluttered her wings irritably.

"I just wanted to remind everyone."

"Well, now you have."

They walked through the front gate, which still had most of the original structure in place.

London huddled under the archway. "Let's stop here for just a minute."

"Why?" Quincy put a hand on her hip. "To get dry? We just left the coffeehouse. And you're going to get soaked again once we walk across the castle. There's no roof left."

"When we walk across the castle?" London looked indignant. "Those are stone decorations on a lawn. This is what's left of the *castle*, Quincy." He slapped the stones behind him.

Thunder boomed overhead, reverberating through their chests.

Natalie shivered. "Shouldn't we get going?"

"When you don't have an umbrella, you take the breaks you can get."

"Why didn't you bring an umbrella?" Natalie twirled hers in her hands.

London shrugged. "I didn't think about it."

"Either that or he assumed that he could share yours." Quincy grinned.

Before either Natalie or London could respond, she had skipped out from the archway and started to navigate the crumbled maze of the castle interior.

Natalie marched behind her without looking at London.

The remaining patches of stone floor must have been too heavy or too damaged for the opportunistic homemakers of Albakirk. Natalie took care to step around the first patch she came to. The castle had already suffered enough abuse. It seemed wrong to disrespect it further.

Her detour led her into a thick puddle of mud. Natalie's left foot slipped out from under her.

"Oh my!" She held out her hands for balance, relying on the wet grass underneath her right foot to remain upright.

Her left leg slipped more, spreading her legs apart. She swayed for a moment—and then toppled backwards.

A hand grabbed hers and pulled her to safety. Surprised, she did a little pirouette on the grass to regain her footing—and London was holding her hand.

They stared at each other.

London let go.

"Sorry." He blinked against the pouring rain.

150

Natalie brushed a curtain of wet red hair out of her face. "Thanks."

Their eyes met again for a brief moment, and then they looked away. London mumbled something incoherent. Then he turned and hurried after Quincy.

Natalie watched him go, feeling the echo of the curious sensation that had swept through her chest when London had held her hand. A less sensible individual might have characterized it as a "flutter."

But, of course, Natalie knew better.

Didn't she?

She put the thought from her mind, and when she reached the next patch of ancient stone, she walked over it without a second thought. After all, it had been a floor once.

Quincy and London were waiting for her at the ruined tower. The boy stood by the tower, looking out at the sea, blinking against the rain that buffeted his face. His leather jacket had turned a dark brown from the downpour.

The sylph glanced at London and smiled knowingly at Natalie, who ignored the look.

"So what now?" Quincy rearranged her expression to a more serious one—but Natalie still caught the hint of a wink.

"We try to find a way in," Natalie answered.

"But it's blocked, see?" London pointed at the base of the tower. "There might have been a staircase or something at one point, but it's covered in rubble now. There's no way in."

Natalie examined the pile of rocks.

"There's got to be a way around." She climbed the rubble and looked for gaps.

"Can't we move the rocks?" Quincy asked.

Natalie tilted her head and considered the question. "I suppose I could try." She closed her umbrella. "Might be a good time for some adjective magic."

Quincy cleared her throat. "Maybe you should let London do that."

Natalie paused, her umbrella poised over the rocks.

"Why?"

"Because your umbrella is new."

"And?"

"And you're new to your umbrella...?" Quincy hesitated.

London stared at the grass and shuffled his feet awkwardly. They made squelching noises in the mud.

151

"Are you saying I can't do this?" Natalie demanded.

Quincy sighed. "This isn't about whether you can do it or not. But it *is* a heavy pile and you might—"

"Not be able to do it?" Natalie narrowed her eyes. With her umbrella closed, the rain was beating against her face. Wet strands of red hair were plastered to her forehead and cheek. She brushed them away irritably. "Come on, isn't that what you're saying? You think I'm going to mess things up like I did with Regina?"

"I didn't say anything about Regina—"

"But you were thinking it, weren't you?"

"Oh, gods." Quincy threw her hands up in frustration. "Fine, Natalie. Do whatever you want."

"All right. I will." Natalie raised her umbrella to tap the rocks. She cleared her throat. "Okay...*light* rocks."

She touched the rock with her umbrella—

—and screamed as the ground collapsed underneath her.

Natalie fell forward into a blur of darkness.

"Natalie!" London rushed forward and climbed over the edge of the newly-made hole.

Natalie was sprawled at the bottom of the rock pile, which was now six or eight feet lower. London stepped down carefully toward her.

"Oh my gods, Natalie!" Quincy leaned over the hole. "Are you all right?"

"I'm fine." Natalie held up her hand wearily.

London ignored her assessment of the situation and took the opportunity to grab Natalie's hand and help her up.

"I'm fine, really. I can help myself up—"

"Just hold on and let me pull you up," London interrupted. He pulled Natalie to the rock he was crouching on, and then pushed her up to the top, where Quincy was waiting.

"Oh my gods!" Quincy held a hand to her mouth. "Are you sure you're okay? You fell!"

"I know, Quincy. I fell. But I'm fine. I just got a little startled, that's all."

"What happened?"

"Well..." Natalie wiped her muddy hands on the grass. "The rocks didn't seem to like the magic very much."

"How so?"

"I felt some negative feedback when I touched them."

Quincy scratched her head. "What does that mean?"

"It means the tower got even more difficult to enter." London pulled himself back onto ground level. "I wouldn't be surprised if that's how this passage got blocked in the first place. Someone else tried to get in with magic and the passage started to seal itself. Natalie must have reactivated it just now." He gave Natalie an appraising look. "You're lucky it wasn't a more aggressive spell. I probably should have known better than to let you try it."

"*Let* me try it?" Natalie raised her eyebrows indignantly. She was on the verge of saying something more, but she thought better of it. Instead, she made a frustrated noise in her throat and looked away.

"But that's the only entrance, right?" Quincy turned to look at the castle from the direction they had come from. "So we're just stuck outside?"

"I guess so." London stood next to the sylph. He crouched and rubbed his elbow on the grass, trying to wipe the mud off. He succeeded in spreading it all over his sleeve.

"Unless there's another entrance we don't know about." He sighed. "Maybe this isn't what Florentina wanted us to look for. The fairy at the coffeehouse did say it was only a legend that the golem army was here."

Quincy stared at the sky. "Well, if we're not making any progress, we might as well find someplace dry while we figure out what to do next."

"And then what?" Natalie demanded. "Find another legend about a different castle?"

Quincy shrugged, staring at the ground to keep the rain from pouring into her eyes.

It started to rain harder. Thick sheets of water surrounded them.

"I think we should get inside," she said.

London nodded. "I agree."

"I can't believe—you're already giving up?" Natalie shouted over the rain. "We just have to be creative in finding the entrance! A buried golem army is too valuable to be hidden in plain sight. We can't give up now—we've come all the way to Albakirk! Florentina needs us—and I need my journal!"

London and Quincy turned around to see Natalie standing under her umbrella on the parapet.

London blinked in shock.

Quincy covered her mouth in horror.

Natalie was perched on the castle *wall.*

One false step and she would plummet into the swirling sea, hundreds of feet below.

London scrambled toward her. "Natalie, get down from there!"

"What in Sol's name are you doing?" Quincy screamed. "It's a sheer drop! You'll fall to your death! Get off this instant!"

"Fine." Natalie stared back at the sylph.

And then she stepped over the edge.

CHAPTER 23:
WRATH

Bellamy flinched when his boot splashed into the puddle. Flecks of the putrid water peppered his face. He had walked in complete silence for over an hour, and he just *had* to let his foot slip now. He held his breath—he was close to one of their nests. The air smelled foul.

Listening intently for the sound of drakes, he quietly scraped the underside of his boot against the tunnel wall. He patted his satchel absentmindedly, just to make sure that *On Creatures Created* was still there. He felt the heavy tome with his fingertips. It hadn't shadowcast with him inside the library, but the protective enchantments were limited to the abbey. The spellbook followed him now.

Below, the passage sloped into a crossing. His current route led to the Colossus Pit, but it passed through a main thoroughfare for the drakes.

Bellamy pressed himself against the wall at the sound of claws scraping along the rocky floor. A half-dozen drakes darted through the tunnel intersection. He waited for their footsteps to fade before moving again. He took a tentative step forward—but then he heard more scurrying. Three more drakes ran into the crossing, stopping to pant and growl at each other.

Bellamy waited a couple of minutes for them to move, but they stayed put. He swore under his breath, wondering if he should track back and find another way. He shook his head at the stupidity of the thought.

There was no other way.

Scraping and growling echoed through the darkness behind him, getting louder each moment. The hair rose on the back of his neck—more drakes! They would run right into him! He tried to swallow, but his tongue felt like cotton. He had to move *now*.

Bellamy closed his eyes.

Go.

He opened his eyes to see his shadow, darker than the tunnel around it, flit down the passage and through the crossing. The shadow slid under the dragons' emaciated feet and long, bony tails.

One of the drakes chose that moment to stop in the intersection. It tilted its head, nostrils flaring, red eyes glinting in the darkness. The dragon's long tongue tasted the cold air. It turned toward Bellamy and took a curious step in his direction.

Behind Bellamy, the drakes were getting closer. The creature in the crossing let out a trilling screech, and its companions joined in the sound. The cacophonous noise filled the tunnel.

Heart pounding, Bellamy closed his eyes to see from his shadow's point of view. It was in an empty stretch of tunnel and looking back at the crossing, where the agitated drakes were scurrying toward Bellamy's body.

He heard the heavy footfalls closing in.

Take me.

Bellamy appeared on the other side of the tunnel, adrenaline coursing through his veins. He stumbled away from the intersection and tripped over a rock. He braced his fall against the tunnel wall and scraped his hand. It made little noise—but he turned around to see if any of the drakes had heard.

The dragons had moved from the crossing to the tunnel Bellamy had just occupied. They ran into the drakes coming from the opposite direction. Harsh cries filled the air.

Bellamy turned away from the jarring screeches and hurried toward the Colossus Pit. He had survived the drakes.

Now he had to convert a colossus.

*

Take me.

Bellamy shadowcast himself into the Colossus Pit. He opened his eyes, pressing himself against the cold stone door, allowing his eyes to adjust to the darkness. He blinked, trying to distinguish the tall columns on either side of the massive aisle.

He licked his lips nervously. The colossus could be anywhere in this massive pit, lurking in the darkness, waiting for the next intruders.

Bellamy only hoped that he could find the colossus before the colossus found *him.*

He took a tentative step toward the center aisle, scanning the pillars for signs of the monster. It wasn't as if a creature of that size could hide itself easily, but the place was huge.

The chamber was perfectly still. He took a cautious step, and then another. Confidence grew, buoying his heart. Maybe he would sneak up on the colossus after all.

In fact, Bellamy went a full ten steps before the lights turned on.

CRACK!

The first tubes of green light blazed into life, sending Bellamy's heart into his throat.

The second pair of tubes ignited—then the third and fourth. Soon the entire chamber was lit with the eerie green glow.

Bellamy's mouth was frozen in a scream. He couldn't believe that he had forgotten the lights.

At that moment, with his foot still poised in the air to take another step, Bellamy wished that he was dead.

That was, undoubtedly, the same wish in the heart of the colossus that had been standing still in the middle of the aisle.

The colossus opened its eyes. Two burning points of red light stared down at Bellamy from behind a titanic helmet.

The boy closed his eyes and sent out his shadow, knowing that he had only seconds to live. The colossus bellowed—a deafening roar that rattled his spine. He wondered if his bones would fall out of their sockets in terror.

Bellamy felt a rush of wind, and even with his eyes closed he could sense darkness overshadow him. The colossus was going to stomp him flat if he didn't move.

So he did.

Take me.

Bellamy opened his eyes to see a thick spike inches from his face. The ground beneath him trembled, and he grabbed hold of the spike. There was another almighty tremor. The colossus was stamping the ground into oblivion.

After a couple more stomps, the monster stopped destroying the floor to survey the remains of its enemy.

From his position on the colossus's back, Bellamy looked down to examine the rubble that could have been his final resting place. The colossus roared in confusion. Bellamy held on tightly as the monster threw back its head in fury. It knew that Bellamy had escaped.

"You're very clever, aren't you?" Bellamy whispered, pulling *On Creatures Created* from his satchel. He carefully reached toward the armored collar at the back of the colossus's neck.

When he had a firm handhold, he stepped away from the spike he had been holding onto.

"Time for some revision," he flipped open the book with his free hand, "to your Script."

*

A strange voice floated to the surface of the colossus's mind.

What is your name?

What was his name? The colossus knew his name.

What is your name?

Who was this strange voice in his head? Why did it want his name?

Tell me your name. I know your Purpose. It is to defend Calypso.

Inside his head, the colossus nodded. His Purpose was to defend Calypso.

You are part of the Golem Army of Calypso.

Yes. He was part of the Golem Army of Calypso.

Your name is...?

Wrath. His name was Wrath. His Purpose was to defend Calypso.

Wrath. Your name is Wrath.

Something shuddered deep within the colossus. The voice had used his name. A strange sensation flooded the pit of the golem's stomach. It was a feeling he had not felt in Many Days.

I will give you a new Purpose, Wrath.

A faint thought of warning washed up on the shores of the golem's mind.

Your new Purpose is to destroy Calypso.

No. Wrath's purpose was to *defend* Calypso, not destroy it.

But this voice knew Wrath's name...

Wrath, your Purpose is to destroy Calypso.

Wrath shuddered violently. He should not have shared his name with this voice.

Deah-leh Tah-bahk...

A primeval groan started in his chest and worked its way up to his formidable jaws.

Spey Es...

This voice was telling lies. It sounded like the Enemy.

Deah-leh...

Wrath knew his Script. He knew his Purpose.

158

Tah-bahk Spey Es...

His Purpose was to defend Calypso. The certainty of his Purpose filled Wrath's head like a fiery cloud—but the voice was an icicle of doubt.

Wrath, your Purpose is no longer to defend Calypso. Deah-leh. Tah-bahk. Spey...

The voice was uttering the Words of the Script that Wrath had not heard in Many Days.

...Es.

Wrath shuddered violently. His red eyes rolled in their sockets.

Your Purpose is to destroy Calypso.

That wasn't his Purpose...was it?

Wrath shook his head. No...no...but what was his Purpose? He thought he knew it, but it was slipping away like water through his fingertips.

Your Purpose is to destroy Calypso.

His Purpose was to destroy Calypso?

Your Purpose is to destroy Calypso.

Or to...defend it?

Fi-hal Sa...

What was it?

Vahs-con Trolis. Fi-hal...

What was his purpose?

Sa Vahs-con Trolis. Fi-hal Sa...

Yes, that was it...

Vahs-con Trolis.

Wrath's Purpose was to destroy Calypso.

CHAPTER 24:
A WAY IN

Quincy was wrong about the sheer drop. There was at least a foot of slick grass and mud on the cliff edge beneath the wall.

She was also wrong about Natalie falling to her death. She had forgotten that Natalie's umbrella was more than just a tool for blocking the rain or casting spells.

Natalie's umbrella could fly.

Or help her through a controlled fall, which was a better way to describe what Natalie had just done.

The red-haired girl folded her umbrella and pressed herself against the rough, wet stone walls. She took slow, deep breaths, but her heart was racing. She had known that the umbrella would fly. She hadn't been worried about falling to her death. It's just that she had never flown with this umbrella before.

And when she jumped, she had been really angry. Consequently, she hadn't been thinking *entirely* straight.

Maybe Abbess Persephone was right about the moodiness, she thought.

"Natalie!" London screamed over the pounding rain.

"Oh my gods! Oh my *gods*! Natalie!"

Quincy started sobbing.

Natalie took another breath to calm herself, and then she raised her voice above the din.

"I'm here! I'm fine!" She looked skyward, blinking furiously against the rain.

"Natalie?" Quincy leaned over the wall and saw her. The sylph swore. "Natalie! Don't you ever pull that stunt again!"

"Natalie? How did—" London leaned over the wall edge. His face was pale, but he relaxed slightly when he saw her.

At the sight of his panicked expression, Natalie felt a rush of guilt in the pit of her stomach. She felt something else too, but not in the gut. It was, again, higher and to the left.

Natalie ignored it. She was still angry, and her emotions needed to be on the same wavelength.

Quincy clasped her hands in front of her face.

161

London trembled and shook his head.

"I'm sorry," Natalie mumbled, but not loud enough for them to hear.

Her hands were getting sore from gripping the stones so tightly.

"Don't you ever do that again!" Quincy's voice was shrill.

"All right."

"You hear?"

"I hear you."

"You hear me good?"

"I said I hear you!"

"All right. Good." Quincy's green eyes flashed. Her wings flapped furiously against the rain, sending drops of water flying in all directions.

"Are you done?" Natalie squinted up at the sylph.

"Yes, I'm done," Quincy answered in a huff.

London's expression was grim. Natalie avoided his gaze.

"Would it interest you to know that there's a cave down here?"

"Yes," London answered shortly. "How do we get down?"

Natalie looked at London, at the slippery rock wall, and then back at London.

"Really slowly."

*

Getting down turned out to be more possible, if not easier, than Natalie would have guessed. Adjective magic worked on the outer stone wall. She was able to make the wall *dry* and even *sticky* so that London and Quincy (after some convincing) could climb down with firm handholds.

"Why didn't you just do that to the rock at the beginning?" Quincy wiped her hands on her jeans after stepping inside the small cave. "Why do you have to be so dramatic?"

Natalie watched drops of water slide down her umbrella handle. Now that they were inside, her rebellious spirit had cooled down. The resulting emotional hole had been flooded with shame. It was as though a reckless Natalie did awful things and then left the conscientious Natalie to deal with the consequences.

Bother.

"I'm sorry, Quincy. I don't know what I was thinking. It was wrong to jump off like that and scare you. I'm sorry." She glanced at London. He was leaning against the wall with his arms crossed.

Natalie slapped a puddle with her rain boot.

Awkward silence reigned until London walked past her to the mouth of a passage.

He pulled a small, glowing salamander from his pocket.

"A luminewt!" Quincy smiled appreciatively. "*Much* cuter than a flashlight."

The orange luminewt scrambled up London's arm and perched itself on his shoulder. London stroked its back. The creature's throat inflated, and it made a noise like a tiny burp.

When the luminewt's throat deflated, it was shining three times brighter than before. London's entire body was bathed with orange light. Natalie could see a good ten yards down the passageway.

"Nicely done, Dwayne." London rubbed the luminewt gently on the head. Dwayne responded with an appreciative gurgle.

"All right. Let's see what secrets the tunnels hold." London motioned for the girls to follow him, and they walked down into the catacombs.

*

"This is disgusting." Quincy wiped the seat of her pants. She looked irritably at the muddy shaft that she had just slid down. "I knew I shouldn't have worn my new green cardigan."

Natalie turned around to examine the filthy back of her yellow raincoat. "Wonderful."

London shrugged. "It's just mud."

Both girls glared at London, who ducked his head to shield himself from their furious stares.

They had gone deeper underground than Natalie had anticipated. Many of the tunnels simply ended in holes with rotted ladders—or no ladders at all—that went straight down to other tunnels. The trio had descended at least five levels in this way.

London continued to lead. The luminewt lit the passage in front of them. They arrived at a three-way split. Natalie expected London to pause and debate which way they should go. He immediately chose the path on the right.

"Why that way?" Natalie asked.

The luminewt swiveled around on London's shoulder and made a gurgling noise. London glanced at Natalie and shrugged.

"One way is as good as the next."

163

The girls followed him down the sloping tunnel. The air grew damper with each passing minute. Mist rose around their feet.

Natalie gasped when a draft of air rushed at her from the left. She stopped, staring into blackness that was thicker than the rest of the tunnel. Reaching out with her umbrella, she walked slowly into the darkness.

There was nothing but empty air, stretching back farther than Natalie dared to go.

She turned around when Quincy gasped to her right.

"Oh my gods." Quincy had lowered her voice to a whisper. "It's *cold.*"

"And it smells disgusting." Natalie pinched her nostrils.

"It's another network of tunnels." London stepped in front of the gap. "A complex network of tunnels."

Natalie glanced at the luminewt on his shoulder. The creature's light made the outer darkness even blacker.

"London, can you can make the newt—"

"Dwayne."

Dwayne gurgled at the sound of his name.

"Can you make Dwayne less bright?"

"Why? I can barely see anything."

"I can barely see anything either." Natalie blinked. "Turn Dwayne down so our eyes can adjust to the darkness."

"Or I could make him brighter and we could see *more.*"

"No—turn him down!" Natalie raised her voice.

Something shifted in the black beyond their vision.

Quincy froze.

"Natalie," she hissed. "I think—"

Natalie ignored her. "Come on, London!"

"Fine. But it's a stupid idea." London stroked Dwayne's back twice, and the luminewt burped. He twitched briefly and dimmed. Now his body was just a glowing shape on London's shoulder.

Natalie blinked to help her eyes adjust to the darkness.

Rustling noises came from their left and right.

Quincy stepped closer to Natalie. "Natalie, I wish you hadn't told London to turn Dwayne down. I think there's something out there."

"Yeah." London licked his lips and swallowed. "I do too."

Natalie clutched her umbrella tightly. The hair rose on the back of her neck.

The commotion grew louder. It sounded like rattling bones.

Quincy grabbed Natalie's shoulder. "There's definitely something out there."

London swallowed. "Maybe lots of somethings."

"I know. But keep it down." Natalie held a finger to her lips. "I'm trying to concentrate."

If Natalie had been honest with herself, she would have admitted that turning Dwayne down was a bad idea. The light might have stopped whatever was out there from getting closer.

Maybe.

Without saying anything, the trio drew close together, standing back-to-back.

"London," Natalie whispered, about to ask him to turn Dwayne back up.

"What?"

Heavy footsteps squelched in soft ground.

"Shh!" Natalie felt a thrill of terror run down her spine.

"What? You just said my—"

"Shut up!"

A dark shape materialized a few feet away from Natalie, barely distinguishable by Dwayne's dim aura.

The figure was very tall. Red eyes peered at Natalie through thin slits. It breathed with a low hissing.

And it smelled foul.

Natalie was the only one who saw it. London and Quincy were looking the other way.

There was a wide variety of things Natalie could have done at this point.

Screaming and running away were out of the question.

Telling Quincy and London might have been useful.

Shooting the newcomer in the face would have been a temporary solution, and not necessarily a good one, because the creature might not be hostile.

Might not be hostile.

But Natalie chose an altogether different option—one that, later on, made her seriously question her own judgment.

She poked it with her umbrella.

The creature screeched in anger.

The air erupted with similar screeches all around them. A dozen pairs of red eyes opened and pierced through the gloom.

None of the others had been poked with umbrellas. But they all sounded upset.

Quincy screamed. London grabbed her and Natalie by the arms and pulled them in the direction they had come from.

Natalie twisted out of his grip and pushed him on. She turned around—and ducked to avoid a bony claw slashing the air where her face had just been.

All light had vanished with the luminewt, but Natalie knew that the monsters were almost on top of her. From a crouching position, she opened her umbrella and sent a flaming blast down the tunnel.

A fiery shockwave billowed through the passage, illuminating the emaciated bodies of huge reptiles. She cried out from the agonizing sting of the bright light.

Fire spilled into the holes on either side. For a brief moment, the light shone on the mangled bodies littering the ground. Then it all went dark.

Natalie blinked rapidly to clear her vision.

Furious cries echoed off in the distance. The noise didn't sound like a retreat.

Sweat flowed down Natalie's brow. She took a deep breath— and then she screamed when something grabbed her shoulders.

"Come on!" London picked up Natalie and half-dragged her, half-steadied her as they ran back up the tunnel.

Natalie heard London swearing under his breath. She glanced at him in surprise.

"London—"

"What do you think you were doing back there?" he shouted.

Natalie flinched. "I was saving our lives—giving you and Quincy a chance to get away. There's no way we could have outrun them." They heard the sound of bony claws scraping on the rock. "And it's not like we'll be able to outrun them now."

"You could have killed us!"

"No, not all of us—because you did what you had to do and made sure Quincy was safe. I took the risk and held up the rear." Natalie glared at London. "It was my choice, I made it, and it worked."

They stumbled up the slope. The monsters' cries rose to follow them. They were louder and more numerous than before.

They turned a corner and Natalie stopped. "I need to seal the tunnel or we're done for."

"You could collapse the whole thing!" London put his hand on her umbrella. "You'll bury us alive!"

166

Natalie glanced around the corner and saw a huge, red-eyed shape scurrying toward them.

"We don't have time to argue!" Natalie yanked her umbrella away from London and fired a blast at the mouth of the tunnel. The fireball hit the ceiling and ricocheted into the creature's face, throwing it against the wall. Its neck snapped with a crack. The beast collapsed to the floor, only to be trodden upon by two more that entered the tunnel.

"Were you trying to bring the tunnel down just then? Because it didn't work."

"No, I—"

"Come on!"

And London dragged Natalie back up the tunnel.

"What is it with you people always grabbing me?" Natalie yelled as they jumped a large rock in the middle of the tunnel. She stumbled and fell as the passage unexpectedly curved down to the right. Planting her hand in the muddy ground, she jumped back to her feet and almost hit her head on a low sloping ceiling.

She tripped again, but London helped her maintain her balance. They navigated the tight passage by ducking their heads and keeping close to the right wall.

Natalie hesitated as they reached one of the shafts with a rotting wood ladder. "Where's Quincy?"

London indicated the level above. "Up there."

A screech caused Natalie to turn around.

More reptilian figures were running at them, their long claws scraping against the floor. The creatures hunched over, scurrying along the ground to avoid the low ceiling.

"Come on, Natalie!"

She shrugged off London's arm and stepped toward the monster. Grasping her umbrella with both hands, she held her breath and sent a glowing white shot through the rock that sloped over the passage. Natalie exhaled and watched the magical projectile pierce through the wall.

Fire and stone shards went everywhere. A rock shot out from the explosion and hit a reptile in the head, breaking its jaw. Then the ceiling collapsed above the pack of creatures, and they were smothered by the rubble.

Natalie held up a hand to protect her eyes and face. Something sharp and bony kicked her in the stomach. She screamed in surprise—and then in pain as the blow threw her against the hard wall. Natalie hit her shoulder against a jutting rock and fell to the ground. She looked up to see red eyes and sharp teeth.

Natalie flinched and pressed herself against the wall to avoid the jaws snapping at her face.

Then the monster's head shuddered and flailed. She screamed again as the drake's teeth scratched her cheek.

The creature gave a gurgled screech. Its red eyes widened. The head jolted once more, and then the long skeletal neck collapsed into Natalie's lap. She trembled and kicked the body off her legs. The head rolled off the neck, which flopped uselessly on the ground. Natalie closed her eyes and crawled away from the monster's corpse.

She took quick, gasping breaths.

"Sorry about that," London said.

Natalie opened her eyes to see him standing next to her. He was holding what looked like a flaming sword.

Natalie's mind felt numb. She couldn't help but state the obvious.

"Your sword's on fire."

"My katana, to be specific." London held the fiery blade in front of him. "And I'm sorry that it wasn't as sharp as it should have been. That beast's head should have come off after the first blow."

Natalie looked the katana up and down. The hilt glowed white in London's hand, but he wasn't burned.

"That last drake made it through the rubble somehow." London lowered the sword and flicked it with his hand. The air shimmered around the blade, which glowed brightly before disappearing. "I almost didn't see it through all the excitement— and then I had to draw up the katana really quick."

"You drew it up?"

"Yeah." London traced a line through the air. He widened his fingers at one end and sharpened them to a point. He moved to the other end and stretched out his hand. London plucked the newly-fashioned fire arrow out of the air and presented it to Natalie. Thin flames burned where the fletching would have been on a normal arrow.

"Impressive." Natalie swallowed. She held a hand to her left shoulder blade and winced. "You said those things were drakes?"

"Yes. A nasty species of underground dragons. Thank Sol they're not fire-breathing." He twirled the arrow and tossed it into the air. The arrow disintegrated into a glowing wisp.

Natalie sighed, trying to ignore the throbbing pain in her shoulder. Her raincoat was stained with mud, and the darkest spots on her blue jeans were almost certainly drake blood. She felt tired. The adrenaline rush was over. Now she was ready for the crash.

Maybe she could just lie here for a while.

Dwayne poked his head out of London's chest pocket. The luminewt's glowing body pulsated rapidly. The amphibian was clearly stressed from the excitement.

Natalie glanced up the shaft. "You said Quincy's up there?"

"Yes. I'm here." A weak voice answered them from the top.

London helped Natalie up the rotting ladder. The red-haired girl expected to see Quincy waiting for them at the edge, but the sylph was curled up against the cold, wet rock.

Quincy's eyes widened at the sight of Natalie. She gave a shaky cry that was halfway between a laugh and a sob. Natalie walked over to her, and the sylph raised her arms to give Natalie a hug.

"I'm so glad you're okay." Quincy was shaking. "I thought you and London were going to get eaten...and I would be left alone, and then they would eat me." Her lip trembled. "And then nobody would ever find our remains down here—"

"Come on, Quincy. It's okay." Natalie stroked the sylph's dirty, blonde hair. "We survived. We're fine."

"But we almost weren't," London said.

Natalie turned around. "What do you mean?"

London shook his head. "You keep on trying to do things by yourself."

"No!" Natalie raised her voice and pointed a finger at him. "Don't act like I was trying to do everything by myself! You're always making it about me!"

"You're the one making everything about you!" London waved his arms in exasperation.

"I had to react quickly, and I did. I would have expected you to do the same. Besides, what was your plan? To keep running away from them? Didn't you see how fast they were? We had to stand and fight!"

London stuttered. "But you don't—you're not listening—"

"Not listening?" Natalie crossed her arms. "To what? You?"

London blushed. "You've been lucky so far, but you're still not ready for this. That's what Abbess Persephone was trying to tell you. You should have listened to *her*, at least."

169

"No, *you* listen. I have ages of experience, okay?" Natalie stepped toward London. "This isn't my first time spelunking."

London moved toward Natalie so that his face was inches from hers.

"You might have ages of experience, but you're not even a year old right now."

"Age is a relative—"

"Oh, just shut *up!*" Quincy got to her feet and stood between Natalie and London. She pushed Natalie back and then tried to push London back. He stepped back of his own accord before she could touch him.

"We almost died, okay?" Quincy glared at them. "Can't you call a truce or something? I know you're both madly in love with each other, but try to show it a little less, okay? It's driving me nuts!"

"Ha! Madly in love with him? I don't know what makes you think that!"

London glared at Natalie. "I don't either."

Then he stomped off down the tunnel.

"Where are you going?" Quincy shouted after him.

"Back where we came from. There are two other tunnels. We'll try one of those." He turned around. "I want to find what we're looking for and leave as soon as possible. This place is dangerous." He glanced at Natalie. "And so is she."

CHAPTER 25:
THE SLEEPING ARMY AWAKES

Bellamy held on tightly to Wrath's collar as the colossus ascended the metal rungs leading out of the Colossus Pit. The golem moved up the ladder with alarming speed.

They finally reached a landing, and Wrath pulled himself over the edge with a deep groan. He rose to his full height, and Bellamy cringed, hoping that Wrath wouldn't smash their heads against the ceiling.

But Wrath's head came short, leaving Bellamy to exhale in relief, grateful for the architects who had designed these passages with Wrath in mind.

Now that he knew the monster's name, Bellamy had started thinking of the golem as "he" and not "it." It was hard to think of something as an object when he had a name.

Bellamy moved around Wrath's armored collar, trying to get a view of where they were. They should be in the Army Chamber, but the map hadn't been precise beyond the Colossus Pit. He wondered if the Golem Army of Calypso would be out in the open, or if he would have to unlock a vault to find them.

When he looked around Wrath's head at what lay below, his jaw dropped in amazement.

Stretched out in front of them were hundreds of golem soldiers, standing in serried ranks on either side of a massive walkway.

The golems were looking away from Bellamy. Wrath tilted his head curiously, examining his motionless comrades.

"Let me down." Bellamy knocked on Wrath's helmet. The metallic sound echoed through the room.

Wrath raised his hand to his neck and Bellamy stepped on. The colossus carefully lowered Bellamy to the ground, and the boy stepped off the huge hand to walk among the armored ranks.

A thrill of excitement ran down his spine. The golems were tall and muscular, with either moon-colored or tan clay skin. Their sculpted cloth robes had faded blue paint. Each soldier had a

171

helmet, breastplate, spear, shield, bracers, and greaves. There must have been a thousand of them.

He looked at the end of the tunnel, where a staircase led to an archway big enough for Wrath to walk through. It had to be the legendary Valkyrie Gate: the portal created to send the golem army to Calypso in time of need.

Bellamy smirked. He was about to send the golem army to Calypso and *create* a time of need.

He pulled out *On Creatures Created,* and a sudden, unpleasant question wiped the smile off his face. Would he have to convert each golem individually, like he had converted Wrath?

He looked at the sea of golems and groaned.

Then the sound of grinding stone at the end of the chamber caught his attention.

A thin bright light shot out at him—a white horizon dawning at the end of the room. Wrath grumbled in displeasure at the light.

Bellamy held up his hand and blinked rapidly, eyes watering. As his sight adjusted, he could see a small figure standing silhouetted against the light. The light was getting bigger and bigger, and Bellamy realized that the Valkyrie Gate was opening. The huge door, hundreds of feet high, was sliding up into the ceiling.

Bellamy watched the tiny figure walk slowly down the aisle, casting an enormous shadow between the ranks of golems. It came to a sudden stop.

"Wrath, what are you doing here?"

Bellamy's stomach turned. His mouth went dry. He recognized that voice.

It was Florentina, the old golem housekeeper from Resurgam Abbey. She had a satchel slung over her shoulder.

What was Florentina doing here?

Bellamy ran to the end of his row, far away from the center aisle that Florentina was walking down. She couldn't know that he was here. He had to convert the golems quickly and quietly.

He placed his hand on the shoulders of a golem and opened *On Creatures Created.*

"What is your name?" he whispered, closing his eyes. "I know your Purpose. It is to defend Calypso."

My name is Ninurta, the golem answered in Bellamy's head, responding much quicker than Wrath had.

"I will give you a new Purpose, Ninurta."

He began the First Sacred Chant of the Rewriting of the Script—but he could hear Florentina's voice echoing through the chamber.

"Wrath, brother, what are you doing here?"

The colossus made no response.

Bellamy's eyes were shut tightly. He muttered softly under his breath. "*Deah-leh Tah-bahk...*"

He heard Florentina stop in her tracks. The echoes of her footsteps faded into silence as Bellamy finished the First Sacred Chant of the Rewriting of the Script.

"*...Spey Es.* Your new Purpose is to destroy Calypso." he whispered urgently to the golem in front of him.

The soldier stirred, and Bellamy froze, wondering if Florentina would see him. He opened his eyes and looked at her. She hadn't seen him—her attention was fixated on the colossus.

"I cannot hear your voice anymore, brother."

Bellamy turned back to the soldier and closed his eyes again. This golem had been much easier to convert than Wrath.

"Your Purpose is to destroy Calypso. *Fi-hal Sa Vahs-con Trolis...*"

Florentina's voice boomed through the Army Chamber.

"The Enemy has changed your Words, brother. Where is the Enemy? Is he here?"

A deep rumble resonated from Wrath's throat.

Bellamy heard Florentina's feet shift on the smooth stone floor. She must have been scanning the room.

"If the Enemy is here, I will find him."

"*...con Trolis.*" Bellamy finished the chant. The golem soldier tilted its head back and forth, as if he were popping his neck. Then he turned to face Bellamy and stood at attention. Bellamy held a finger to his lips for the golem to be quiet. The soldier nodded silently.

Bellamy moved to the next golem to start the process over again—but he froze when he saw Florentina out of the corner of his eye.

Across the aisle, the golem housekeeper had stopped at the end of a row. She placed her hand on a golem's shoulder. The soldier stirred and snapped to attention. Florentina pointed to the golem beside the awakened one. The first golem slung his shield over his back and put his hand on the golem beside him, who also awakened. This continued down the line. Meanwhile, the first awakened golems turned to the golems in front of them, putting their hands on their shoulders and waking them up.

Bellamy swore under his breath. He couldn't change the golems' Scripts at that rate. He had to stop Florentina.

He crouched low and began sneaking toward the aisle. Meanwhile, Florentina had crossed to his side. She stopped at the end of a row and placed her hand on the first soldier.

"Mr. Bellamy Hart. I thought you were no more."

Bellamy froze.

Florentina turned and looked directly at the boy through the rows of soldiers.

His mouth opened and closed. No words came to his lips.

"What are you doing with my brother, Mr. Hart?"

Bellamy put the codex back into his satchel. He stood slowly and walked into the aisle, positioning his body so that the light of the Valkyrie Gate didn't blind him.

"You have changed my brother's Script." Florentina's eyes flashed. "I cannot hear his voice anymore."

"Yes, I changed his Script." Bellamy's lower lip was trembling, and he couldn't stop it. He didn't want to have this conversation. "I need him."

Florentina shook her head slowly. "No, Mr. Hart. You need help from your friends. I am your friend."

"You were my friend, Florentina." Bellamy took a step back toward Wrath. "But things have changed. You can't help me. And Wrath has been given a higher purpose. This is bigger than you or me."

The housekeeper tilted her head—only she didn't look like a housekeeper now. She carried herself with a confidence that Bellamy had never seen before.

"This is bigger than you, Mr. Hart, but not in the way that you think. You have made bad decisions, but you can still be helped. You are the Enemy now, but I do not think you are the Enemy for the same reasons as the other Enemies. You were a good boy. Now you are confused. You are making bad decisions."

She looked up at Wrath, who had remained eerily still this entire time. "You have corrupted my brother, but it is not too late for him or for you. He can still be saved. You can also be saved if you surrender. Come back to the light. Obey your Script, son of Sayornis."

"I don't have a Script, Florentina."

174

"We all have a Script, Mr. Hart. It gives us the Purpose that burns within us."

"I have a new purpose now." Bellamy clenched his jaw. "I'm not surrendering, and Wrath is coming with me."

Florentina dropped her head in disappointment. "Then I must kill you."

She raised her hands. Bellamy stumbled back and raised his arms defensively. But Florentina pointed at the awakening ranks of golems on either side.

"Go to Calypso and await my command." She turned around and pointed at the Valkyrie Gate.

"What are you doing?" Bellamy's stomach tied in knots. "You can't send them to Calypso! The gods will destroy them! They'll think an invasion is coming!"

"No." Florentina shook her head. "I will explain the Situation to them. My brothers and sisters will be safer in Calypso than here." She gazed sadly at Wrath. "Here there will be destruction."

Bellamy looked at the scores of soldiers walking toward the Valkyrie Gate. More and more were waking up to join the loyal Golem Army of Calypso. He glanced to the right at the only golem that he had converted.

Anxiety tightened his chest. In less than twelve hours, the Arcadian Games would start and the Forerunners would attack Calypso.

The Forerunners' entire plan rested on using the golem army, not fighting it!

Florentina motioned at a golem, who tossed a spear toward her. She caught it deftly and pointed it toward the boy.

"Come forward, Mr. Hart," she commanded. "Face me and die with honor."

"I'm not going to fight you, Florentina." Bellamy stepped away from the golem. "We were friends. I don't want to hurt you."

"Do not worry, Mr. Hart. You cannot hurt me."

"I can, Florentina. Don't test me. Regina wouldn't want me to kill her old housekeeper."

Florentina's eyes flashed. "How dare you mention Miss Regina Primaver to me, Mr. Hart! You are a disgrace to your Purpose and to hers. I will kill you and end this dishonor!"

She jumped at Bellamy, spear poised to plunge into his chest.

Bellamy dropped into a roll to avoid her. The golem slammed onto the stone floor and spun around, ready to strike again.

"Wrath!" Bellamy shouted from the floor. "Grab her!"

He ducked as the colossus swiped at Florentina with a deafening roar.

"Don't kill her! Just grab her!" Bellamy screamed.

But Florentina had dodged Wrath's lumbering arms. She ran toward the left block of golems. Wrath responded with a backhand that shattered the bodies of a dozen soldiers. Their pieces flew away and scattered among the other ranks, breaking off more heads and limbs. Clouds of dust rose from the dead golems.

Bellamy clutched his head in horror. "No! Don't destroy them!"

Wrath stopped in mid-swing, confused. Beneath him crumbled the remains of golems who would never wake up.

Bellamy spun around, trying to find Florentina. He swore as the blinding light of the Valkyrie Gate hit him full in the face. He stumbled to the ground, hitting his forehead against Wrath's massive foot.

"Attack!" Florentina's voice boomed through the chamber.

Bellamy had never heard such a terrifying cry from her lips.

He rolled on the floor, squinting down the aisle to see what she was doing. He swore again—she was leading a charge of golems toward them.

"No!" Bellamy screamed. His mind raced. If they started to fight, Wrath would destroy hundreds of the golems. He could kill them all if he needed to—but then there would be no army.

And he didn't want to kill Florentina if he could help it. He had to protect her—for Regina's sake.

Bellamy spun around and waved frantically at the colossus. "Wrath! Pick me up!"

A moment later, he had been swept up in Wrath's gigantic hand, and he was rising through the air. Once atop the golem's shoulders, he looked down at the dozens of soldiers running toward them. Florentina motioned toward the golem soldier that Bellamy had converted, and one of her warriors broke off from the group after him. Bellamy was going to lose his only soldier.

Florentina brought her troops to a halt a few feet away from Wrath.

"What is your move, Mr. Hart? My brothers and sisters will die here fighting you."

"That's not what I want," Bellamy shouted. "I want the army. Surrender now and I won't destroy *you*."

Florentina laughed.

"You could never kill me, Mr. Hart."

"You think so?" Bellamy tried to keep his voice steady. "You want to test me?"

"I will test you and win." Florentina's eyes glinted. "You could never tell Miss Primaver that you killed me."

Bellamy swore under his breath.

"You cannot kill me, and you cannot convert the Golem Army of Calypso!" Florentina raised her spear defiantly. "You cannot win here."

"Maybe not here," Bellamy hesitated, and then a thought rose to the surface of his mind.

It could work.

Yes. That was how he was going to do it.

"Maybe not here," Bellamy said, and he actually laughed. "But I'll win where it matters. I always do!"

He grabbed hold of Wrath's armored collar.

"Wrath, grab some of the sleeping golems—but be gentle!"

Wrath grunted in response, and Bellamy held on for dear life as the colossus turned to his right and scooped up a handful of golems. Some of the soldiers broke into fragments at his powerful touch, but at least a dozen remained intact.

"No!" Florentina screamed from down below. Bellamy ignored her. His heart was pounding. This could work.

"Now stack them in your arm—your left arm—hold them gently!" Bellamy gestured frantically. "Gently! Don't break them!"

Wrath carefully slid a collection of broken and whole golem soldiers into his left arm, which he cradled against his armored chest. He suddenly roared of displeasure and looked down— Florentina and her golems were stabbing his feet with spears.

Bellamy laughed again in spite of himself. They wouldn't make a dent in his armor with their weapons.

"Don't worry about them!" He banged on Wrath's helmet to grab his attention. "They can't hurt you! Scoop up some more with your right hand—and remember, gently!"

Something sharp and sleek shot past Bellamy's ear—and he almost fell off Wrath's shoulders. He glanced down to see that the golems had abandoned their first strategy. Now they were trying to pick Bellamy off with spears.

He pressed himself against Wrath's helmet, blocking their angle of attack while the colossus bellowed angrily at the spears hitting his head.

But then the golems circled around Wrath's back. A spear flew up and smashed against his helmet where Bellamy's head had been a moment before. He ducked to avoid the shaft, and then he slipped and fell painfully against one of Wrath's back spikes. Two more spears narrowly missed him. They clattered against Wrath's heavy armor, bouncing between his spikes on their fall back to the ground.

One of their spears was sure to hit Bellamy eventually.

"One more scoop, Wrath!" he yelled, bracing himself against the spikes, using them to block the spears. "One more scoop and then we're going through the Valkyrie Gate."

They had collected a few dozen golems by now. That would have to do. Bellamy would just convert them on the other side—provided that they didn't break in transit.

Wrath stood after gathering more golems into his arms.

"Let's go!" Bellamy shouted. "Take us to the Valkyrie Gate!"

The boy held on tight as Wrath lumbered forward, picking up speed with each step. Both of Wrath's arms were clasped in front of his chest as he cradled dozens of his sleeping brothers and sisters.

Florentina's voice echoed around the cavern.

"You have corrupted my brother, but you will not force him to betray his Purpose! You will not send him to Calypso!"

Bellamy looked around, trying to locate the housekeeper.

"And how are you going to stop me, Florentina? Your spears can't harm his armor. You can't save your brother, and you can't save Calypso!"

"I will save the city, Mr. Hart," Florentina raised her voice.

Where was she?

"My brother will die before he attacks Calypso!"

"It's already too late, Florentina!" Bellamy raised his hand to block the light of the Valkyrie Gate. "I will win."

"You will drown first."

A loud crack echoed through the room—and there was a brilliant flash of light from the ceiling. Bellamy finally spotted Florentina—she was standing at the top of a walkway that trailed from the ceiling to the floor. She pulled a glowing green crystal spike from her satchel.

Bellamy's heart dropped into his stomach. "Oh...no."

Florentina shoved the spike into the ceiling, where it flashed again and began to pulsate. She hurried back down the walkway.

Bellamy flattened himself against Wrath's shoulders. "Run, Wrath! Run!"

178

The entire cavern shook violently. Chunks of rock fell from the ceiling—right toward Bellamy. They cracked against Wrath's shoulders and slid down his back.

A huge rushing noise, like water streaming down a pipe, filled the cavern.

Bellamy looked back to see the huge hole that Florentina's explosive-spike had created. A stream of water shot from the hole—and then a river spilled forth.

Water gushed from the ceiling, cracking more of the rock and sending chunks of boulders down to the floor. It flooded the chamber—crashing on the ranks of golems and sweeping them toward the cliff edge.

Bellamy shuddered at Florentina's resolve. She would rather drown the soldiers than let them betray their Purpose.

The ceiling was breaking apart, and more water was streaming from the widening hole. Streams of water splashed against Wrath's back, threatening to knock Bellamy off. A feeling of dread gripped Bellamy's heart, and he wondered if the golems would fall from Wrath's arms.

They surely would if Wrath didn't get them out soon. The gate was getting closer, but the water was rising from below and pouring from above.

Wrath's long strides made huge splashes in the torrent. He needed to go faster.

"Wrath! Hurry! Take us through the Valkyrie Arch!"

Water gushed around Bellamy, splashing against his face and weakening his grip.

Then there was a blinding flash of white light. A rushing noise filled Bellamy's ears until there was no sound. Bellamy's world went dark—his heart skipped a beat—

—and then they were through the Valkyrie Gate.

CHAPTER 26:
THE LAKE

"Oh my gosh, this is *disgusting!*" Quincy pulled something wet and indescribable from her hair. She flicked it onto the floor. "That was *not* water! What was that?"

London wrinkled his nose at the smelly water running along the ground. Drops of the putrid liquid splashed onto his hair from the ceiling.

"Best not to think about it." He pointed to a spot on her shoulder. "And you missed some."

"Ew!"

Natalie walked next to them in silence. She hadn't spoken since their last argument. She distracted herself by wondering why the water level was slowly rising. She was splashing through water with each step.

"Are we in any danger of drowning down here?" Natalie asked.

London shook his head. "I don't think so."

Quincy pointed up ahead. "Unless we fall in there."

The tunnel had opened up to a huge space. London stroked Dwayne's back, and the luminewt brightened with a burp. Dwayne's orange light revealed the murky black waters of an enormous underground lake.

A walkway of stone stretched out from the shore, weaving through a forest of stalactites and out of sight. The lake's far shore was impossible to see through the thick rock columns puncturing the surface of the water.

"This looks promising." London stepped out of the wet tunnel onto dry rock.

"Are you serious? You can't even see the other side. We don't know what's over there." Quincy drew her green cardigan closer. "And it's so cold down here."

"I agree with London," Natalie said, stepping after him onto the rocky shore. "Let's take the path."

They followed the smooth walkway over the water. It was only wide enough to walk single-file.

Quincy brushed her hand against the cool limestone columns on either side. "This seems too well-made to be natural."

"Yeah. But I wonder why they went through the trouble of weaving it through all of these stalactites?" Natalie walked around a bend in the path. She glanced down at the black, placid water, which was five or six feet below them.

"Did you see how perfectly it connected to the shore? It's one solid piece of rock." London pointed to the thick pillars around them. "Some of the stalactites are connected to the path, but none of them block it."

The trio turned around another bend and saw a stalactite that had been cut to make room for the walkway.

"Maybe this is the path to the golem army!" Quincy clapped her hands together in excitement. The sound echoed, booming around the cavern.

CLAP...Clap...Clap...Clap...

London and Natalie whipped around to look at Quincy, whose mouth gaped in horror.

When silence fell again, London breathed a sigh of relief.

"I was afraid the echo might—"

BOOM!

The sound and the resulting shock knocked them off their feet. London fell forward and hit his knee on the rock. He swore.

Natalie fell backwards with a yelp. "London! You swore again!"

"Sorry." He grimaced and rubbed his knee. "I—"

"What was *that*?" Quincy quivered against a stalactite. "And what's that noise?"

A tremendous bellow rose up from the depths of the lake, shaking the limestone pillars around them.

Natalie crawled to the edge of the walkway and peeked over the side to look at the water. The lake wasn't calm anymore.

It was *churning*.

"Oh, dear." She gripped her umbrella and rose unsteadily to her feet. The ceiling rattled overhead. A stalactite broke off to crash into the lake, splashing them with icy water.

"We need to get back to shore now!" Natalie stumbled over to Quincy and pulled the sylph to her feet. "Run!"

"What's happening?" London crouched at the stone's edge. His voice was shaky. "What's the water doing?"

Natalie looked at the water from the light of the luminewt. The lake was circling faster and faster.

182

"What does it look like? It's a whirlpool!" She grabbed London and pulled him away. Her voice rose to a scream when another stalactite smashed into the ground behind them.

They ran down the winding path. Natalie tried not to look at the lake, but she couldn't help noticing the way the water level was dropping underneath them and gathering at the edges.

Through the collapsing forest of stalactites, Natalie could distinguish a long trail of water running down the center of the whirlpool.

"Oh my gods! The entire lake is draining!" Quincy shrieked. She and Natalie ran ahead of London, who had to slow his pace to keep from running into them.

They weaved in and out of the stalactites surrounding the pathway while the cacophonous sounds of breaking rock and rushing water filled their ears. Limestone cracked and crashed into the receding waters on either side.

"Oh my gods!" Quincy continued to scream hysterically. "The cavern is collapsing! We're going to be buried alive!"

"Quincy! Shut up!" Natalie gripped her umbrella, a grim expression on her face. "We're almost at the shore!"

She could see it through the forest of limestone. Just one more bend and they would be on the final stretch—

CRACK!

A heavy column of limestone snapped from the roof and broke through the pathway, cutting them off from land.

Cold water splashed onto their faces as Natalie and Quincy came to an abrupt stop on the edge. They teetered for a moment over the yawning whirlpool—but London pulled them back to safety.

They collapsed back onto the path together.

Natalie brushed a wet tangle of red hair out of her eyes. She scrambled to her feet with London's aid, and the two of them helped Quincy up.

"My arm!" Quincy bent over in pain. "I think it's broken!"

London took Quincy's arm in his hands and examined it. Natalie looked at the huge gap between them and safety. Another thought occurred to her—and she glanced at the ground beneath their feet in sudden dread.

"What's holding us up?" She turned to London, her eyes wide.

He was helping Quincy flex her arm. "It's not broken, see? You can move it."

"It hurts so much!" Quincy cried, her face shining with lake water and tears.

"What's holding us up?" Natalie repeated.

London looked at her, confused. "What are you talking about?"

"We're not connected to the shore anymore." Natalie pointed at the break. "What's keeping the path from collapsing?"

London gulped. "The stalactites?" Another thunderous boom shook the cavern. "Best not to worry about that—how are we getting back to the shore?"

"I don't know! I—my umbrella!" Natalie held it up. "I'll fly us!"

Quincy stopped crying to give Natalie an incredulous look.

"Are you crazy?" she shouted over the rushing water and crumbling stone.

"Yes!" Natalie opened her umbrella in her right hand—and before London or Quincy could protest, she wrapped both arms around the pair and jumped off the edge.

They plummeted into the darkness. Quincy screamed in Natalie's ear, and the red-haired girl winced in pain. The trio fell down, down, down. Just as their feet brushed against the draining whirlpool, which threatened to drag them under, they shot up with a jolt.

They soared up toward the underside of the path—on course to hit it.

Natalie twisted the handle between her fingertips, swinging them around the walkway to avoid a collision.

"Natalie!" Quincy screamed at the sound of a stalactite breaking right above them.

Natalie whipped them back the way they had come—and London yelped in fright. She barely maneuvered them around the falling rock, which sent a rush of air against them as it whooshed past.

She had flown over the path, and they were about to touch down when she kicked off again.

"What are you doing?" London yelled, his eyes wide.

"Look!" She gave a restricted nod to the shoreline, which was crumbling into the lake. They flew over collapsing ground toward the tunnel mouth, trying to find a safe place to land on the shrinking shoreline.

Another crack boomed overhead. Natalie swung them hard to the right to avoid the falling stalactite, but she was too late. It

184

clipped the edge of the umbrella, and they fell hard onto wet, shifting ground.

Natalie scrambled to her feet, her mind dizzy and her vision blurred. She spun on the spot, trying to locate London and Quincy through the black chaos.

Quincy screamed again.

Natalie shot a flare toward the ceiling to illuminate her surroundings. Quincy was holding desperately onto a boulder while the churning waters tugged at her legs and waist, threatening to drag her away.

Natalie ran toward her just as Quincy lost her grip. She threw herself at the sylph and grabbed her wet forearm. Something wrapped itself around Natalie's feet.

Quincy's arm slipped out from Natalie's grasp. The sylph screamed and fell away—

"No!" Natalie shrieked. She swung her umbrella at her friend and whispered an urgent spell. Quincy's flailing hand brushed against the magically glowing tip.

With unnatural speed, Quincy's hand wrapped around the umbrella and locked onto it—caught in the spell's Irresistible Grip. Natalie screamed in surprise as something dragged her backwards—taking Quincy with her.

They slid along the ground, away from the churning water and crumbling rock.

London pulled them back to the tunnel mouth. He dropped to the mud, chest heaving with exertion and eyes wide with fright. Natalie wiped water and hair from her face and nodded her exhausted thanks. Beside them, Quincy doubled over and threw up.

There was another great, shuddering boom, and the water receded from the edges.

"Up the tunnel!" London shouted. He grabbed Quincy's hand and pushed Natalie up the slope. They sprinted along the path while the ground continued to shake beneath them.

After rounding a corner, they came to a wide stretch of tunnel. Another almighty tremor boomed. Natalie groaned—the stalactites cracked and began to fall.

She motioned to the other two. "Hurry!"

They quickened their pace through the tunnel. An exit yawned up ahead. Natalie hoped they would be safe if they could just get past this stretch.

"London!" she screamed.

He looked up to see a needle-sharp stalactite hurtling toward his face.

In a blur of movement, Natalie opened her umbrella and threw herself at London. She tackled him to the ground and held her umbrella overhead as the stalactite slammed into them.

She felt the rock break against the umbrella canopy.

London and Natalie coughed from the dust rising around them. Natalie opened her eyes to find that she was lying next to London with her face against his shoulder.

She jumped to her feet and brushed herself off. London did the same.

A sob escaped from Quincy's throat.

"We're going to die down here!"

The tunnel had been blocked. Mud and earth covered the exit, and the air felt thick and dirty in their lungs.

They were trapped.

CHAPTER 27:
THE GARGOYLE GUARD

In the late hours of the night, so late that it was early morning, the gargoyle guard stood watch in the dock.

Technically, he *crouched* watch.

Gargoyles are excellent guards because they never sleep. They never move from their post. They never get bored.

This gargoyle's name was Tim. He was very ugly. Gargoyles should be ugly. Tim wasn't a paragon of gargoyle ugliness, but he would have held his own in an ugly contest.

If he had a mother, his mother would have been proud. As it was, Tim didn't have a mother because he was carved from stone. Not many gargoyles have mothers. Tim, for one, didn't mind. He never had a mother, so he didn't notice her absence.

He did, however, notice the seagull droppings that covered him from chipped horns to weatherworn pedestal. And he noticed the foliage that had overgrown his body. No one had trimmed it in ages.

He also noticed the massive ship breaking through the fog.

It was a flying frigate, but it was skimming the surface of the water. The ship came to a halt in the empty dock, where it loomed menacingly.

Tim had been assigned to this station to observe unusual activity. He observed that it was most unusual for a frigate to come into this dock, which had been used by small-time fishermen before the piers fell into disrepair. It was near the outskirts of old-town Calypso. Not many people came around here anymore.

A boy suddenly materialized out of the shadows.

That was unusual too. Tim frowned.

The boy dropped to a crouch, twitching his head left and right, as if making sure that no one was watching. Tim stayed still—something he was quite good at. The boy looked directly at the gargoyle, but must not have seen him. Tim fancied that he excelled at not being seen when he wanted to remain hidden.

187

But he admitted that the overgrown foliage made for really good cover.

Either way, the boy seemed satisfied that he was alone, and he hurried across the sand to the shoreline.

A small boat descended from the frigate. The boy watched it, shifting from one leg to the other. Tim thought he looked nervous.

When the boat landed, a dark silhouette detached from the shadow and stepped onto the beach.

This newcomer was tall and thin. He towered over the boy.

"Do you have it?" he asked coldly.

The boy handed him an object.

Tim screwed up his eyes in concentration, trying to decipher the shape through the gloom.

"This book is very powerful," the boy said, a hint of warning in his voice.

"Yes," the tall one said impatiently. "That's why you were instructed to steal it."

"Just be careful."

"It will be used well."

"And make sure the Pantheon doesn't find out who gave it to you," the boy hissed. "Or all of my work will be compromised."

"I am well aware of the sensitive nature of this operation," the tall one snarled. "I have no intention of being captured."

"I just want to make sure—"

"I will make sure," the tall one interrupted. "Now, I don't have much time. Are the golems in place?"

"As instructed."

"Good. Are you coming aboard?"

"No. I have business elsewhere."

"I hope for your sake that it's not in Calypso. If I were you, I would get away from here as soon as possible."

"Duly noted."

The tall one raised the book to his forehead in an ironic salute. Then he got into his boat, which became a black silhouette before the frigate's shadow absorbed it.

Moments later, the ship disappeared into the fog.

The boy watched it fade away, and then he too disappeared.

Tim frowned. He scratched his stone chin thoughtfully.

All of this seemed very important. Surely, the Pantheon would want to know.

If only Tim had been sculpted with legs, he could go and tell someone what he had heard.

As it was, Tim had no legs.

So he settled in and waited for someone important to come and ask if he had seen anything unusual.

CHAPTER 28:
THE OPENING CEREMONY

The sky exploded in a burst of fireworks.

"It must be three thirty now!" Clare shouted, clapping her hands excitedly. "Less than an hour until sunrise!"

"I can't believe we've been here since eight. I'm dead." Arthur ran a hand through his long, sweaty hair. "As soon as they light the Undying Fire and this ends, I'm going to sleep."

"No!" Clare yanked playfully on Arthur's red hoodie. "We need to stay for the post-ceremony concert!"

Arthur rubbed his bleary eyes. "I don't think so. After that dwarf metal band, I don't want to hear any more music for the rest of the week. They were terrible."

"That's because they're dwarves." Clare rolled her eyes, brushing a strand of blonde hair behind her pointed ear.

Arthur shrugged. "Feldspar is an okay band. So are the Quake Brothers. They're dwarves."

Clare stuck out her tongue in disgust. "That's a loose definition of the word 'okay.'"

"You're okay. I guess." Arthur grinned, tickling Clare under the arm. She laughed and swatted his hand away.

A bald gnome in overalls rolled his eyes and leaned away from the elves' public display of affection. The gnome's wife shook her head, stroking her ginger beard and watching the elves disapprovingly.

Down below, the field was dominated by an enormous stage shaped like a mountain. A series of steps ascended to the top, where the Golden Bowl of Undying Fire gleamed in the early morning darkness.

The streets outside were packed with the hundreds of thousands who didn't have tickets to the opening ceremony but wanted to imbibe the atmosphere. For blocks all around the stadium, Calypso was full of cheering, singing, dancing, and drinking.

Arthur and Clare sat at the top eastern end of the Arcadian Stadium, a bowl arena which seated over 120,000 people. To the southwest they could see people lined shoulder-to-shoulder on the Calypso Bridge, which had been decorated with lights.

"Look! It's the gods!" Clare pointed at a small ship approaching the stadium. It was a fancy skiff with golden sails. Two clipper ships flanked the vessel as it descended to the west end of the field.

The stadium lights dimmed, and huge spotlights illuminated the early morning sky. An enthusiastic male voice boomed through the stadium.

"All rise for the arrival of the gods!"

"Figures they would wait until it's about to start." Arthur yawned. "They have to make a big entrance."

"Shh." Clare kicked Arthur in the shins.

"Ow!" he protested. She ignored his whining and pulled him up to join everyone who had risen to their feet.

The spotlights centered on the skiff. Dozens of armored angels walked out to the ship, forming a guard of honor that led to a luxuriously furnished section in the west stands.

A herald in shining silver descended from the skiff on a floating platform. His long black hair billowed in the early morning breeze. He tossed the trail of his robe over his shoulder and blew three loud trumpet blasts.

All of the mortals in the stands bowed their heads in respect. Even Arthur dropped his head a few degrees. A procession of gods descended from the skiff, looking like a rainbow parade in shining robes of amber, emerald, lapis lazuli, ruby, and sapphire. A long red carpet rolled out from the luxury seating. The carpet unfurled on the ground, reaching the skiff just before the first gods stepped onto the lush green field.

"Huh. Look at who came." Arthur snorted. "Anyone who's anyone is at the wedding in Parlemagne. We got the dregs. Ahumaz is the only god who looks like he really wants to be here."

"Arthur!" Clare hissed.

The stadium was silent while the gods walked from the skiff to their section. Once they were seated, they waved their hands at the audience, who applauded.

"What are we doing? Applauding them for sitting down?" Arthur asked sarcastically.

"Arthur, shut up!" Clare tried to kick him in the shin again, but he moved out of the way. "It's about respect."

Arthur winked at his girlfriend. "I have lots of respect for them. It must be hard to walk in those ridiculous costumes."

The herald blew his trumpet again, and the crowd fell silent. He took a minute to ascend the mountainous stage, where he stood next to the Golden Bowl of Undying Fire. Then he unfurled a scroll, his voice magically amplified throughout the stadium.

"Welcome, gods and goddess, to the opening ceremony of the Arcadian Games!" He bowed toward the gods' section, who responded with a small round of polite applause.

"Welcome, mortal residents and visitors of Arcadia, to the opening ceremony of the Arcadian Games!"

The stadium and the surrounding blocks erupted with noise.

"We celebrate the Arcadian Games as a testament to the strength and virtue of the Pantheon. The Undying Fire is a symbol of the Goddess Sayornis, the brave and mighty First Goddess who sacrificed her life in the Battle of Three Suns to defeat the Titans and save the universe!"

A huge cheer went up around the stadium.

"To light the Undying Fire and begin the Arcadian Games, I present to you the winner of two dozen gold medals! The remarkable, the stunning, the only—Io!"

The herald pointed to the southwest corner of the stadium, where a handsome tan god with flowing black hair was running down a ramp.

Io held the Torch of Sayornis in his right hand, and he blew kisses at the audience with his left. Even from the top of the stadium, Arthur could hear the squeals of girls lining the ramp. They tossed bouquets of flowers at their idol. The entire stadium chanted "Io! Io!" in step with the god's run toward the Golden Bowl.

As Io ran closer to the stage, the roaring got louder until the stadium shook with the cheering.

Io reached the mountain and ascended the steps, passing the herald, who hurried down to stand by the gods' section.

Arthur and Clare clapped their hands in time with the other fans. The roar was deafening. They looked at each other and shared a kiss, which lasted longer than Clare had anticipated. But she didn't mind.

When they finally broke apart, Io was a dozen steps away from the Golden Bowl. The stadium trembled beneath the roar.

The god stopped next to the bowl, his chest heaving, his muscular arms glistening with sweat. He held the torch aloft and raised a hand to his ear. The crowd elevated their screaming to another decibel level. Io was enjoying every moment.

Arthur clapped his hands over his ringing ears. Clare did the same.

Then Io lowered the Torch of Sayornis to light the Undying Fire—and the stadium literally erupted.

An explosion boomed from the center of the field, and the stage collapsed in on itself.

Io disappeared in a shower of debris. The torch disappeared in an avalanche of rocks.

Clare grabbed Arthur's arm, and he held her close.

Smoke covered the field. Screams filled the air.

The spotlights searched for Io through the clouds of dust. They stopped on a figure that was climbing out of the rubble. It was Io. He reached down, pulled the Golden Bowl out from beneath a rock, and held it aloft. The crowd went wild.

"Absolutely amazing!" the herald stuttered. "I give you...*Io!*"

Clare laughed with relief and clapped a hand over her mouth. "Was that supposed to happen?"

"I don't know." Arthur hugged her tightly. He glanced at the aisles, checking to see how crowded they were in case they had to leave immediately. "But the field is in total ruins."

"Well, if they planned it, I'm sure they can—"

BOOM.

The entire stadium shook again. Arthur looked at Io, who was staring at the ground. The god stepped back slowly.

Then he dropped the Golden Bowl and ran.

BOOM!

A huge hand burst out of the rubble. Io disappeared between the titanic fingers. An enormous arm followed the hand, and then another arm burst out of the ground, sending a shower of rocks onto the lower levels of the stadium.

Heavy debris crushed entire sections, burying thousands of fans. The remaining crowd panicked, screaming and shouting in dismay.

"What—what is that?" Clare cried.

"I don't know—but we need to get out of here!" Arthur took her by the shoulders and led her toward the aisle, which was full of people jostling to leave.

Then there was a spine-tingling, earth-shaking roar, and a monstrous body pulled itself out of the ground. A colossal figure, covered from head to foot in spiked armor, emerged from the clouds of dust to stand over the hole he had created.

The hand that had grabbed Io was still clenched. Arthur cringed and tried not to think about what would happen to the god.

The colossus threw back his head and bellowed. He squeezed his hand tightly and tossed something messy and indistinguishable to the ground. Arthur was grateful to be standing so far away.

The crowd was in pandemonium. Tens of thousands of people had evacuated their seats and were fighting to get down the ramps. The gods scrambled from their stands to board the skiff, which was hovering overhead. The two clippers circled around the stadium, but they couldn't fire at the colossus without hitting the people in the stands.

"Look! It's Ahumaz!"

"It's Ahumaz!"

Arthur turned his head at the shouts. He felt Clare tug his sleeve desperately.

"Arthur! We need to go!"

He pointed down at the field. "Ahumaz is going to fight it!"

A bolt of lightning shot from the sky to the field and coiled in the god's hand. Thunder cracked, and a shining two-handed sword formed in Ahumaz's hands. Curly blonde locks fell over his brilliant red robes. He faced the colossus, feet apart, standing his ground while the gods around him fled.

He held the sword aloft and shouted in a stern voice that boomed throughout the stadium.

"Surrender, golem! Yield to Ahumaz!"

The colossus tilted his head, considering the god. He let loose a furious roar and swung a long arm.

Ahumaz jumped into the air with a mighty leap that carried him up to the colossus's face. He swung his glowing sword at the golem, slicing across its cheek. The sword found its target with a shattering blow that forced the colossus back. The monster staggered, swatting at the air in vain.

Ahumaz landed feet-first a dozen yards from the colossus, balancing himself with a hand on the ground.

Arthur clapped a hand to his mouth, mesmerized by the sight.

"What a warrior! He's going to beat that colossus! Did you see what he did with the first blow?"

"Arthur, we need to—"

The colossus roared and swung around clumsily, trying to find who had wounded his face. Down on the ruined field,

Ahumaz was running around to the colossus's back, swinging his sword in a furious circle.

The sun had finally risen—and a ray of light broke over the edge of the stadium to illuminate the colossus's back.

Arthur looked at the gods' stand to see that most of the gods had climbed into their skiff.

"Why don't more of the gods stand and fight with Ahumaz?" he asked out loud.

"Didn't you see what that creature did to Io?"

Arthur turned around to see a female gnome watching the battle intently. She had red hair, long eyelashes, and a thick ginger beard. "I wouldn't want to face that beastie either. But Ahumaz seems to be doing all right by himself."

There was another thunderclap, and Arthur turned around to see a deep gash on the crown of the colossus's helmet. Ahumaz spiraled through the air and landed on the field. The golem staggered with heavy steps, clutching his head wound. His armor was thick, but he was no match for Ahumaz's speed.

Ahumaz paused a moment to take a breath while the colossus looked around for him. He started swinging his sword again and was about to jump when the ground blew up.

Arthur gasped and felt Clare tighten her grip. An enormous ship had flown over the south end of the stadium. It was concentrating a broadside at Ahumaz.

The glowing-white cannonballs peppered the ground, rendering the field unrecognizable.

Arthur's heart plummeted. When the barrage finally stopped, he could see a faint red shape crumpled in the rubble. It was difficult to distinguish between Ahumaz's red robes and his mangled body. Arthur felt nauseated.

He thought he saw the god stir—but then an enormous foot crushed the body, driving it deep into the ground.

The colossus raised his leg and stomped again—and again.

Then he roared and beat his chest.

Another explosion tore Arthur's eyes away from that horrifying sight to another—he looked at the west end to see the large ship unleash a merciless salvo of cannonballs on the gods' defenseless skiff, which had lingered to watch Ahumaz fight. The skiff spun in the air before crashing into the stands.

A trail of smoke poured from the wrecked vessel—but then the colossus slammed his fist and extinguished the flames. He pummeled it with another blow, creating a hole in the stadium, burying the remains of the skiff and the gods it had carried.

"Oh my gods," Arthur gasped.

"They're dead," the female gnome said. "And we will be too if we don't run! *Run!*"

CHAPTER 29:
THE BLINDING LIGHT

Natalie looked at the pile of boulders blocking their way to the surface. Her heart sank.

"What are we going to do?" Quincy asked.

Natalie didn't answer. London looked stunned. Wordlessly, he turned around and walked back to the cavern they had just left. He stepped around the massive fragments of fallen limestone, staring at the empty bowl that had once held a lake.

He licked his lips nervously. "Our only option is to go down."

"Down? Farther into the cave?" Quincy clasped her hands in horror. "There could be more of those creatures down there! Who knows if there's any way out? We could be trapped down here forever!" She collapsed to the ground and started to cry.

Natalie knelt by Quincy and held her shoulders. "Now is not the time to panic."

"I don't want to die down here! I don't want to suffocate!"

"It's going to be okay," Natalie said.

"You don't know that!" Quincy yelled.

Natalie flinched at Quincy's scream in her ear. She waited a minute while Quincy calmed down. Then she stood and wiped her dirty hands on her jeans. "London's right. All we can do is go down."

"And how will we do that?" Quincy sniffed and looked at the gaping mouth that plunged into darkness. "It's just a big hole where the lake drained."

Natalie lifted her umbrella. "I'll have to fly us down."

London sighed.

"You know it's the only way."

"I know. But I don't like it."

"I don't want to go." Quincy sat on the ground with her arms crossed. "I've had enough."

"Quincy, we need to go on. Florentina could be down there."

Quincy scowled. "Don't talk to me about Florentina. She's the one who sent us here in the first place."

"Oh, come on." Natalie grabbed Quincy's forearm and lifted her up. The sylph stood reluctantly.

"*Fine.*" Quincy wiped her bottom with her hands. "Ick. This is disgusting-disgusting-*disgusting!* Florentina owes me big for this. She better clean my room spotless."

"That's your idea of a reward?" Natalie opened her umbrella with a flourish. "I would settle for Florentina leaving my room alone for a day."

A few moments later, the trio was holding onto each other while Natalie navigated them "down the drain," as Quincy put it. They descended through the tunnel, trying to avoid the slick muddy walls, until they reached a hole that was too small for the umbrella to fit through.

"Here," Natalie landed on the sloshy surface, "hold onto the—whoa!" Her feet slipped out from underneath her, and she slid toward the hole.

London grabbed her raincoat and yanked her back just in time.

"Hold onto the wall, you mean?" He helped Natalie to her feet. Her yellow raincoat was covered in mud.

"Thanks." Natalie brushed hair out of her eyes, leaving a streak of mud across her forehead. She took a deep breath. "I'll go down first and see if I can find another landing where you can follow me."

"You don't know what's down there!" Quincy leaned away from the wall to peer down the hole.

"I should go first," London said.

Natalie rolled her eyes. "Yeah, and do what? Fall all the way to the bottom? I'm the one who flies the umbrella."

"I can—"

"I'm going down." Natalie closed her umbrella and stepped forward.

"Wait!" Quincy grabbed Natalie. "How are you going to get us down after you go through the hole?"

"Slide down after me." Natalie plucked her raincoat sleeve from Quincy's grasp. "And don't grab me just before I'm about to jump down a tunnel. It's dangerous."

"Well, speaking of *dangerous*," Quincy put her muddy hands on her hips, "what's going to happen when we slide down? Are you going to catch us?"

Natalie hesitated. "Well—"

"Yeah. It sounds dumb when you say it out loud, right?" Quincy flashed a humorless smile. "Because it *is* dumb. Let's just make the hole bigger. Come on." She pushed away from the wall and began kicking at the ground. "Then we'll—all—go—through."

"Quincy, stop!" Natalie's eyes widened. "You don't know how loose—Quincy!"

The ground collapsed beneath the sylph's feet. Quincy screamed and plummeted out of sight.

"Quincy!" she yelled. "Oh—we're coming!"

Natalie grabbed a startled London around the waist.

"What are you—" London began, but he was cut off when they jumped after the sylph.

They fell down a thin hole, slipping and sliding along a winding tunnel. They fell down, down, down—Quincy's screams echoing back up to them. A cold blast of air told Natalie they were about to enter a larger space. A moment later, they shot into a huge chamber.

"What is that?" Natalie screamed, but her words were lost to the rushing wind.

To her right, a blazing white light shone from the cavern's floor to its towering ceiling. She twisted her body away from the light, blinking to erase the blinding scene. She could still hear Quincy screaming—and then the screams were cut off by a loud splash.

"What was—" Natalie started to ask, but then she and London plummeted into a frigid river.

She swallowed a mouthful of cold, foul water. It forced her umbrella open, and Natalie felt the drag of her umbrella protesting the plunge, pulling them back up to the surface. A strong current whipped her and London around, dragging them off in a new direction. Natalie felt London lose his grip on her.

A moment later, she surfaced. The bright white light was behind her, illuminating the shapes of London and Quincy bobbing on the surface. The river was sweeping them toward what looked like a waterfall.

Then Natalie realized that this wasn't a river. It was the lake they had seen earlier.

And it was still draining.

With an effort, she dragged her umbrella out of the current and raised it into the air. She burst out of the water and flew toward London. Holding onto the handle with her right hand, she strained to reach him with her left. He grabbed at it but missed.

"Get Quincy!" he shouted, paddling in vain against the current.

Natalie turned around and steered herself toward Quincy, who was dangerously close to the waterfall. The sylph screamed hysterically against the dark waves.

Over the edge of the waterfall, Natalie could see scores of red dots lining the walls.

The red dots were organized into pairs.

Oh dear, she thought.

Drakes were climbing the walls.

Natalie hoped that the dragons weren't good swimmers. The last thing she wanted was for drakes to drop onto her.

She was getting close to Quincy. Natalie held up her umbrella to decelerate. She had to time this perfectly. There would only be one chance to save Quincy.

The waterfall's roar filled her ears. The draining lake rushed over the edge and into the abyss.

Natalie dropped to the waves, stretching down her hand to grab Quincy's.

"Quincy!" she screamed.

The terrified sylph turned around to see Natalie sweeping toward her. Quincy had just enough presence of mind to raise a hand for help—and Natalie snatched it. She pulled Quincy out of the water, yelling with the effort. The sylph's hands were slippery and wet. Quincy started to lose her grip, but Natalie dug her fingernails into Quincy's skin. Quincy screamed in pain, but she was able to throw her arm around Natalie's waist and hold on.

Quincy's sudden weight almost sent the two girls back into the water, but Natalie kept them above the surface, sweeping them around in time to see London rushing toward them. She had to squint against the blinding light at the end of the cavern.

Where was that light coming from?

Above her, she heard the harsh cries of the drakes. She tried not to think about what would happen if the dragons jumped on her conspicuous red umbrella.

Meanwhile, Quincy was strangling Natalie's waist in a desperate attempt to hold on. The draining lake swept London towards them. How was Natalie going to save *him*?

An idea struck her.

She shook her right foot. "London!"

His face kept disappearing and reappearing amid the tossing waves, but she thought she saw him respond with a thumbs-up.

She hoped it would work.

London came closer and closer. Natalie bit her lip hard. If he missed, she wouldn't be able to turn around in time to save him from going over the edge.

He was less than fifteen yards away. Natalie stretched her foot down as far as she could, hoping that London wouldn't take her rain boot off or pull them into the water.

He raised both arms to grab her.

She passed over him—

—and London wrapped himself around her leg.

For a terrifying moment, the weight almost pulled them under. A huge wave caught Natalie in the chest, and Quincy screamed. But then they were flying up and toward the light.

They flew faster and higher, away from the waves. The wind rushed against Natalie, whipping her red hair about her face. She flew them away from the walls, which were dotted with the red eyes of drakes.

She was taking them toward the light—but, with a sinking feeling, she realized that she didn't know why. It was away from the waterfall, but what was it?

Quincy seemed to be thinking the same thing. "How are we going to get out of here?" Her voice was slow and exhausted.

As they drew closer, Natalie realized that the painfully bright light was shaped like an arch.

"I think it's a portal," Natalie said.

"What if it's dangerous?" Quincy asked.

"Why wouldn't it be?" London called from below.

They flew closer and closer. Natalie glanced at the walls behind her. They were teeming with drakes. The beasts were scurrying along the walls toward the arch.

There was only one way to go.

Natalie swallowed nervously. Then she closed her eyes and they passed into the light.

CHAPTER 30:
MIXED COMPANY

Natalie collapsed onto hard ground. She heard London groan as he hit the ground beside her. Quincy gave a little scream and stumbled into both of them.

The red-haired girl rolled over and closed her eyes. She lay against the coarse ground, feeling it with her fingertips. It was cement.

No, it was tarmac. It was a road. That was interesting.

She opened her eyes to see a spear pointed in her face.

She sighed. When could she get a moment's rest?

"Are you Miss Bliss?" a deep, resonant voice asked.

Natalie glanced at the figure holding the spear and saw that it was a heavily-armored golem.

"Yes," she answered weakly. "I'm Natalie Bliss."

"Welcome, Miss Bliss. My name is Eamon." The golem withdrew his spear and extended a hand toward Natalie. She took it and Eamon helped her up. She whimpered as a dozen sharp pains registered their complaints with her nervous system.

"These are your friends?" Eamon pointed his spear at London and Quincy, who were surrounded by armored golems.

"Yes!" Natalie said quickly. "Don't hurt them!"

The golems lowered their spears and helped London and Quincy to their feet. The sylph shot a dark look at the soldier who had pointed a spear at her. His white eyes stared back impassively.

"I am sorry to alarm you," Eamon said. "Florentina ordered us to wait here for Miss Bliss."

"Florentina?" Natalie said excitedly. "She was here? When did she get here? How did she—"

Natalie was cut off by a terrifying screech. She turned around to see a drake flying toward her, mouth open, sharp talons flailing.

A heavy hand shoved Natalie to the ground. Her forehead hit the tarmac. Liquid splashed onto her right arm.

Dazed, Natalie opened her eyes to see that her right arm was covered in black blood. She glanced up and saw Eamon's spear sticking through the drake's chest.

The golem lifted the drake and shook the creature off his spear. The dragon crumpled onto the ground, limbs splayed out at awkward angles.

Eamon pointed at another soldier. "Close the Valkyrie Gate. There will be more of them."

The golem nodded and lifted a heavy key off the ground. Using both hands, he shoved the key into a hole beside the arch. He gripped the end of the key and rotated it hand-over-hand. There was a heavy ratcheting noise, and then the Valkyrie Gate flashed brighter.

"We must back away," Eamon said.

Without waiting for a response, he picked up Natalie and carried her away from the arch, which flickered violently. Natalie closed her eyes.

The ground trembled beneath her feet for a long moment, and then it was still. When Natalie opened her eyes, she saw an ornate mural where the white light of the Valkyrie Gate had been. Countless ranks of heavily-armored golems filled the mural. Some of the golems near the front carried banners. Beside them were important-looking golems that Natalie assumed were officers. One of them had curly brown hair and a finely-sculpted face. She looked remarkably familiar.

Eamon set Natalie on the ground.

"We must join the battle," he said, walking down the long, stone-walled tunnel. "Our brothers and sisters are already fighting."

"Where are they?" Natalie hurried behind the golem and his soldiers. London and Quincy followed.

"They are by the Arcadian Stadium."

Natalie clapped a hand over her mouth. "And does the enemy have the colossus?"

"Yes. They have rewritten Wrath's Script." Eamon's eyes flashed. "He has lost his Purpose. He has killed many of our brothers and sisters."

"Florentina said that he could be brought back to our side." Natalie quickened her pace to keep up with the golems, who had broken into a small run, their armor rattling with each step.

"It can be done if Florentina says it can be done."

206

"How far is the Arcadian Stadium?" Natalie examined the huge tunnel. "And what is this place?"

"This place is called the Tunnel. The Arcadian Stadium is many miles away."

"Many miles?" Natalie's heart sank. "Are we walking all the way there?"

"We are not walking. We are running. But we will not run the whole way. The Tunnel leads to many places. It was built so the Golem Army of Calypso could move quickly to any part of Calypso. We will run to the train station. We will take the train to the Arcadian Stadium."

"If there's fighting going on, will the trains still be running?" London asked.

Eamon's head swiveled around backwards to look at London. His body continued to run ahead in a straight line.

"We will take the train. It will run for us."

*

"That was a lot of steps," Quincy gasped. They had reached the top of a staircase that had started down at the Tunnel, which was now far below them.

Natalie blinked in the light filtering through the ceiling grates. "Where are we?"

"We are at the train station. Follow me." Eamon led them through a culvert and into a small room.

It seemed to be a dead end. There was nothing in front of them but smooth marble walls.

They could hear lots of people moving around and talking excitedly on the other side, but there didn't seem to be a way through.

"What now?" Quincy panted, holding her hips.

"The Tunnel has not been used in many years." Eamon stepped up to the wall. "People have built around the exits. We will make a way."

Then the golem punched a hole through the wall.

A small cloud of dust settled to the ground as he drew back his fist for another blow. Screams and shouts came from the other side.

The golems joined Eamon, punching the walls and pulling chunks of marble away until they had created a hole big enough to walk through.

Natalie thought the golems must have looked terrifying as they emerged from the hole. They were massive, armored, clay warriors with shining white eyes, covered in dirt and dust. Then she examined herself and realized that she was covered in sweat, mud, dust, and a good deal of drake blood.

A hush fell over the Calypso Train Station. People stopped and stared. A few women stifled screams. One woman just screamed.

Eamon stepped forward. "We require a train to the Arcadian Stadium."

After a stunned silence, someone shouted, "We're all trying to get *away* from the stadium! There's no trains running *to* the stadium!"

Eamon's voice rumbled, sending a shiver down Natalie's spine. "We require a train to the Arcadian Stadium. We will provide a driver if needed."

"We can send an automated train to the stadium if we need to," a conductor with a billed cap and jean trousers shoved his way through the crowd, "but why in Sol's name do you want to go to the stadium?"

"We go to the stadium to fight!" someone called out over the crowd.

Natalie turned at the voice, which had come from the tall entrance to their right. It sounded familiar.

The crowded parted to make way for thirteen golems. Some of them were wearing blue aprons. Others had smocks. They were armed with mops, rakes, shovels, and clenched fists. All of them looked dirty and worn, but their white eyes shone fiercely.

"Florence!" Natalie ran forward and hugged the golem at the front of the group.

"Florence?" London repeated in disbelief. He and Quincy joined Natalie.

"Hello, Miss Bliss. Hello, Miss Taylor. Hello, Mr. Montgomery. I am glad to meet you here at the train station."

Natalie looked up at the golem's stern ceramic features. "How did you know about the battle?"

"The Clay speaks, Miss Bliss," Florence answered. "Florentina told me. She said the battle is going poorly."

"So Florentina is alive!" Natalie's heart skipped a beat. Relief flooded her chest.

"Yes. She is alive. But we must hurry, or Wrath will kill everyone in the city."

Florence stepped toward Eamon.

"Captain Florence." The golem gave Florence a stiff salute. "I am glad to see you."

Florence returned the salute. "I am glad to see you, Lieutenant Eamon."

"I feared that the gods had melted you down when you did not come with the rest of us." Eamon's eyes flickered.

"I was afraid you had become a myth." Florence put his hand on Eamon's shoulder. "But we are here. And we must go. We fight for our brothers."

"We fight for our sisters." Eamon put his hand on Florence's shoulder.

"We fight for each other."

All of the golems stood at attention.

"You are Clay of My Clay," the golems chanted together while hundreds of train passengers watched in stunned silence. "I am Clay of Your Clay."

"Who are you?" Florence asked.

A chorus of golems responded.

"We are the Golem Army of Calypso."

CHAPTER 31:
INTO THE STORM

Natalie looked out of the train window. Lightning streaked across the clouds. Raindrops pelted against the glass. The train rose up through clusters of skytowers and skybergs en route to the Arcadian Stadium.

They passed over a small park on a skyberg. Natalie glanced down to see an empty playground. Swings flailed back and forth in the heavy wind.

She looked around the train, which was empty except for Quincy, London, and the golems. She closed her eyes and played with her umbrella handle. Her chest tightened with anxiety when she thought about what lay ahead. She forced herself to take a deep breath and let it out slowly.

Hugging her legs close to her chest, she tried to clear her mind. She soon felt pleasantly warm, and she realized how much she wanted to sleep. She wanted to wake up with Florentina knocking on her door, ready to clean her room. To keep the dust and stains away.

The red-haired girl managed a smile. That would be a welcome sight—to open the door and see Florentina with her blue apron and bucket. Natalie needed some normalcy in her life again. After all, she had only come back from Mithris a few days ago. She just needed to find Florentina and sort this mess out, and then they could all go home.

She and Florentina could go back home...

Natalie's eye twitched.

Florentina had her journal...

Natalie jerked forward with a gasp. Her umbrella clattered on the floor. Her heart beat wildly against her chest.

"Are you all right?" Quincy's eyes widened at Natalie's sudden movement. She put a hand on Natalie's shoulder.

"I'm fine," Natalie lied. She leaned back in her seat.

London poked his head into the aisle to see what was wrong. He and Quincy stared at Natalie, who avoided their gaze and looked out the window.

If Florentina died in the battle...if the journal was destroyed...

An image of Regina and her wild, panicked eyes shot through Natalie's head like a bullet. She shook her head and shuddered.

No, that isn't going to happen to me.

"Natalie?" London sounded distant. Panic pounded in Natalie's mind, blocking the drumbeat of the rain against the window. She bit her lip. Her hands clenched the armrests.

I don't want to perish—

Natalie gasped again when a hand closed around hers. She turned away from the window to see Quincy smiling at her. Warmth spread from the sylph's touch. Natalie squeezed Quincy's hand.

"It's going to be okay," Quincy whispered.

Natalie nodded mutely.

"Oh my—look at that!" London shouted.

The girls rose from their seats, and London motioned for them to join him.

"Look at that! Oh gods..." He shook his head.

Quincy gasped. Natalie pressed her hands against the cold glass.

Through the wind and rain, they could distinguish a gigantic shape lumbering through the skyscrapers by the stadium.

It was Wrath.

He was smashing walls and showering debris onto the streets. In the clouds above him, they could see ships shooting white streaks of light at each other. Thunderous booms rippled through the air moments after the glowing cannonballs found their targets—or missed and smashed into buildings.

"Why are the ships fighting each other?" Quincy asked.

"There is an Enemy ship," Florence answered from the front of the train car. "Florentina told me it is called the *Marcion*. It is a frigate."

The train slowed to a halt.

"We have reached the Arcadian Stadium." Florence and the golems stood. "It is time to join the fight. Fight for honor. Fight for your friends."

The golems slid the door open. The rain swept inside, beating their faces. Cannonballs screamed across the sky. Wrath's roars boomed through the air, competing with the thunder, sending shivers down Natalie's spine. She gripped her umbrella tightly and looked at London. He nodded grimly.

The golems stepped onto the platform. Florence turned around and raised his voice to be heard above the storm.

"Are you coming with us?"

"Yes." Natalie nodded. She glanced at London and Quincy. "I'm going to find Florentina."

"I need to tell the Pantheon about the golems." London held up a hand to shield his eyes from the rain.

Quincy pointed at the ships. "I think they already know about them."

"Yes, but they don't really know what they're up against. I'll try to get on a ship and bring reinforcements for Florentina and her troops."

Natalie and London looked at Quincy.

"Quincy," Natalie began, "you should—"

"Find somewhere safe to stay."

"—yes."

They stood on the edge of the train, shivering in the rain.

"Miss Bliss, we must hurry." Florence held out a hand, beckoning Natalie to join him.

"Right." Natalie swallowed. She started to step off the train, but London put a hand on her shoulder.

"Natalie," London said hesitantly.

"What?"

"Be safe."

The red-haired girl arched an eyebrow. "Do you want me to be safe? Or do you want me to save Florentina?"

London swallowed. "It's dangerous out there."

"I know." The hint of a smile trembled at the corner of Natalie's mouth. "But I'm dangerous too, remember?"

She hopped off the train.

Then Natalie and the golems hurried down a covered staircase toward the battle.

*

Minutes later, Natalie and the golems were running through the streets toward the sounds of destruction. A few panicked civilians ran the other way. They shot the golems looks of terror and Natalie looks of confusion—if they noticed her at all. She almost laughed. They *were* running the wrong way, weren't they?

But she was a Phoenix Guardian, and she ran toward the chaos. That's what she had wanted to do, wasn't it? Help people?

Well, now she was going to help people.

She tried to distinguish landmarks that would tell her how close they were to the stadium. The fighting had moved away from the stadium, and the golems were tracking through the streets toward Wrath's deep roars. The colossus kept moving, probably to escape the Pantheon ships. The thick clouds over Calypso made it hard to see Wrath or the ships, leaving them no choice but to follow the sounds of battle and the trail of destruction.

Here on the streets, the fog was thick and the rain was even thicker. It beat upon Natalie's umbrella and swept down against her raincoat. It was, however, washing some of the mud and blood away. She hurried past red phone booths and damaged storefronts, stepping around broken glass and bricks. Fallen trees filled the streets between abandoned cars and buses. People had left the area in a hurry.

Looking to her left, Natalie could see why. A twenty-story building was missing a dozen or so floors, as if someone had taken a massive scoop down the middle. Wrath had probably kicked through the building in his attempt to get away from the ships.

She was wondering what other damage the colossus had done to the street when she tripped over an unexpected edge. She fell hard into a pile of leaves, branches, and shattered pavement.

"Miss Bliss!" Florence called down. "Are you all right?"

"I think I'm..." Natalie stumbled to her feet, only to hit her forehead against a wall. She spun away, dazed, and fell to the muddy ground.

"Miss Bliss, you have fallen into a footprint." Florence jumped into the massive depression. "My brother has been through here." He pointed to the tell-tale signs of destruction where Wrath had carved a path through stone and brick.

He pulled Natalie to her feet. "You must be careful where you step, Miss Bliss. If you are not careful, you will fall again."

"Thanks, Florence." Natalie massaged her head and brushed the backside of her pants. She walked to the far side of the depression, past pancaked cars and the remains of a bus. The bright turquoise of a tattered dress caught her attention. A long strip of the dress flapped violently in the wind from a crushed window. A knot twisted in Natalie's stomach. She approached the bus slowly.

"Do not look, Miss Bliss."

214

Natalie turned around to see Eamon behind her. The golem shook his head.

"There are no survivors."

Natalie bit her lip. She looked back at the flattened bus. If someone had survived, they would need immediate help.

"Miss Bliss—"

"I know." She waved her hand to show that she had heard. "But I need to double-check."

She got down on her knees to look into the bus—and turned away in horror. She blinked in shock, stumbling to her feet and tripping over a shattered tree stump.

"Miss Bliss!" Eamon helped Natalie away from the mess of wet, wooden splinters. He held her in his thick arms, and she stared blankly into white eyes.

There were no survivors.

She nodded and patted his arms to indicate that he could let her down. He did, and Natalie swayed on the spot.

Her back convulsed. Then she threw up.

*

Natalie staggered through the rainy, wrecked streets of Calypso, following the golems and getting closer to the sounds of battle. Lightning and cannonballs streaked overhead, crackling menacingly through the clouds. Wrath's roars were coming from the river. She could only guess that he was going toward the Calypso Bridge.

Then the empty shops and restaurants parted to reveal Selene Square, a massive river-side area dotted with statues, monuments, and benches. Usually a place for families to gather and enjoy a picnic, the square was now host to the chaos of golem warfare.

Standing at the top of a staircase, Natalie surveyed the ferocious hand-to-hand combat below. She couldn't tell the golems apart, but the clay warriors seemed able to distinguish friend from foe. Their deep battle cries resounded through the curtains of rain.

And there in the distance, standing tall through the fog and the rain, Wrath waded in the water toward the Calypso Bridge. The silhouettes of ships floated high above, shooting glowing white cannonballs at him. Wrath swatted at the projectiles and bellowed in fury.

Florence put his hand on Natalie's shoulder.

"Miss Bliss, you must stay here. I will find Florentina."

Natalie's heart beat faster at the terrifying scene before her.

"Is Florentina in there?"

"Yes, Miss Bliss. My sister is leading her troops."

"How do you know?"

"I hear her voice through the Clay, Miss Bliss. I will find her. We will defeat our brothers and sisters who have been corrupted. You must wait for us."

"I need to fight too! I can help!"

Florence shook his head. "No, Miss Bliss. Stay here."

The housekeeper nodded to his golems, and they hurried down the stairs. They raised their assorted weapons high and shouted.

"We are the Golem Army of Calypso!"

Natalie watched them crash into the churning sea of golems. They split apart, identifying enemy golems and throwing themselves into combat.

Within a few moments, she had lost sight of Florence, Eamon, and their golems in the whirling mass of clay soldiers.

Natalie gripped her umbrella handle and scowled.

She wasn't just going to stay here, waiting to see if the loyal golems won the battle. She needed to find Florentina now—before anything happened to the golem.

She closed her umbrella and hurried down the stairs. Most of the fighting was concentrated at the center of the square. Natalie walked along the court wall, where she was afforded some protection from the wind. She pointed her umbrella toward the melee, ready to fire at any enemies that broke away from the fight.

She scanned the soldiers locked in combat. A golem with a spear—perhaps Eamon?–skewered another golem and lifted him high into the air before smashing him into the stone ground. A stream of dust poured from the victim's broken body.

An explosion behind Natalie caused her to turn around. There was a blaze of white, and the front of a department store crumbled to the streets in an avalanche of glass and cement. It might have been a stray cannonball shot, but it packed a powerful punch.

Natalie looked up at Wrath to see him standing by the river. He swatted in vain at the ships. The colossus was positioned between two Pantheon ships and Selene Square. Any stray shots would inevitably land amidst the golems or the buildings behind them.

A shiver ran down the girl's spine. There was no time to lose. She would either find Florentina in the battle, or Florentina would find her.

Or they would die.

Natalie sighed. Was there any chance that the golem would still be wearing her blue apron?

It was time to find out.

She ran into the chaos, darting past a row of statues and around a tangle of golems. One of them broke off from the fight and chased after Natalie, who grunted in satisfaction. She had identified a hostile.

Natalie stopped, smiling grimly, and swung her umbrella around to face her attacker, who was faster than she had anticipated. The golem thrust his spear at Natalie, who jumped out of the way. The golem spun and hit Natalie in the chest with his shield.

She fell to the ground, the wind knocked out of her. Natalie rolled under the golem and thrust her umbrella into the soldier's thigh. The umbrella ignited into white flames and pierced the clay, coming out through the other side. Natalie pulled the umbrella out, and a mist of golden-white dust streamed from the wound. The golem bellowed and threw a wild punch at Natalie's face. She dodged the blow and got to her feet, pushing her umbrella through the golem's chest.

The golem head-butted Natalie in the face. Her vision went dark. She staggered back, and a heavy weight dropped onto her knees.

She blinked, feeling dazed, and saw a dead golem lying on her legs. The umbrella to the chest had done enough. She shrugged the body off and crawled away from him.

The hair tingled on the back of her neck, and she side-stepped left. A spear narrowly missed her head. Natalie twisted around to face her new attacker.

The golem thrust his spear at Natalie's face, but she rolled away. She jumped to her feet and swung her flaming umbrella, cutting through the soldier's spear. The golem tossed the broken shaft away and grabbed his shield with both hands. He raised it aloft and slammed it toward her head.

She held up her umbrella defensively. It cut through the center of the shield, but the broken slabs hammered her face and chest. Natalie winced in pain, closing her eyes and losing sight of her enemy for a brief moment.

The brief moment lasted too long. Something slammed into her face.

Natalie fell to the hard ground.

Her shoulder throbbed and her mind spun. She had enough grasp of consciousness to know that the golem would deliver the final blow at any moment.

But she heard a sickening crunch above her. Something bounced and cracked on the ground, and then a heavier object collapsed beside her.

"Miss Bliss?"

Natalie opened her blurry eyes. The golem's severed head was lying on the ground next to her. She turned away from the soldier's sightless eyes and looked at the person standing over her.

She saw a beautiful face—perhaps the most beautiful face she had ever seen.

Rain dripped from the stone ringlets in Florentina's hair. Her white eyes sparkled. She reached down to offer Natalie a hand.

"Florentina!" Natalie pointed over the golem's shoulder.

The housekeeper whirled around and grabbed the tip of the spear before it punctured her forehead. She kicked the enemy golem in the knee and yanked the spear out of his hands. The surprised golem dropped to the ground, dust streaming from a crack in his leg. Florentina spun the spear around and plunged it into the back of the golem's neck. His shoulders shattered, dropping his head to the ground.

She looked back at Natalie and was about to say something when the girl screamed and pointed again. The housekeeper turned and spotted the broad-shouldered golem running toward them. This one swung a menacing-looking chain over its head. In mid-stride, he whipped the chain at the face of another golem, shattering his head like a pot.

The enemy golem was ten yards from Florentina, but she stood her ground. Natalie thought she saw a brief shake of the head—a flicker of sadness in the eyes—and then Florentina twisted the spear around in her hand and threw it.

The spear shot through the unlucky golem's neck, tangling the heavy chain around his waist and legs. The dead warrior tripped, his body sliding on the stone before coming to a halt at Florentina's feet.

Her shoulders rose and fell in that unnatural movement that Natalie recognized as a sigh. The former housekeeper turned to face her.

"Miss Bliss." She extended her hand once more. "It is good to see—"

But then the screaming sound of a cannonball filled Natalie's ears. She saw it explode behind Florentina, and then the blinding light forced her eyes shut.

CHAPTER 32:
GOLDEN-WHITE DUST

Something heavy flew past Natalie. She turned away from the explosion and opened her eyes to see Florentina thrown upside down against a statue. There was a sickening crack. The housekeeper crumpled to the ground, leaving a large chunk of broken porcelain at the base of the statue.

Natalie ran to Florentina's side. The golem's back was bent at an unnatural angle. Her white eyes flickered in the light rain.

"Florentina!" Natalie brushed red hair out of her eyes. "Florentina, are you all right?"

"No, Miss Bliss." The golem's eyes looked down to her thigh. "I am not all right."

Natalie followed her gaze and saw a gaping hole that revealed the hollow interior of Florentina's body. A cloud of golden-white dust rose out of the hole and dissipated in the air.

"How does your back feel?"

Florentina shook her head slowly.

Natalie looked behind Florentina to see the damage. She turned away and closed her eyes in horror. Florentina's back had been reduced to moon-colored shards and clay powder.

The red-haired girl stumbled back onto her elbows, feeling dizzy. She looked around the square, where shattered bodies littered the slick stones. Some golems were stumbling to their feet again, but very few had survived the cannon blast.

Overhead, a large ship sailed between skybergs and skytowers, shooting at two other ships that seemed hesitant to fire back.

Wrath was by the Calypso Bridge, fighting the remnants of the golem army. He swatted at the golems with his long arms, crushing soldiers with each blow, but they were relentless in their attack.

All this Natalie noticed in a brief moment while her mind tried to register what was happening.

"Miss Bliss. You must go now. You must keep up the fight."

Florentina's words broke Natalie out of her reverie. She blinked at the golem, whose eyes were dimming. Then Natalie realized what Florentina had said. The red-haired girl felt a rush of anger.

"I can't leave you now! I have to help you!"

"Miss Bliss, I am broken. You cannot help me."

"We'll get you fixed up! We just have to get out of here."

"No." Florentina held her hand against Natalie's chest to stop the girl from picking her up. "There is no time. You must go now. Stop my brother. Stop Wrath."

"*Other* people are fighting!" Natalie screamed. "London is bringing help! The golems are fighting—that's why we brought them here. I'm staying here with you."

"No, Miss Bliss. I have given everything to save my brothers and sisters. You must finish this for me. You must save Wrath."

Natalie watched Wrath slam his fist into a group of golems, leaving a pile of dust and shattered clay.

"I'm not sure if Wrath deserves it."

"You must save him." Florentina grabbed Natalie's arm with her smooth, cool hands. "The traitor who destroys the city is not Wrath! His True Script is more powerful than the False Script written by the Enemy."

Natalie hesitated. She noted the desperation in Florentina's face.

"Miss Bliss, Wrath is trapped inside. He is struggling to break free. You cannot defeat him in battle. You must free him." Her flickering eyes shone bright and clear for a moment. "Our souls cannot be destroyed by the rewriting of our Scripts. Our souls are deeper than lies."

Natalie clasped Florentina's hand. "But I need to save you first!"

Florentina shook her head. Natalie shook hers harder, feeling angry.

"No, Florentina! I came back to life and met you again! We're friends! Everyone dies and leaves, or they change and lose themselves! And now you're going to leave me too?"

Florentina tilted her head. "I am sorry, Miss Bliss. It is not my choice. I did not mean to hurt you. But I hurt you when I stole your journal and put you in danger." Florentina pointed to the satchel at her waist. "Take it."

"Florentina—"

"Take your journal, Miss Bliss!"

Natalie reached into the satchel and found her leather-bound journal. It was safe and whole. With a shuddering sigh of relief, Natalie put the journal inside her raincoat.

"I was wrong to steal your journal, Miss Bliss. I put you in great danger."

Natalie was about to respond, but Florentina interrupted again.

"No. Listen to me, Miss Bliss. I am sorry that I put your memories in danger. But I was afraid that you would not come without the theft. I did wrong. I stole the memories of the people you love."

"Florentina, I...you *are* one of the people I love."

"I love you too, Miss Bliss. You have been a great friend to my people."

"I'm glad for that, Florentina. But please don't go. Not when I'm getting to know you again." Natalie bit her lip. "Don't leave me alone."

"You are not alone. London and Quincy are your friends. You have many friends. But I am done. I am complete."

Natalie looked at the gaping hole in Florentina's side. Thin clouds of golden-white dust floated from the wound. Florentina smiled at Natalie's confused expression.

"Is there any better fate than to fulfill your Purpose? I followed my Script. I followed the True Words written on my soul. I defended the city. I served the Golem Army of Calypso once more." Florentina looked at the spear lying at her side. "I am broken. But I am complete."

She touched Natalie's hand and held it. The red-haired girl trembled.

"It's not right." Natalie closed her eyes and shook her head. She didn't want to cry, but tears rolled down the side of her face. "I hate crying—I'm tired of crying! I'm tired of losing people! Why does it always end this way?"

A stunning boom shook the air above them, and Natalie glanced up to see the large ship fire at a skytower, blowing off the roof and showering the building in flames. The ship disappeared behind a skyberg before the Pantheon clippers could retaliate.

"Ask questions later." Florentina squeezed Natalie's hand. "Now you must fight. Love me by fighting for my brothers and sisters." Her eyes, faint points of light, gazed skyward. "You must destroy the frigate if we are to prevail."

223

"The frigate?" Natalie glanced at the ship, which had circled around the skyberg toward them.

"It is called the *Marcion*. It is powerful."

She looked back at Florentina. The golem's eyes were darkening. But then they flared brightly.

"Oh, Miss Bliss!" She gripped Natalie's hand tightly.

"What?" Natalie leaned close. "What is it, Florentina?"

"When I was in the Army Chamber, I saw—"

A terrifying noise split the air.

Natalie looked up in time to see the frigate shoot a skytower just above the ground. The blazing-white cannonball hit the building like a hammer smashing an egg. Glass exploded everywhere. Fire poured onto Selene Square.

Natalie raised her umbrella to protect her and Florentina from the blast. Chunks of metal flew around them. From under her umbrella, Natalie saw a beam land on a golem and split his porcelain body in half. Any golems that had stayed in the square were surely dead now.

"Florentina—" The red-haired girl looked back at the golem. What she saw cut her words short.

Where light had shone moments ago, empty blackness now stared at Natalie.

She stretched out a hand toward her friend and former housekeeper—but then she hesitated, her fingers inches away from the golem's face. Florentina had no eyelids to close.

Natalie was struck by how much Florentina looked like a hollow, broken shell. The last trail of dust rose through the air and brushed Natalie's ear. Thoughts sprang unbidden to her mind, and she remembered the words of Oswald Canteloupes.

Hope is for the living.

Natalie stepped away from Florentina's body. Darkness swallowed the ground around her. The *Marcion* passed directly overhead, casting the street and the surrounding buildings into shadow.

Natalie stared up at the frigate's thick hull. Then she surveyed the damage around her. Fires licked the ruined buildings. The broken bodies of golems and statues littered Selene Square. Dust and ashes mingled in the thickening rain.

Natalie took a deep breath. She swept out her arm and opened her umbrella with a defiant flourish.

Then, with a final glance at Florentina, she took to the air and rejoined the battle.

CHAPTER 33:
THE *MARCION*

Natalie rose through the air, confronted by heavy rain. Fierce drops of water pelted against her umbrella. She put on an extra burst of speed as a cannonball sailed toward her—a wayward shot from a Pantheon clipper. She swung her legs up and narrowly avoided the shot. But the sudden movement threw off the flight of her umbrella, exposing her face to the rain.

Natalie blinked against the harsh raindrops that slapped her eyes. She regained control in time to realize that she was still speeding toward the *Marcion*. She tugged on the umbrella to slow her ascent but was already moving too quickly. The frigate grew larger, filling her vision—meeting her too hard and too fast.

She collided with the hull and bounced painfully. Her umbrella sprang back to hit her in the face. Natalie slipped along the wooden surface, carried by momentum, before flying out under the stern.

She looked up in time to see the enormous sterncastle and glowing cabin lights. Her red umbrella and yellow raincoat must have caught someone's attention, because she saw frantic pointing and yelling from the sailors inside.

So much for a stealthy entrance.

Elven sailors in black uniforms rushed onto the deck of the frigate and began shooting at Natalie with repeating crossbows.

Stupid elves, Natalie thought as the first fiery blue bolt flew over her umbrella. The second almost went straight through it—Natalie had to raise the umbrella to avoid a dangerous hole in the canopy. The third shot flew straight toward Natalie's head—

—along with shots four through sixteen.

Reacting quickly, Natalie half-closed her umbrella to drop away from the shots.

The result was more dramatic than she had intended. She plummeted toward the earth like a stone.

The bolts sailed high overhead. She would have breathed a sigh of relief—but the needle-sharp spire of a skytower waited to meet her mid-fall.

She opened her umbrella and spun around to avoid sudden impalement. Her momentum carried her away from the tip and around to hit the shaft. Natalie's left hand slipped off her umbrella handle, and a gust of wind blew her away from the building. She struggled to regain her two-handed grip on the umbrella.

By this time, the *Marcion* had moved out of a group of skytowers to cross the river. Wrath was still causing havoc at the Calypso Bridge.

A Pantheon clipper weaved through the skytowers, trailing after the frigate and trying desperately to get a clear shot. One clipper had been floating near the river, almost hidden in the mist. When the *Marcion* pulled out of the cluster of air-buildings, the clipper rose to meet it and loosed a fearsome broadside into the frigate's prow.

Bright blue cannon balls slammed into the *Marcion's* forecastle and hull. Some unlucky elves on the deck were tossed overboard by the shock. Other sailors grabbed hold of rigging or braced themselves against the railings. A few took crossbow shots at the clipper's crew. The Pantheon elves returned fire.

Natalie navigated her umbrella in the frigate's direction, hoping to find a good wind that could carry her. She flew over the river and found the current she needed. She gripped her umbrella tightly and was swept toward the enemy ship.

As she approached the frigate's port side, Natalie breathed a sigh of relief. The enemy sailors were occupied with the clipper. She descended to land gently on the deck—but fell out of the current with a cry of surprise.

The unexpected drop sent her short of the frigate. Natalie flung out a desperate arm to grab a railing. She missed—but her umbrella caught a line.

She swung awkwardly in the air. The entire hull shuddered, and Natalie's umbrella almost came free. The Pantheon clipper had circled the frigate and launched another broadside—this time into the *Marcion's* stern.

Natalie bit her lip and pulled herself up by her umbrella—wanting to get onboard before the clipper's fire successfully knocked her off the ship. Grunting with the effort, Natalie pulled herself over the railing, closed her umbrella, and collapsed onto the deck.

She rolled into a pair of tall black boots. An elven sailor stepped back.

"You're a girl!" he exclaimed, staring down at Natalie with a look of surprise. Then he pointed his crossbow at her forehead.

Natalie had no retort—and no choice but to swing her umbrella up at the sailor's chest. A billowing wave of heat exploded from her umbrella, blasting the elf across the deck and over the side.

Thundering footsteps warned Natalie that more sailors were closing in. She jumped to her feet and spun around, trailing a stream of fire from the tip of her umbrella. The flaming arc flew outward and consumed the elves that had come too close.

Natalie turned around to complete a circle of fire, clearing a wide space. She backed up toward the cabin.

A few crossbow bolts found their way through Natalie's firewall. She dropped low to the ground to avoid them, and the stream of flame dropped with her, revealing at least two dozen sailors on deck. With a terrible sinking feeling, Natalie realized that she could not win against an entire crew—especially not if they all backed away and shot at her.

The sailors seemed to be thinking the same thing. Elves were climbing up the rigging to shoot from above.

Natalie cut off the flow of fire and opened her umbrella to protect herself from the inevitable shower of crossbow bolts. She hurried toward the cabin, high-stepping to avoid the blazing blue bolts hitting the deck at her feet.

When she got to the cabin door, she rattled it frantically. It was locked.

How predictable.

In any other situation, Natalie would have just used adjective magic to unlock the door. A simple prefix for a useful adjective— *un*locked—and a tap from the umbrella would have done the trick. But now her umbrella was occupied with other important tasks, like saving Natalie from becoming a pincushion.

She crouched against the cabin door to shield her body. A merciless onslaught of bolts peppered the umbrella.

Natalie's stomach twisted in knots. What she really needed right now was help.

She bit her lip—and flinched as a particularly strong bolt made a small indentation in the umbrella fabric. Natalie prayed a silent prayer of thanks for the umbrella-makers. They knew how to make a durable umbrella for the Phoenix Guardian who led a rough life.

227

Natalie strained to listen—the shots were hitting harder and harder. She heard the sound of people trying (unsuccessfully) to disguise their footsteps by walking very slowly and quietly.

The crew was getting closer. They were going to surround her, take away her umbrella, and kill her. They had probably been moving in since she had crouched against the door.

Natalie's heart raced. She really needed help right now.

But *Natalie* was supposed to be the help. She was the Phoenix Guardian who people called to solve their planet's problems. Or, as the case might be, the Phoenix Guardian who came unbidden to solve the planet's problems.

But now *she* needed help.

And much to her horror, her thoughts turned to...

...London.

If her heart wasn't beating its final, desperate rhythm to this new and all-too-brief life, it might have *fluttered*.

In the midst of her stress, Natalie still managed to roll her eyes.

Stupid traitor heart.

The footsteps were getting closer.

But Natalie wasn't going down without a fight.

She closed her eyes and squeezed her umbrella handle, shooting a wall of fire at the advancing sailors. Natalie peeked around her umbrella to see burning bodies thrown back against the deck. One sailor flew through the air, screaming as the hungry flames consumed him. His round metal helmet flew off at an inopportune moment—just before his head collided with the mizzenmast. Natalie winced at the sight and the sound.

Life would be so much better if they could all just get along.

Another shot flew past Natalie's face and almost punctured her cheek. She ducked behind the umbrella.

They weren't going to get along.

Natalie flinched at the impact of another crossbow volley. She had reminded the crew that she was dangerous with the umbrella—but she wasn't any closer to getting inside the cabin. And now she couldn't leave the ship, even if she wanted to.

It was a stalemate.

BOOM!

An enormous blast started a series of explosions that rocked the frigate under Natalie's feet. Fighting to keep her balance, she almost dropped her umbrella and exposed herself to enemy fire.

She crouched closer to the deck and braced herself against the door.

Bother.

What was it she had just been saying about help?

She thought of London again.

Double bother.

Natalie heard the whining sounds of projectiles flying through the air. But this new volley wasn't aimed at her. She could hear screams from the ship's stern, where the sailors were congregated.

Something heavy slammed into the deck in front of Natalie. It was followed by a host of more heavy-somethings.

Natalie peered out from behind her umbrella to see tall elves in blue uniforms with tri-cornered hats. A shorter figure in a leather jacket stood in the middle. Beyond them, enemy sailors lay dead on the forecastle. Others hung lifeless from the rigging.

The newcomer in the brown leather jacket turned and looked at Natalie. A look of relief passed over his face.

It was London.

CHAPTER 34:
THE CANDLE OF THE WICKED

"Natalie! You're alive!" London hurried toward her.

Natalie rose to her feet, using the cabin door for support. London made a strange movement with his arms, like he was going to hug her. Natalie raised her eyebrows in surprise, and London hesitated.

He patted her awkwardly on the shoulder. "I thought I had lost you there."

Natalie crossed her arms. "You thought you had lost me?"

"I—I thought *we* had lost you," London stammered. He pointed at the elven marines, who were searching the bodies of the enemy sailors. "We spotted you flying up from the square. You were about to land on the deck and then you disappeared from view."

London was talking very fast, but his eyes were fixed on hers. Natalie felt a smile start at the corner of her lips. She ran a hand through her hair and let a loose strand fall across her eyes. He must have noticed. He swallowed and stammered again.

"I—I thought you had fallen into the river. We kept firing at the *Marcion* to make sure it didn't shoot you. Then I saw you on deck, so we moved in close and boarded her."

"How did you know it was me?"

London managed a smile. "How many other girls fly around the city with red umbrellas and yellow raincoats?"

"Not many." Natalie grinned, but the expression faded when she saw the deck, which was wet with blood and rain. She looked at the cabin behind her. "We should see to the *Marcion*'s captain and accept his surrender."

"You think he's going to surrender?"

"What other choice does he have?" Natalie asked. She walked up to the door and tapped it with her umbrella. "*Unlocked*." There was a click, and Natalie grabbed the handle—

"You should let the marines go in first."

"I can handle whatever's inside—oh, London!" she snapped.

London was waving at the marines, who ran over to join them. They stepped lightly over the dead sailors and through the crimson water staining the deck.

London pulled Natalie away from the door. Two elves took up position next to the cabin and drew swords. A tall elf stood a few feet from the door and brought his crossbow up to his shoulder. He nodded at another marine, who kicked the door open. The marines poured inside—and Natalie heard screams and the slaps of bolts hitting flesh.

A marine staggered backwards into the doorframe, sliding down and clutching his stomach. His sword clattered to the deck. Natalie jumped forward to join the fight, but London yanked her back as a stray projectile ricocheted off the threshold.

She rounded on him. "What are you doing?"

"Keeping you safe!"

"I belong in there!" She tried to pull away, but he tightened his grip.

She heard a wild yell and turned around in time to see an elf sailor running out of the cabin, swinging his sword. He was stopped at the doorway by the fallen marine, who summoned enough strength to thrust his sword into the sailor's chest. The sailor fell to his knees and plunged his own sword into the wounded marine. For a brief moment they stared at each other, clutching their sword hilts tightly, eyes full of fear and hatred. Then their grips slackened and they crumpled to the deck.

Natalie stood frozen, staring at the two dead elves. London was still holding her arm. He relaxed his grip.

"Mr. Montgomery," a marine called from inside the cabin. "Everything's sorted in here. And there's someone you should see."

London and Natalie walked inside cautiously.

Papers and shattered glass covered the cabin. A few shelves had broken and strewn their contents everywhere. Books, maps, and models littered the rubble. A vase of red roses had shattered and spilled water on the polished wood floor.

Elves from both sides lay dead.

A tall elf in a black, golden-trimmed captain's uniform lay against a desk, clutching his ribs with his left hand. Sweat stained his sharp nose and handsome features, plastering strands of black hair to his forehead. His chin was covered in stubble. Blood shone between his fingers from a grisly wound at his side.

Four Pantheon marines watched the captain, swords and crossbows at the ready.

The wounded captain scowled at them. "Who are you?"

"I'm Natalie Bliss. Who are you?"

"Captain Barias." He curled his bloody lip in disgust. "You killed my crew and disabled my ship. Were you commanding the *Arete*?"

"That would be Captain Hall," London answered. "I will accept your surrender on his behalf."

"Accept my surrender?" the captain laughed. A trickle of blood ran down his lip.

London crossed his arms. "You have no other choice."

"Allow me to surprise you."

"Where's your spell-book?" Natalie interrupted, looking around the wreckage of the cabin.

Barias narrowed his eyes. "What?"

"You changed the golems' Script to turn them against the Pantheon. You must have used a codex. I want it." Natalie pointed out of the window, where broken panes of glass let in the wind and rain. Down the river, Wrath could be seen on the Calypso Bridge. "The colossus has to be stopped. I want to save innocent lives."

"Save innocent lives? I do too." Barias made a gurgling noise in his throat. He winced. "But let me know if you find any in Calypso."

"Calypso is full of normal people living their lives." Natalie's eyes flashed angrily. "Elves, dwarves, fairies, gnomes—ordinary people. And you've murdered hundreds of them today."

"'Murdered.' 'Normal.'" Barias spat a mixture of blood and saliva. "Normal people living their lives to support a throne of wickedness. Preserving the order of the First Gods."

"The Pantheon isn't perfect, but it works."

"'It works'?" Barias scoffed, licking his dry lips. "Is that the same as doing good? No. But keep telling yourself that 'it works.' Meanwhile, they'll continue to commit crimes while 'normal' people stand by...because it all works."

"What crimes?"

"There are three powers at work in this universe, Miss Bliss. Those that want to return the First Gods to power, those that want to keep the First Gods from waking up—"

"Why would anyone want to do that?" Natalie interrupted.

Barias laughed.

233

"You think everyone wants to awaken the First Gods and let them take charge again? Many gods in the Pantheon *like* being in charge. It's a big universe out there. Gods love power, and the Pantheon is made of gods who lust for it." He coughed violently. "But other gods want the First Gods to come back. They want to be rewarded for their loyalty. They'll pay any price for the First Gods' return. And they'll hurt anyone who gets in their way."

"You're one to talk about hurting people. You unleashed a golem colossus on the Arcadian Stadium!" London said, trembling with fury.

"I could freeze your blood with stories of what the Pantheon has done." Barias glared at London. "But first I must tell you about the third great power in the universe. Some of us want to bring the *Titans* back. We want a return to justice—"

"A return to chaos, you mean," London scowled.

"You speak out of ignorance." Barias's lip curled into a sneer. "The Pantheon wrote the history books. You have no concept of how the Titans ruled. All you know are the tales of your beloved First Gods. But they're all asleep, aren't they? Except for Sol. He's gone. No one knows where he is, do they? He's left this universe to fend for itself. So all of the First Gods are missing...each in their own way." A mocking smile spread across Barias's trembling lips. "Your mighty First Gods aren't so mighty after all, are they?"

Natalie was silent. Sweat trickled down her brow. She didn't want to listen to Barias any longer.

"We need to stop the golem colossus. Give me the spell-book— or do I have to find it myself?" She began kicking aside books and papers on the floor.

"Forget about the spell-book!" The captain shuddered with a spasm of pain. "You have bigger things to worry about. Like the fact that you're fighting for the wrong side."

London reached down and grabbed Barias's collar. "If you wanted any credibility, you should have thought twice about slaughtering the innocents of this city!"

"London! Let him go!" Natalie grabbed London's shoulder, but he shrugged her off.

"This attack is nothing more than a statement!" Barias spat at London. "And you should think long and hard about who is really responsible for the deaths today. Who created the golems? The First Gods! The Pantheon! They may be victorious today, they may destroy their own wretched creations, but what kind of saviors create the very danger that they save you from?"

Natalie shook her head in disgust and resumed her search for the spell-book. How could they reason with someone like this?

Barias took a deep, shuddering breath. "I'm sorry that those people had to die, but sacrifices must be made in war. The Arcadian Games are a symbol of the First Gods' enduring tyranny. The lighting of the Undying Fire is a constant reminder that the flame of the wicked still burns. And it must be put out!"

Natalie looked up from a fallen pile of books. "The Undying Fire is a symbol of Sayornis, the goddess who sacrificed herself to defeat the Titans. She's the ancestor of the Phoenix Guardians—our ancestor." She scowled at Barias. "You're talking to the wrong people about the Undying Fire. It's a symbol of love, hope—"

Barias waved a dismissive hand. "What you think it means is irrelevant. But *you* are relevant. You and your Phoenix Guardian friends are powerful. There's still time to fight on the right side." He grimaced. "Now, you *must* listen to me. The Pantheon can't awaken the First Gods without powerful magic."

London arched an eyebrow. "The Pantheon *has* powerful magic."

"Not this kind." Barias wiped blood and spit from his mouth. "The First Gods are caught in something more than just sleep—they're between life and death. The Pantheon needs a power that can only be collected by one means."

"And what is that?" London asked skeptically.

Barias swallowed, looking earnestly into his eyes. "Harvesting souls."

"That's nonsense." London snorted. "You're a fool."

"You think I'm a fool, boy? Wait until your own friends—"

"I found the spell-book!" Natalie held up a thick tome beside the window. She examined the cover. "Wow. That's a long title."

"Take your book." Barias glared at her. "Convert your colossus. But our work has already been done. The line has been drawn."

"Yes, it has, hasn't it?" London grabbed Barias by the collar again. "You've killed thousands of people today!"

The captain winced in agony. "Thousands of lives aren't important when you're talking about the entire universe! We didn't set out to kill civilians. We set out to make a statement. To give people hope."

"Hope?" Natalie stepped carefully over debris to stand next to the captain. "What hope is there from terrorism?"

"Terrorism is perspective, Miss Bliss. Today the Forerunners made a statement against the Pantheon. A spark of light shines in a world of darkness. We let the Pantheon know that their reign of wickedness isn't secure—even at the foot of their iron throne in Calypso. And we let the universe know that the Pantheon can't keep them down forever."

"You're not a light of hope." London looked at the captain with disgust. "Killing people deepens the darkness."

Barias narrowed his eyes at London. "You were willing to kill my crew."

"They were killing innocent people—"

"*Other* people." The captain growled. "They were killing *other* people. But your 'innocent' people weren't better than my elves. My elves fought for a cause—a new age of order, benevolence, and equality. Your people were glutting themselves on food and games."

"But you killed thousands."

"Would you have been willing to kill thousands of my elves?"

London shook his head in disgust. "What?"

"Don't you get it?" Barias closed his eyes, clutching his side tightly. "It's not about numbers. The numbers don't make the heroes or the villains. The cause does. And you're on the wrong side." He glanced at Natalie. "Now get out of my sight and let me die."

The red-haired girl crouched next to him and raised her umbrella.

"What are you doing?" Barias looked nervously at the umbrella pointing at him.

"I'm going to heal you." Natalie poised the umbrella over his ribs and took Barias's hand, trying to move it so she could have a good look at the wound.

"And then we're going to arrest you." London motioned to the marines. "You can tell all of this to the Pantheon."

"You're not arresting me." Barias shook his head slowly. "I wanted to tell *you* this, not the Pantheon. You can pass along my sentiments if you'd like. But I'm not going anywhere." He reached across his chest with his other hand and pushed Natalie's hand away. "I appreciate your kindness, Miss Bliss, but I'm going to die right here. You're welcome to join me. I started a self-destruct sequence when your marines blasted their way into my cabin. By my reckoning you have..." He glanced at a watch pressed against his ribs. "...less than a minute to get off my ship."

CHAPTER 35:
COLLATERAL DAMAGE

"Go!" London shouted. "Everyone, back to the *Arete*!"

He grabbed Natalie and pulled her out of the cabin. They stumbled against the doorframe and onto the slick wooden deck. Natalie held *On Creatures Created* tightly in her hands. London grabbed a grappling line and handed it to Natalie, helping her start the climb before getting on himself. The marines moved quickly up the other lines.

Natalie grabbed a handhold on the Pantheon clipper, and a marine helped her over the railing. London followed close behind and shouted urgently toward the bridge deck.

"Captain Hall, get down the river to the bridge! The *Marcion* is about to explode!"

"Hard to port!" Captain Hall shouted at the helmsman, who turned the wheel quickly. The captain hurried down to the weather deck to stand by London. He took off his tri-cornered hat, dripping water onto his blue uniform. His pointy ears stood out amidst ruffled brown hair.

"How soon is 'about to'?" the elf asked London.

"Their captain said less than a minute—but that was when we were still in his cabin."

Captain Hall's gaze hardened. "Understood."

Sailors and marines scurried along the deck as the *Arete* moved away from the *Marcion* and turned around.

Natalie clutched the railing, waiting in fascinated horror for the frigate to explode. London pulled her away from the edge.

"Come on, Natalie. We need to get you down below—away from the blast."

Natalie pulled her hand free of his grasp. "If we don't get away quickly, it's not going to make a difference if I'm above or below deck."

The deck beneath her tilted as the clipper turned hard to port. Natalie screamed in surprise and fell against the railing, which caught her hard in the stomach. London helped Natalie to her feet, and this time she didn't shrug him off.

The *Arete* rounded the curve in its trajectory and accelerated toward the Calypso Bridge. Wind whipped Natalie's hair about her face. She turned away from the stinging rain to look back at the *Marcion*.

The frigate floated off to her left, silent and deadly. Natalie glanced at her watch to see how much time had passed—more than a minute, surely. Then she saw the maze of numbers and hands on her watch and remembered that it didn't tell time.

While they pulled away from the *Marcion*, a tall skytower floated down to the river between them and the frigate. Plumes of smoke billowed from the top floors of the air-building.

"Oh no." Natalie held her hand to her mouth. "Those are apartments!"

The residents were leaning out of the windows. They waved desperately at the *Arete*. A blonde god in a toga made eye contact with Natalie and yelled something. His glistening tan face was a mask of fear. He indicated the burning apartment above him, and then he pointed in the direction of the frigate.

Natalie couldn't hear what he was saying, but it was easy to guess: *Help us.*

The skytower dropped in front of the *Marcion's* bow, blocking the entire ship from view.

A cacophony of noise erupted from behind the air-building. For a brief moment, a burst of light illuminated the skytower—and then the building dissolved into a burning cloud. The blonde god and his neighbors disappeared in the flames. Stone, steel, and plaster showered the air.

Natalie fell back from the railing. She heard shouts from the sailors around her.

She watched the largest piece of the building crash into the river, trailing a thick plume of black smoke. The frigate and the skytower were gone.

London stood next to Natalie.

"All those people..." She bit her lip.

"More people are going to die if we don't stop the colossus." London turned to the captain. "Can you take us over the golem, sir?"

Captain Hall wiped his brow with the back of his hand. "To do what?"

Natalie held up *On Creatures Created.*

"Drop down on it," she said. "I have a plan."

Captain Hall touched his tri-cornered hat. "I'll see how close I can get."

Rain rattled on the *Arete*, which rose higher as they flew toward the bridge. The clipper had to get a good position above Wrath and his dangerously long arms.

As they approached the bridge, Natalie got a better appreciation for the sheer size of the colossus. Wrath towered above the Calypso Bridge and the surrounding buildings.

The colossus looked up at the approaching clipper.

"Why hasn't he destroyed the bridge, I wonder?" London asked.

"Don't know." Natalie shrugged. "Maybe he likes bridges."

They flew closer to Wrath, who ripped a chunk of brick wall from a Parlemagnian restaurant and hurled it at the *Arete*. The makeshift projectile tore through a sail and slammed into the foremast. The huge wooden beam broke in two, splitting the air with a terrible crack. The foremast creaked and fell backward. Lines snapped and whipped about their heads.

"Move!" London grabbed Natalie to get her out of the way, but she yanked him under her umbrella instead. A tremendous weight slammed against the edge of the umbrella and buried itself against the deck.

Mind spinning, Natalie raised her umbrella and recovered her feet. Chaos reigned on deck. Sailors worked to cut the torn sail, which billowed in the wind like a wild thing. A dead elf hung from a tangle of broken lines.

Captain Hall shouted orders for the clipper to turn around. He grabbed another officer.

"Tell the guns to be ready on my command. This time we'll blast him to the Abyss!"

"No! You can't do that!" Natalie tripped over the fallen mast and fell onto the deck. She pushed herself up and stumbled toward the bridge deck. "Our only chance is to win him back to our side."

The captain shook his head. "Young lady, he is a dangerous weapon. I will remove him by any means necessary. We don't have time for you to magic him out of being a monster."

The clipper circled around, presenting its starboard side to the colossus.

"Open fire!" Captain Hall signaled with a wave of his hand.

The deck shook as the starboard guns erupted. Cannonballs glowed blue in their flight toward Wrath.

The golem turned his enormous head at the sound. His shining red eyes narrowed. With surprising agility, he crouched low and rolled out of the volley's range. His momentum carried him into brown-brick apartments, which he smashed into rubble.

The stray cannonballs exploded into the Calypso Bridge and the surrounding shops. Golem soldiers scrambled for cover on the ground. Some were not lucky enough to escape the damage, and shards of dead golems scattered across the street.

Wrath regained his footing and ripped out the remains of a clothing store. He threw the building's second story toward the clipper, but the ruins fell apart before they had gone far. Moments later, a harmless cluster of debris bounced off the ship's hull.

The colossus shook his armored head and bellowed. It was a hollow, booming noise that sent shivers down Natalie's spine.

"You can't stop him this way, Captain!" Natalie turned back to the elf. "You'll destroy the entire city before you can destroy him."

Captain Hall ran a hand across his face. "You have a recommendation?"

"Get me closer to the bridge so I can fly onto the colossus and change his Script."

The captain shook his head. "I can't do that. You saw what happened the first time."

"But—"

He held up a hand to stop her. "I can distract the colossus with a few more rounds—lighter rounds that will cause less collateral damage. But you have to get yourself to him."

Natalie scowled.

"That's the best I can do. I won't risk my crew or my ship. I can't stop the colossus if I'm dead at the bottom of the river. Neither can you."

Natalie took a breath and clutched her umbrella.

"All right then. Thank you, sir."

"We'll follow your flight and give you as much cover fire as we can."

Natalie nodded and walked toward the railing.

"Natalie, wait!"

She turned around, her expression strained.

"London, I don't want to hear anything from you about how I can't do this or I'm not ready. There's no one else who can—"

"Natalie—" London grabbed her arm.

"London." There was a low, dangerous undertone to her voice. She glared at the boy's hand on her raincoat sleeve. "Let me go."

London's gaze darted from her to the colossus on the bridge. She looked up at him, trembling in anger.

Then his eyes softened, and he sighed deeply. He released his grip and stepped away from her.

"I always let you go."

Natalie blinked. She swayed next to the railing, caught in the wind. "What?"

London nodded at the bridge. "Go."

Natalie hesitated for a moment. Then she opened her umbrella and jumped off the clipper.

CHAPTER 36:
CLAY OF MY CLAY

Rain pelted against Natalie's umbrella. Her legs swayed in the wind as she flew toward the bridge under grim, gray clouds.

What did London mean that he always let her go?

She shook her head to clear her mind. She could think long and hard about London's words if she survived. But now she had to focus on the battle.

And right now she was sailing through the air, drifting unprotected toward a golem colossus.

Thankfully, Wrath was paying her no attention. He was occupied with the scores of golem soldiers at his feet, who attacked him relentlessly. Natalie marveled at the golems' unwavering dedication to their Purpose.

She glanced back at the clipper. London stood by the railing, looking after her. She didn't want to admit it, but knowing that he was watching...

Well, it was...

It gave her a kind of...that is to say...

...it gave her strength.

Natalie finished the thought quietly and reluctantly in her head.

She cleared her throat and glanced at *On Creatures Created*, which she held in her left hand. With a start, she realized that she hadn't actually found the passage with the Golem Script in it. She didn't know what to do.

Did she have to write a new Script in his head?

Or did she merely have to tap into the True Script that was there, locked deep down in his mind?

Florentina had never explained it to her. Natalie was floating toward Wrath for her final act, and she didn't even know the lines.

Bother.

So Natalie did what any sensible girl would do if she was flying an umbrella toward a golem colossus in the middle of a storm: she carefully opened the spell-book with one hand and began to read.

She braced the book against her knee to turn the pages with her thumb and forefinger. She had to maintain a good grip, otherwise the book would slip and *fall into the river—*

Natalie caught the book between her boots just before it dropped out of reach.

She took a deep shuddering breath. A warm wave of stress washed down her throat and into her chest. She lifted her legs and plucked the book from between her feet. Then she held it firmly with one hand and kept it closed.

Maybe she would just look at it when she landed on the colossus.

Maybe there would be an index to help her find the right page.

Maybe the colossus would acknowledge her good-faith effort to redeem him and just surrender.

Natalie was less than one hundred yards from the colossus now. She gripped her umbrella tightly, hoping for a good wind that wouldn't send her straight into the golem's destructive hands or terrifying face.

A current picked up her umbrella and carried her directly over the golem.

Natalie held her breath, wondering at her good luck. Traditionally, travel in the skies had been unkind to her— particularly when she was dropping from very high altitudes.

She would have to blow out a candle at the Temple of the Wind Gods tomorrow.

She was within twenty yards of the colossus—she closed her umbrella and pointed it down at Wrath. She hurtled through the air and ignited the umbrella tip, positioning it between her legs.

The ridged spikes lining the colossus's shoulders rose up to meet her. Natalie made herself as thin as possible and fell through a gap. She bounced off the side of a spike and scraped her elbow. Then she landed on the back of the colossus with a jolt—and almost hit her head on her umbrella handle.

The umbrella tip glowed white as she magically anchored herself to the colossus's back. He trembled and swayed beneath her feet. She braced herself against a massive spike jutting up from his right shoulder. Then she held her breath and stood still.

Wrath hadn't noticed her yet. He was still busy stomping the golem soldiers at his feet.

Natalie barely managed to stifle a scream when the colossus stooped low to swat some golems with his long arms. She almost lost her grip and fell into the golems' forest of spears.

Their tactics didn't seem any more complicated than rushing the colossus and trying to overwhelm it with sheer numbers. Their strategy was brave, determined, and stupid. Clearly, these were not the maneuvers that had made them the best army of the ancient past.

Her thoughts were interrupted when Wrath suddenly stooped to grab a hunk of brick wall and throw it at the *Arete*. The colossus's overhand throw tossed Natalie against the back of his hunched neck.

She screamed and held out a forearm to save her head from cracking against his armored collar. When she had recovered her balance, Natalie chided herself for screaming. Wrath might have heard her.

It turned out that he had.

After seeing the brick wall drop short of the clipper, he turned around and swatted a thick hand at his right shoulder, trying to knock her off his back. Natalie crouched close to her umbrella and narrowly avoided the blow.

She made herself as flat as possible while the colossus swept his hand over two more times. Then he must have been satisfied that whatever had bothered him was gone, because he turned his attention back to the street.

Natalie allowed herself a deep breath. She looked down at the handle to realize that she was holding onto the umbrella with both hands. Her relief turned to horror.

Where was the spell-book?

Natalie braced herself against the shoulder spike, desperately scanning Wrath's back to see if she had dropped it on him...or if it had fallen to the ground below.

She peered over his shoulder in time to see him pulverize a golem soldier into powder. The ground was littered with broken clay. Even the streets beneath the dead golems were cracked from the colossus's heavy blows.

If she had dropped the book, there was no way she would get it back.

Natalie clasped her head, fighting to control the panic building in her chest.

Out of the corner of her eye, she saw the book lodged between Wrath's neck and armored collar.

Natalie unanchored her umbrella and stumbled across the enormous shoulder toward the book.

It was at that moment the colossus saw Natalie out of the corner of *his* eye. She froze, her feet braced against his armored collar and shoulder spike. His glowing red eyes widened.

He stood still for a second, and then he twisted around sharply to throw her off.

In a clumsy movement, Natalie fell forward, lit her umbrella tip, and plunged it into his neck just above the book.

Wrath roared in anger. Natalie ducked as he slapped the back of his neck. The blow removed a thick chunk of clay from his skin, dislodging the umbrella.

Natalie slipped backwards toward a spike in the golem's rear armor. With one boot outstretched, she braced herself against the ridge.

But her single foot, braced against the sharp edge, was the only thing holding her upright.

The ridge cut into Natalie's boot. For a brief moment she wondered if it would severe her foot.

Then she lost her balance and fell.

She landed against a thick trunk that had probably been another spike before cannon-fire had damaged it.

At least the Pantheon clippers had landed *one* good shot.

Natalie lodged herself against the broken piece and the tall spike she had fallen from. She wedged her legs in the gap to keep from falling off and held onto the damaged armor.

There was no point in anchoring here—she might have to jump off and fly away if Wrath decided to start slapping his back. And he certainly had the reach.

But the colossus was back to stomping on the golem soldiers. She had a brief moment to recover the book!

Natalie almost slipped when the colossus crouched and stood quickly to throw a handful of golems at the *Arete*. The move dislodged *On Creatures Created* from his armored collar.

Natalie reached out with her free hand to grab the falling book. From her cramped position, the stretch was sudden and painful. She bit her tongue to stop from screaming again.

But she caught it. Again.

She looked at the back of the golem's head. Time was running out.

She opened the book to see if there was an index.

There was not.

Bother.

All she had to do now was flip through a few hundred pages to find the right spell...and then use it immediately.

This was going to be hard.

"I need help." Natalie bit her lip.

"How may I help you?"

Natalie nearly fell off again.

"Who's there?" she whispered.

"I am. The book in your hand."

"You can talk?"

"Unless you are talking to yourself."

"Why didn't you talk before?"

"If you had been through what I have been through in the last few days, you would feel shy too."

"I'm standing on the back of a golem colossus who's trying to destroy Calypso. There's no time to be shy."

There was a pause.

"Understood. But in my defense, you did not ask for help until just now."

"Well, I'm asking for it."

"What kind of help?"

"I need to rewrite the Script of a golem colossus."

"Ah, golems. One moment, please."

The book shot open and the pages glowed, flipping forward, turned fiercely by an invisible hand.

About two-thirds of the way through the book, the pages stopped abruptly.

Natalie examined the chapter header: *On Golems.* She began to read but quickly realized that this was an exhaustive history of golem origins. She flipped through the chapter with a sense of rising panic.

"Where do I find out about golem Scripts?"

"Do I have to do everything for you? Just look for the section, 'On Golems and Their Script.'"

She kept flipping until she found it.

"Oh, thanks."

Section II
On Golems and Their Script:
The Script is a simple collection of commands that gives the golem its purpose. The Script:
I. Names the golem.

II. Provides the golem with the general or specific instructions needed to accomplish its purpose.

III. Sustains the golem's sense of purpose and devotion to its duty throughout the duration of its usage.

A golem's Script may be written or spoken. It is received into the golem's interior, which is hollow. The Script "fills" the golem, after a sort.

She tried to read as quickly as possible. Her eyes skimmed across the page.

It is possible to erase or write over the original Script. However, this can only be done by a master with the power and force of will proportionate to the tasking of rewriting the Script. In order to rewrite the Script, the new master must carefully follow these sacred instructions:

I. Invoke the golem's name.

II. Utter the First Sacred Chant of the Rewriting of the Script three times. The first chant is as follows:

Deah-leh Tah-bahk Spey Es

III. Write or speak the new Script.

IV. Utter the Second Sacred Chant of the Rewriting of the Script three times. The second chant is as follows:

Fi-hal Sa Vahs-con Trolis

It must be noted, however, that even if the new master has sufficient power to rewrite the golem's Script, the original Script will still retain some measure of potency. The original Script, or "True Script," as some scholars call it, can never be completely erased from the golem. Therefore, it is possible that the original Script may be accessed by a master with the power to sift through the Words inside the golem.

Natalie closed the book. That would be enough.

"Thanks," she whispered to the book.

"You are welcome."

"By the way, I just have to ask—"

"Yes?"

"If you're such an old book, how come you don't speak in a funny accent—or one of those dead languages that I keep hearing about?"

"I like to update myself for the modern reader. I find it helps me to stay relevant."

"Oh. Right. Well, thanks."

Natalie folded the corner of the page and shoved the heavy book into her raincoat pocket—something she should have done the first time she got it.

She unanchored her umbrella and climbed toward Wrath's neck. Natalie wondered at Wrath's insensitivity to movement on its body. Maybe his brain could only focus on a few physical sensations at a time.

Like the golem soldiers below, who relentlessly attacked Wrath in a futile frontal assault, intelligence was not one of Wrath's strengths.

Natalie reached the top and anchored her umbrella, bracing herself against the colossus's left shoulder spike. Then, hoping that the colossus would *be still for a moment*, she pulled out the book and followed the instructions.

"Wrath!" Natalie invoked the golem's name.

Wrath hesitated in mid-stomp—and then he brought his foot down to crush a golem soldier.

"I...I am giving you a new Script. Your True Script!" Natalie struggled to stay upright. "You must protect the city of Calypso! Your current Script is a lie! *Deah-leh Tah-Bahk...*um...*Spey Es...*"

Wrath roared, sending shivers down Natalie's spine and raising the hair on the back of her neck.

"*Deah-leh Tah-Bahk Spey-Es!*"

Wrath shuddered violently. Natalie braced herself against the shoulder spike to avoid being thrown off again. She raised her voice.

"*...Tah-Bahk Spey—*"

Wrath dropped into a sudden crouch. Natalie held on desperately to her umbrella, the book caught between her hand and the shoulder spike. She was losing her grip—

—and then Wrath reared to his full height, throwing back his head and bellowing in fury.

On Creatures Created slipped out from beneath Natalie's fingers. With a faint cry of dismay, the book bounced on Wrath's chest and was lost to the destruction at his feet.

Natalie fell over the golem's shoulder, her anchored umbrella was all that prevented her from joining the spell-book.

She bit her lip to keep from screaming. Muscles burning, she pulled herself back onto Wrath's shoulder and braced herself against his collar. She crouched against his armor, breathing hard.

The colossus stomped on the pavement, destroying more golems and the codex that might have saved him.

Natalie felt numb. The rain beat against her face. She had absolutely nothing to go on now. She had lost the spell-book, the sacred chants, and the magic words.

Wrath was going to knock her off, and she was going to die.

Tears traced their way down her cheek. She had let everyone down. She closed her eyes, feeling the shock of Wrath's powerful movements beneath her feet.

She had let Florentina down. Florentina had trusted her to save her brother...

"Our souls cannot be destroyed by the rewriting of our Scripts. Our souls are deeper than lies."

Natalie gasped at the memory of Florentina's words.

The True Script! It was buried deep within the colossus. She could still awaken it!

"Wrath!" Natalie screamed over the chaos. "Your Purpose is to defend Calypso! That's your True Script! The lies in your head don't define you. You fight for your brothers and sisters—*for* your brothers and sisters!" Natalie pounded her fist on Wrath's shoulder as he crushed more golems beneath his feet. "Your brothers and sisters are who you are! They are Clay of Your Clay! Florentina was Clay of Your Clay!"

Wrath froze, his arms poised for another blow. They hung in the air, perfectly still.

For a moment, Natalie could hear the shouts from the golem soldiers shuffling below. But they quieted down.

Everyone held their breath, unsure of what to do next. They waited on Wrath.

Natalie's voice trembled.

"The Golem Army of Calypso is Clay of Your Clay. Florentina was Clay of Your Clay. She was broken for you. She fulfilled her Purpose and fought to protect Calypso. Return to your True Script!"

Wrath roared again. The sound started at a low, rumbling bass, and then it rose higher, like the clanging of a heavy bell.

Wrath clutched his head—and Natalie ducked as the two huge hands clamped together on his helmet. He shook his head and shuddered, bellowing in his strange, deafening tones.

250

The sound was inhuman, but it was universal: confusion and anguish. Natalie cringed from the noise—and yet, her words were clearly resonating in Wrath's mind. His soul was locked in a terrible struggle.

Natalie yelped in alarm when she dropped suddenly—but then she realized that Wrath himself was dropping. He dropped into a crouch with a boom that shook the street.

And then, all of a sudden, Wrath fell silent.

He stopped shuddering, and then he raised his drooping head. His shoulders sagged, as if he was relaxing. Natalie felt a tingling of magic beneath her feet, coming up through Wrath's armor. It felt like a torrent of tension releasing from his body.

Her chest constricted with a sudden rush of stress, and then she breathed a deep sigh.

Her shoulders relaxed. She leaned against his left shoulder spike. It was over.

An enormous hand closed around her body and pulled her into the air.

CHAPTER 37:
THE TRUE SCRIPT

Darkness surrounded Natalie.

She felt the power in Wrath's fingers—larger than her waist—that enclosed her body. They were poised to ground her into powder.

She screamed against the smothering thickness of the clay hand. She was turned upside-down. Blood rushed to her head. Then the fingers pulled back and she blinked against a sudden shower of rain.

Natalie felt the sensation of weightlessness.

She was falling.

Wrath had dropped her to her death!

She fell into another hand of clay.

Natalie's cheek pressed against the wet armor on Wrath's enormous palm. The cold metal stung her skin. She raised her head slowly and gazed into her captor's face.

Wrath's red eyes pierced through the curtain of rain, locked onto hers.

Natalie raised a hand to shield her face from the rain. She looked at the umbrella shaking in her trembling hands.

Wrath followed her gaze to the umbrella. Natalie felt a lump in her throat. Was he going to crush her?

A low rumble sounded from behind Wrath's faceguard.

"Words."

Natalie blinked, taken aback. "Words?"

"Words...Script." He tapped the top of his enormous head with a thick finger. He was surprisingly articulate.

"Yes."

The red eyes blinked. "Bad Script."

Natalie nodded fervently. "Very bad."

"Script..." He moved his hand to the back of his head, feeling it carefully. "True Script inside."

"Yes, True Script." Natalie tensed, feeling light-headed with anxiety.

"True Script." Wrath nodded slowly. "Soul. Purpose. Defend Calypso."

Natalie's face broke into a smile. She laughed, trembling with relief. "Yes! Yes—True Script! Your Purpose—"

"My Purpose." The colossus looked at the destruction around him. Hundreds of glowing white eyes pierced through the gloom on the street below, gazing up at their estranged brother.

The red eyes softened and flickered.

"My Purpose. Broken."

"But fixed!" Natalie held up a hand to shield her eyes from the rain. "We fixed it! You fought against the Bad Words in your head! You're back to normal!"

"Bad Script...written by Others." His gaze drifted up to the *Arete* floating beside the bridge, and then to the skytowers. "Script always for Others. Not for Wrath. Not for Golems. Others not care."

"But I care. And Florentina cared."

"Florentina." Wrath's eyes shone brighter at the sound of her name. His gaze swept the wreckage around him. "Florentina?"

Natalie shook her head. "Broken."

The colossus looked at Natalie. His eyes flickered.

"Broken? Fix?"

"No fix."

"Fix!" Wrath's voice boomed with urgency.

"No fix. Broken." Tears welled up in Natalie's eyes. "Her soul...the dust...it's gone."

Wrath's eyes flickered out for a long moment.

"Florentina..." His voice was deep and hollow.

Natalie looked at the bridge and the *Arete*. Rain continued to fall.

"Write."

Natalie turned back to Wrath. "Sorry?"

His eyes narrowed in concentration. His words were slow and deliberate.

"Others write Good Words for Wrath. Others write Bad Words for Wrath. Now Wrath choose Powerful Word for Wrath."

Natalie was impressed. That was probably the longest speech of his life.

"You want to write Words for yourself?" she asked.

"You write Word."

"What Word?"

"Florentina."

Natalie held up her umbrella. "Florentina?"

Wrath nodded and pointed to his chest. "Florentina. Write on heart."

He carefully raised Natalie up to his chest so she could write on the breastplate. She lifted her umbrella to begin, but then she hesitated.

"On your heart?" The question came out before Natalie could stop herself. She immediately regretted it.

But Wrath just stared at her.

"Wrath have Heart."

"Of course." Natalie nodded. "Just like Florentina."

Wrath stared up into the pouring rain. "Like Florentina."

*

After Natalie finished inscribing Florentina's name on Wrath's chest, she turned around to see the *Arete* drifting toward them.

London stood atop the ship's forecastle, looking at Natalie with a mixture of concern and reverence.

Natalie crossed her arms. "It took you awhile to show up."

London looked from Natalie to Wrath. "It looked like you had everything under control."

Natalie couldn't prevent a smile from spreading across her face.

"Friend?" The golem's rumbling tones made Natalie turn around on his palm.

"Yes." Natalie raised a hand to shield her eyes from the rain.

"Many friends." Wrath gazed at the clipper. He looked down at the golems assembled on the streets. They hadn't moved the entire time. They were waiting to see what would happen.

"Many broken."

Natalie nodded. "Yes."

"Wrath lost Purpose." His eyes flickered.

"Yes. But Florentina knew that you could be saved."

"Florentina." He traced her name on his chest. "On Heart and Soul."

Natalie nodded. She looked at London, who held out his hand over the railing. She took a tentative step toward him and glanced back at the colossus.

Wrath seemed to understand the idea. Natalie stood still while he raised his hand level with the *Arete*.

Natalie took London's hand and stepped lightly onto the bow.

255

"Nice to have you aboard again, Miss Bliss." Captain Hall took off his hat with a flourish. "You are a remarkable young lady."

"Thank you, sir."

Natalie glanced at London, who still hadn't let go of her hand. She cleared her throat.

He let go of her hand and blushed.

Natalie turned away and allowed herself a smile that London couldn't see. She was about to ask Wrath what he was going to do now—but a shout from the *Arete's* stern stole her attention.

A cover of clouds rolled away to reveal the starboard side of the *Marcion*. Guns gleamed through the veil of rain.

A shiver ran down Natalie's spine. That was impossible. The frigate had been destroyed.

Hadn't it?

The sky erupted as the *Marcion* unleashed a hail of glowing cannonballs straight toward them.

CHAPTER 38:
RECKONING

The *Marcion*'s broadside slammed into the *Arete*'s hull, shaking the deck beneath Natalie and London's feet.

Natalie held out a hand for balance and scraped her forearm against the railing. She stumbled to the ground, clutching the stinging cut. London shouted something but was drowned out.

Glowing cannonballs pelted against Wrath, who bellowed angrily. His armor was strong, but the shock from the salvo pushed him toward the river. The golem soldiers at his feet scurried away, afraid of being crushed like so many of their comrades.

Wrath heard the golems' shouts below and stood still to let them evacuate the area. The *Marcion* took the advantage to concentrate an entire broadside on Wrath.

Shots screamed across the sky, cutting through the rain and exploding against his face and chest. The frigate drifted closer to Wrath. At this range, the cannon-fire was devastating, even against a golem colossus. Chunks of Wrath's armor crumpled and broke under the barrage. A cannonball dented the breastplate bearing Florentina's name, erasing half of the word.

Wrath roared in anger. He scraped his hand against his chest in a vain effort to repair the damage. The *Marcion*'s course took it directly over the golem and the clipper, allowing the frigate's fire to pour onto the *Arete*'s unprotected deck.

Natalie crouched against the front of the forecastle, holding her umbrella overhead. There was a knock on her umbrella, and she raised it to see London peeking underneath.

Natalie motioned for him to crawl under the canopy. "Get in!"

"Are you crazy?" London pointed at the frigate flying above them.

A cannonball broke the surface of the deck, sending a shower of flaming wood into the air. London raised his arms to shield himself from the debris. The clipper trembled underfoot.

"We need to get off the ship!" London yelled.

257

Natalie closed her umbrella and took in the scene of destruction before her. Sailors scrambled for cover amid the fallen masts, the tangled lines, and the splintered deck. Captain Hall strode calmly through the chaos, stepping around the hole and barking orders to his crew.

London put a hand on Natalie's shoulder. "We need to go. The ship is going dow—"

As if to confirm his words, the *Arete* shuddered with a terrifying jolt and tilted toward the starboard side. Captain Hall grabbed hold of a line to stay on his feet.

Natalie anchored her umbrella against the deck to keep from slipping down to her left.

"No!" London shouted when Natalie's umbrella tip glowed with the anchoring-spell. "We need to leave *now!*"

"Sorry, just habit!" Natalie released the umbrella and stood— then she *did* slip when another explosion rocked the ship. She tumbled against the railing at the same time that London lost his balance. Natalie caught her leg between the railings, but London tripped over a sliding box and fell overboard.

"Natalie!" He plummeted head over heels, hands outstretched for help. Natalie threw back her hand with the umbrella. London's left hand grabbed onto the umbrella's Irresistible Grip—and then Natalie screamed as his weight pulled her off the ship railing.

They plunged toward the river.

With London holding the end of her umbrella, there was no way that Natalie could fly.

Their eyes met. London seemed to be making a decision.

He glanced at the river rushing up to meet them, and then at the flaming wreck breaking apart overhead.

"No!" Natalie shouted.

London shook his head, a sad look in his eyes. He swung up his right hand to grab his left, which was locked to the umbrella. There was a green flash and a popping noise—and London's counter-spell released the Irresistible Grip.

He plummeted toward the river.

Natalie's umbrella opened immediately. She screamed incoherently at London before a strong draft of wind picked her up and away from the river. She glanced over her shoulder to see London, but a fiery blur had blocked him. The *Arete's* hull exploded, smothering the surface of the river with flames.

A moment later, the *Arete* was stolen from view as the wind turned Natalie around and whisked her toward the Calypso Bridge.

She looked down at the river, desperate for any sign of London. All she could see was flaming wreckage and falling debris. The wind twisted her around and around, making it harder to scan the surface of the water.

She flew against one of the bridge cables and wrapped her free arm around it. Then she slid down the cable, the thick wire scraping against her raincoat sleeve. Wind pulled at her umbrella and threatened to blow her off the bridge, but Natalie managed to swing the umbrella down and close it.

Her descent accelerated. A moment later, Natalie stumbled onto the bridge.

She rolled onto her back, sore and panting for air. Raindrops poured down her gasping throat, making her choke. She struggled to her knees and coughed violently. Then her back convulsed and she threw up.

Natalie groaned and wiped her mouth with her sleeve. She knelt there, shivering in the rain on wet cement. Tension gripped her chest. She threw up again.

The frigate's booming cannon-fire competed with Wrath's heavy roars. The cacophony of destruction echoed in her head and disoriented her.

When Natalie had finished being sick, she looked up to see the battle's final combatants. The *Marcion's* volleys pounded Wrath mercilessly, pinning him to the ground beside the river. Stray shots exploded against the ruined buildings lining the riverside. Unlike the Pantheon clippers, the *Marcion* didn't care about collateral damage.

Natalie searched the sky, wondering what had happened to the second clipper. And where was the rest of the Pantheon's fleet? All she could see were the *Marcion* and the colossus.

The golem soldiers couldn't do anything against the frigate. It looked like the *Marcion* was going to unload all of its ammunition upon Wrath. The colossus lay crouched against the ground, protecting his face with his arms. Even in this position, his height was still greater than most of the surrounding buildings. He could do little against the *Marcion's* merciless ranged attack.

Flaming white-hot projectiles lit up the air around the colossus, cutting through his armor and tearing holes in his clay body.

Natalie felt like she was going to be sick again. She rose unsteadily to her feet. Wrath's red eyes pierced through the rain, locked onto hers. She gripped her umbrella tightly. Her left forearm, legs, and head throbbed with pain. She glanced down at the surging river, where London had—

She forced herself to look away.

You can't think about that right now. Focus on the battle.

The frigate drifted closer to the colossus, pouring white cannonballs into his towering body. Captain Barias was closing in for the kill.

Natalie had been in tight corners before, but she wasn't the one in the corner now. Even if she could fly onto the frigate *again*, she was too weak to take on the crew.

Her shin throbbed with pain. She tried to ignore it.

She gazed at Wrath's face, at the two points of red light peering from under the heavy helmet and hulking armor.

The golem knew his sins, but he had been redeemed.

Natalie could see a fragment of armor with the letters "NTINA" hanging from Wrath's chest. It was the last remnant of Florentina's name.

Her mind swam in suppressed pain and fatigue. At the abbey library, she had read an old word for flower—from one of the dead languages that made common words sound smarter. The word was *flore*: the missing part of Florentina's name.

Natalie waved a hand at the black spots erupting in front of her eyes. Her mind spun dizzily. Why was she thinking about flowers?

Her knees buckled beneath her. She didn't have much strength left.

The colossus had strength. If only he had a little bit more to overcome the *Marcion's* onslaught.

Natalie blinked and forced herself to stand up straight. Maybe thinking about flowers wasn't such a silly thing after all.

Flore...ntina.

Natalie closed her eyes against the booming cannons and flashing lights. She raised her umbrella and focused.

A sparkle of flame sputtered from her umbrella and sizzled into vapor at her feet.

She bit her lip and concentrated harder. She thought of Florentina. She thought of London too—but she shut her mind from the image of him falling into the river.

Hope is for the living.

A long torrent of flame burst from her umbrella and shot into the air, trailing an arc through the sky.

The fiery stream fell far short of the *Marcion*.

But as the flames dropped toward the river, they traced into the letters, "FLORE."

Natalie watched the glowing shapes spread into glowing petals and disintegrate. It was the first half of Florentina's name. It was a flower, beautiful and alive.

It was just a word. Something for the heart—but it was all Natalie had left.

Fortunately for her, golems put a lot of stock in words.

Wrath watched the word trace its way through the sky. He saw the petals fade into the rain. His red eyes burned brightly, and he staggered to his feet with a terrifying roar. He stumbled toward the river as the frigate's volley ripped through his weakened armor and decimated his exposed body. Golden-white mist streamed from holes in his clay flesh.

Natalie held a hand to her mouth. He was dying.

But the colossus lumbered forward. Wrath was not to be stopped this time.

With surprising agility, he ducked low and prepared to jump. A stream of cannonballs missed his head to slam into the ruins far behind. The *Marcion* put on a last-ditch burst of speed to move away from the shore, but it was too late. Captain Barias had been too eager to take advantage of the tempting close range.

It had almost worked.

Almost.

With a spine-tingling roar, Wrath leapt from the shore's edge. His lumbering arms flailed through the air. Colossal hands slammed into the frigate's stern and bow. He gripped the ends of the ship and sunk his fingers into the hull.

The colossus wrapped himself against the *Marcion* while the cannons continued to fire. White-hot projectiles blasted through his body, punching holes in his thick clay flesh. A flood of golden-white dust flowed from the gaps in his riddled body.

But he held on.

Then the frigate shuddered and tore apart with an almighty crack. For a brief moment, colossus and frigate fell through the air, plummeting toward the river.

In a passing moment, Natalie saw Wrath turn to look at her. His red eyes shone.

Then his destructive fingers found the frigate's magazine, and a ball of fire exploded in the disemboweled ship. Natalie blinked against the inferno that enveloped frigate and colossus.

There was no doubt this time. The *Marcion* was gone.

And Wrath was fulfilled.

CHAPTER 39:
ALL YOU EVER HAVE IS TODAY

Natalie watched the remnants of Wrath's body sink into the depths of the river. Within moments, he was gone. Rain peppered the surface of the waters where the colossus had disappeared.

Ship wreckage floated on the river, passing underneath the Calypso Bridge. Natalie shivered. She looked around, waiting for some kind of confirmation that the battle was over.

There was no announcement. There were no flashing lights. There was no roar of celebration from an enraptured crowd.

The Arcadian Games had ended prematurely. Natalie wondered if they would be able to continue. Surely they had to continue—Arcadia had always seen the games through to completion. Calypso would carry on.

Emptiness filled Natalie's chest. That was the best and the worst part of it: people would carry on.

But some lives would never be the same. Natalie bit her lip and shook her head bitterly.

Florentina was gone. London was gone. Even Wrath was gone.

Who knew where Quincy was?

Florentina said that Natalie had friends, but memories might truly be all she had now.

She was alone again.

She finally succumbed to her fatigue and half-sat, half-fell onto the bridge. She dangled her feet over the edge, letting the rain pour down her face. Strands of wet hair fell over her eyes and brushed against her lips.

An eerie silence reigned over Calypso. Up and down the streets, survivors were poking their heads out of ruined shops and homes, drawn by the sudden calm. The golems had lined up in ranks along the shore. They stared down into the waters. As one, they each raised a fist to their chests in a form of salute. Then they stood there in the rain, waiting for further orders.

Natalie sighed, wondering what the Pantheon would do with the golems. It would probably be the same as before: gods would

263

argue that the golems should be destroyed because they might fall into the wrong hands.

And, as much as Natalie hated to admit it, there was truth to that argument.

A pained scream broke the silence. Natalie's head jerked up to see where the noise was coming from. An elf woman was wandering down the street by the bridge. She stumbled over the rubble, carrying a small bundle wrapped in white. There were red stains on the cloth.

The mother turned her head back and forth in desperation. Natalie had seen that look before. It was when you were searching for someone who could make everything right again, someone who could provide an explanation for what had happened. You wouldn't find anyone, but you looked.

Perhaps the person she was really looking for was in her arms.

The mother's cries were joined by others, as though the city had been given permission to start mourning. Screams and sobs rose up along the streets, punctuated by the shout of names as people searched for relatives and friends.

Natalie gazed across the city toward the bay, trying to see the Pantheon Palatium. High above the ocean, she caught a glimpse of the skyland through a break in the clouds. Then it was covered up again.

For the first time since her return, Natalie felt that there was a terrible irony to Arcadia. Even on their home planet, the Pantheon remained aloof from the wounds of the world.

No golem colossus could fly to the skyland, bursting through the sacred ground and besmirching the divine floors of the Pantheon. No enemy frigate would come close to the Palatium— not without an entire fleet and the spells to breach the skyland's magical defenses.

No, Calypso might be set ablaze, and it might burn for a time, but the Pantheon itself would never smell smoke.

But would the cries of mortal mothers reach the ears of the gods?

Natalie shook her head. Maybe she wasn't thinking straight. Maybe she was just being emotional.

Well...she *was* being emotional.

She wiped away the thick strands of wet hair falling over her eyes. Perhaps she should feel thankful that the Pantheon had sent two clippers to the games.

The clippers...

A knot tied in her stomach.

London was right. They should have jumped from the *Arete* sooner.

"...Natalie..."

She closed her eyes, remembering the sound of London's voice calling her name. The memory sounded faint in her head. She replayed the image of him falling into the river—of the fiery blur that had covered him from view. It was the fall that had taken him from her...maybe forever.

"...Natalie..."

How could she hear his voice so clearly now? It almost sounded real.

"Natalie!"

She turned around, looking down the ruined bridge to see a shape caught in a dangling web of cables.

It looked like London.

The figure threw back his head and shouted at the top of his strained voice. "Natalie!"

It *was* London!

"I'm coming!" Natalie sprinted down the road, white rain boots slapping against the slick pavement. Her tired legs slipped in a puddle, but she kept her balance with an outstretched hand. She ducked under a railing and reached the edge.

"How did you—you're alive—what happened?" Natalie got down on her knees and held her umbrella toward London.

"Yep...m'alive." He grunted. He pushed a hand through the cables and stretched out to grab the umbrella. It was just beyond reach.

Natalie leaned down farther. "What happened?"

"A lifeboat from the *Ptolemy* rescued me. It had taken too much damage so it had to withdraw from the battle—ow!" London winced. The cable had cut into his skin when he reached for the umbrella, and his movement was swaying the cable back and forth. He slid down farther.

"Oh, what am I doing?" Natalie pulled her umbrella back up.

London's eyes widened. "What are you doing?" His voice cracked from fatigue.

Natalie jumped to her feet. Her knees wobbled, and she almost lost her balance again, but she caught herself in time. Then she opened her umbrella and stepped off the bridge.

She floated down level with London, who slowly worked himself free of the steel net. His leg dangled over the edge of the tangled cable.

"What now?"

"Come on." Natalie spread out her arm, indicating that London should hold onto her.

"Uh..." London looked at the skinny girl offering her a ride. "You want me to...?"

"Oh, London." Natalie grabbed London's arm with surprising strength and pulled him close. He wrapped his arms around her waist. Natalie cringed.

"What?" he asked.

"My leg. It hurts."

"You're hurt? Then how are you carrying me?"

"I can manage. But I'd like to drop you off as soon as possible."

"Right. Yeah. Me too."

Their faces were inches away. London was looking determinedly at the river.

"London, when we were on the ship, before I—"

He cleared his throat. "Don't tell anyone you've been carrying *me*, okay?"

Natalie made an impatient noise and floated them back up onto the bridge. She dropped him onto the pavement—a few feet higher than she needed to. Then she landed herself and turned around angrily.

"Don't tell anyone I've been carrying you? You stupid—" She cast about for the worst word she could think of. "You stupid *boy*! I was *worried* about you!"

London looked at Natalie with a mixture of surprise and incredulity.

"Worried—what? Of course you were! I was worried about you too!"

"But you don't underst—ah!" Natalie winced again. Her angry landing had wrenched her leg painfully.

"Are you okay?"

"No, I'm not okay! I'm a long way from okay!"

London stepped closer. "You were about to say something. What is it that I don't understand?"

"You don't..." Natalie sighed and shook her head.

"You're hurt." London took her cut forearm and examined it. She flinched from the touch, but she didn't pull away.

"Yes, I'm hurt! This whole city is full of hurt right now!"

Tears filled her eyes.

Great. *Now* she was going to cry? In front of London?

"I know. I'm sorry. It's all messed up." London stared at the ground, and Natalie noticed the crusted blood on his forehead and cheek. "But we're still together, right?"

Natalie arched an eyebrow. "Whatever *that* means."

London pulled away. "I had to let you go—twice! Twice *today!* I saved your life!"

"And I saved yours." Natalie crossed her arms. She breathed heavily, muttering under her breath. "And now you say ridiculous things like, 'We're still together.'"

"We are! We still have each other."

"But what does—"

"I thought there was going to be a happy ending to this miserable day, where you two held hands and kissed or something—but instead you just started arguing again."

London and Natalie turned. Quincy poked her head around the pillar behind them.

"Quincy!" Natalie redirected her anger at the sylph. "How long have you been standing there?"

"Long enough to see you fly London up to the bridge." Quincy grinned. "You were holding each other very tightly."

"Quincy, this isn't funny—" London began, but Natalie interrupted him.

"No, it's not funny. It's also private, Quincy, so if we want to argue, that's our decision. And we'll argue by ourselves, thank you."

"No more arguing." Quincy shook her head. Natalie noticed how exhausted the sylph looked behind her fading smile. "There's been enough fighting today." She pointed at the ruined city around them. "They're hurting! I'm hurting—and I know you are too!" Her voice broke, and she started to cry. "And what this world does *not* need right now is *more fighting!*" She punched Natalie in the shoulder.

Natalie flinched, more from surprise than anything else.

"It hurts me that you can't be with each other for two minutes without fighting!" Quincy took a deep breath. Her wings fluttered as she exhaled. "Listen, I don't care if the two of you are in love or not. I think it's cute."

Natalie crossed her arms. "What makes you—"

"Don't be naïve, Natalie. But it's not my business if you like each other or not. It *is* my business that we're all friends, and I need to see you two getting along. Because you do love each other, even if you're just friends."

Natalie stared at the pavement. Then she stole a glance at London, who had stolen a glance at her. They both looked down.

"Life's not all about memories, Natalie," Quincy said quietly. "In fact, it's really about what's going on right now. All you ever have is today—not yesterday, not tomorrow. And today, we're here together. Okay?"

Natalie swallowed. "Okay."

The girls looked at London, who nodded.

"Yeah, okay," he said. He turned to Natalie. "I'm sorry."

She brushed a strand of red hair behind her ear. "Me too."

Quincy stared at both of them until she was satisfied.

"Good. Now you need to come with me." She turned on her heel and started walking away.

"Where are we—" Natalie started to ask, but Quincy interrupted her.

"Oh, London—is Dwayne okay?"

"Huh?" London reached inside his soaked leather jacket and pulled out the small luminewt. Dwayne's eyes were wide, and his body pulsed a faint orange.

London managed a smile. "Yeah, he's fine."

"Oh, good." Quincy sighed in relief. Then she started walking off the bridge again. "Now follow me. Abbess Persephone sent me to find you. She's with the golems, helping to clean up the city."

"Wait a minute." London carefully put Dwayne back inside his jacket. "You ask if Dwayne is okay, but not me?"

"Oh, I knew you were fine, London. Come on!"

CHAPTER 40:
PICKING UP THE PIECES

"Arthur!" Clare screamed, stumbling through a ruined street by the Calypso Bridge. The rain had finally stopped, allowing the city a small measure of relief.

All around her, people were digging through mounds of rubble to find loved ones. Cars and buses lay buried underneath bricks and mangled steel. Blood stained the streets.

Heavily-armored golems were helping to move the wreckage and look for survivors. They did their work silently, lifting heavy beams, clearing tangles of wire, and pulling victims from the wreckage. People gave the golems a wide berth, eyeing them suspiciously.

"Arthur!" Clare called again, holding her limp, bloody hand close to her stomach.

She and Arthur had come across the Calypso Bridge after fleeing the Arcadian Stadium. But the colossus had moved to the river too.

The elf couple had been running down the street when the colossus had tossed a chunk of restaurant at one of the ships. Shards of glass and broken bricks had rained down on them. Clare had watched people disappear all around her, crushed by falling debris.

Arthur had disappeared too. He had been holding her hand— but a hail of bricks had hit her arm and separated them. Then there had been darkness.

When Clare came to, she had seen thick rain and collapsed buildings. People had been pushing and shoving in their desperation to escape. The terrifying colossus had stood by the bridge, fighting the ships and the girl with the umbrella.

And in all the chaos, Clare hadn't found Arthur.

She stumbled to the ground and sat against a smooth slab of cement, favoring her injured left hand. Beside her, an elf woman cradled her small child. The boy wasn't moving.

Trembling with rage and grief, Clare continued to whisper his name. "Arthur..."

"Over here, Florence."

Clare turned around to see a short woman in a plain black overcoat leading more golems into the street. One of the golems had a blue apron.

The woman's face was pale. She walked through the devastated city block, clutching a black umbrella in one hand.

She stopped by the elf mother and gazed soberly at the motionless child. The elf looked up at her with pleading eyes, and the woman placed her hand on the boy's forehead. She held it there for a long moment.

"I'm so sorry," she finally said.

Tears slid down the mother's cheeks. She bent over her son, holding him closer, shaking her head in disbelief.

The woman in the black overcoat stood by the elf, head bowed and eyes closed. When she looked up again, she caught Clare's eye.

"Hello, dear. Are you hurt?"

"No, it's my boyfriend—I think he's buried somewhere in the rubble." Clare's voice broke. "I was running with him, and then it was like a building fell on us, and then—"

"Where?" the woman interrupted. "Where did you lose him?"

"Over there." Clare pointed at a brick wall resting on a pile of plaster and dirt. "I thought maybe he had gotten out, but I don't know. I don't know..." She dropped her head, tears sliding down her nose.

She felt a hand on her shoulder.

"I see," the woman said, examining the indicated pile. "Florence, I'm going to need help."

One of the golems brought two more over, and together they joined the black-haired woman at the fallen brick wall.

"Let's make sure this doesn't crumble while we're trying to lift it." The lady tapped her umbrella twice. "*Solid* and *light* brick wall."

Three golems surrounded the wall and lifted it. The lady moved out of the way so the golems could drop it onto the street.

An elf covered in soot and dirt lay in the rubble. He was motionless.

Clare jumped up and stumbled toward him. "Arthur!"

"Just a moment, dear." The woman held out a hand. She knelt by Arthur and brushed the dirt from his face. She placed the tip of her umbrella on his chest, where it glowed faintly. Then she cradled his head in her arms, whispering softly for a minute.

Arthur coughed violently.

Clare dropped to her knees and embraced her boyfriend, tears of joy streaming down her face.

"Give him some air," the woman said gently.

She and Clare helped Arthur up to a sitting position. He blinked, shaking his head and gasping. His breathing finally settled down, and then he smiled at Clare. They hugged each other tightly, ignoring the dirt on their clothes and tear-stained faces.

"Thank you!" Clare cried to the woman, who nodded and stood.

Persephone turned away from the couple and glanced at the Calypso Bridge to see three figures walking her way. They broke into a run when they saw her.

She embraced them all in a hug. "Thank goodness you're all right."

"You too," London said. "When did you get here?"

A shadow passed over Persephone's face. "As soon as I heard the news. Not quickly enough, I'm afraid." She indicated the devastation around them. "But the golems and I are doing what we can." She looked down at Natalie. "I see that you did what you could. And more."

Natalie swallowed. It looked, for once, like the red-haired girl didn't know what to say.

"Hello, Miss Bliss." Florence appeared next to them. "I am glad that you are alive and not dead. You were very brave."

Natalie hugged the golem housekeeper around his dusty apron.

"Thank you, Florence. So were you. But I—I need to tell you that Florentina—"

"Is dead," he finished. "I know, Miss Bliss. But I also know that you were with her at the end. That is good. She loved you."

Florence patted Natalie's back in a stiff movement. Then he turned away, his white eyes flickering.

"I don't understand how the colossus could have caused this much damage in Calypso." London shook his head bitterly. "Why wasn't the city better defended—especially at the start of the Arcadian Games? Why weren't there more Pantheon ships?"

Abbess Persephone put a hand on his shoulder. "There will be a full inquiry into all of this, believe me. The thin security measures are already being blamed on the Divine Wedding in

271

Parlemagne, but that excuse is weak. It is unacceptable that only two Pantheon ships were engaged in the battle. The admiral of the fleet won't be admiral after today, I can assure you that." She brushed a strand of curly black hair out of her eyes. "But I'm afraid that today revealed more than just incompetence. There's something sinister afoot."

"The captain on the *Marcion* called himself a Forerunner," Natalie said.

A wave of concern passed over Persephone's face.

"You've heard of them?" Natalie asked.

"Oh, yes." Persephone's eyes narrowed. "I know about the Forerunners. So do many in the Pantheon. Those who didn't believe in their existence have received a most severe education today." At the questioning look on Natalie's face, Persephone added, "There were gods who thought that the Forerunners were an imaginary threat—rather like the Golem Army of Calypso, which clearly took me by surprise." Her blue eyes flashed angrily. "Serious questions must be raised about our intelligence. I don't know the point of being on the Security Council if the members are ignorant of the weapons buried underneath our feet."

"What will happen to the golems?" Natalie asked.

Persephone sighed. "Oh, it will be like last time, I suppose. But I'll do what I can for them."

They stood silently for a long moment. London left quietly to help the golems sift through the rubble. Quincy wandered over to the riverside.

Natalie stayed by Persephone, looking deep in thought. Her arms were crossed.

"Something bothering you, dear?" Persephone asked.

"About the Forerunners—the captain said they wanted to bring the Titans back."

Persephone nodded gravely. "They do."

"He said today was just a statement against the Pantheon."

"It was a statement. It proved that the Titans still have powerful friends, and that the Pantheon is not invincible." She frowned. "But this attack may have been premature. We can use it to strengthen our position against the Titans. The public will demand that the Pantheon be ready next time. And there will be a next time."

Persephone twirled her black umbrella on the ground. "What really worries me is that there are Forerunner agents inside the Pantheon. And in high positions too."

"How do you know??"

"I trust the inquiry will provide the details. I don't believe for a moment that the inadequate military response was a mistake. It's not a simple failure by a fool—although the Forerunner agents will try to paint it that way. So will the gods who want to brush the Forerunner issue under the rug—but!" She sighed, waving a dismissive hand. "Enough of politics right now. For the moment, I want you to know that I'm very proud of you." The abbess arched an eyebrow. "And you surprised me."

Natalie's expression was neutral. They both knew that a rebuke was waiting when the other shoe dropped.

"You were right about the golem army. You were stronger than I expected you to be this early in life. But," she fixed Natalie with a stern gaze, and the other shoe dropped, "don't make a habit of disobeying me."

Natalie nodded soberly.

Persephone's expression softened. She put a comforting hand on Natalie's shoulder. "I made at least two crucial mistakes about this situation—about the golem army and about you. That is a humbling experience for me. I learned something. I hope you did too."

Then the abbess patted her on the shoulder and started toward the golems.

"You know," Natalie began, and Persephone stopped. "When we talked in your office, I thought I was a lot stronger than I really was. You didn't underestimate me. I just got stronger when I needed to—with London and Quincy helping me along the way. Florentina, Florence, London, Quincy—we all helped each other." Natalie adjusted the sleeves on her raincoat. "We carried each other, even."

Persephone smiled. "You did learn something."

Then she walked back to join Florence and London.

Natalie turned toward the river, where Quincy was standing by the shore. The sylph's blonde hair blew gently about her head. Her wings glistened faintly in the dying sunset.

"Hey." Natalie put an arm around Quincy's shoulder.

"Hey. You all right?"

Natalie nodded.

To the northeast, they could see the ruins of the Arcadian Stadium. Entire sections of stands had been demolished. None of the surrounding buildings were still standing.

Quincy sighed. "I wonder if they're going to continue the Arcadian Games."

"I don't know. Probably. Arcadia is going to need something to cheer about when this mess is cleaned up."

"Yeah." Quincy's lip quivered. "I heard that Io was killed by Wrath."

"Oh. I'm really sorry to hear that."

"It's a shame—it's a terrible shame about all of them. Thousands of people died." Quincy wiped away the tears flowing down her cheeks. "And it's a shame about the Torch of Sayornis too. The Undying Fire wasn't even lit. Io was killed before he could light it." She gave a shuddering sigh. "The torch isn't ever supposed to go out."

"Yeah." Natalie pulled a handkerchief out of her raincoat and gave it to the sylph. "But maybe it's not as important that the torch got blown out."

"What?" Quincy blew her nose and sniffed loudly. "What do you mean?"

"I think what matters is that there will always be someone to light it again." Natalie pointed to the ruins of the Arcadian Stadium. "And there will be—look!"

From across the river, they saw a faint light flickering atop the rubble. The Golden Bowl of Sayornis gleamed in the fading sunlight.

"The rescue workers must have lit the fire." Natalie smiled as a tear traced its way down her cheek. She leaned her head on Quincy's shoulder. "See? Hope in the midst of despair."

Quincy nodded quietly, wiping her eyes with the back of her hand.

They gazed at the stadium until the sun went down.

When Natalie and Quincy finally left, they knew the Undying Fire would continue to burn brightly—through darkness to the dawn.

EPILOGUE

Regina opened her eyes wearily, feeling the comfortable weight of her green bedspread. She had slept for a long time. Her arms felt sore. She pushed back her covers and examined her forearms, brushing her fingers against the smooth, pale skin. She didn't know why they were sore. They looked fine.

She had the nagging feeling that something had happened before she had fallen asleep—or while she had been sleeping. But she couldn't remember what it was.

She looked around the dark room, wondering whether it was morning or night. Rolling onto her side, she pressed her face against her warm pillow and tried to fall asleep again.

The carpeted floor by her bed creaked, as if sudden weight had pressed against it.

She heard a soft intake of air.

Regina froze. Was someone in the room? She held her breath and heard the faint breathing of another person.

Her chest tightened with anxiety. Regina opened her eyes and gasped.

An olive-skinned, black-haired boy stood next to the bed, smiling warmly at her.

"How are you feeling, my love?" he asked, brushing long black hair out of his eyes.

Her heart skipped a beat. She didn't recognize him, but a surprising feeling of security washed over her at the sound of his voice.

Was he a hallucination?

She blinked and shook her head, but the boy didn't disappear. She waved her hand at his face, trying to see if he was a mirage. He took her hand gently into his own, pressing it against his face. She felt the smooth skin on his cheek. The touch sent a strange, soft feeling through her chest.

"I missed you, my love," he said.

Regina blinked, feeling confused.

"Who are you?" she whispered.

The boy's smile flickered.

275

"I'm Bellamy." He cleared his throat. "Don't you remember me, Regina?"

She gazed into his hazel eyes. She didn't remember him, but she liked it when he said her name.

Regina nodded slowly.

The boy almost laughed with relief.

"Good. I'm so glad." Tears shone at the edges of his eyes.

Regina didn't understand why he was crying.

He gently picked up her other hand, holding both together in his own. "I love you, Regina. I love you so much."

He gazed eagerly into her eyes. She stared back.

A broad smile spread across the boy's face. Regina eventually realized that she was smiling too.

"You haven't smiled in a long time," he said. "You have a beautiful smile."

Regina felt a strange warmth on her cheeks. She was blushing.

The moment lasted for a long time. Regina wanted it to last longer.

But then her eyelids felt heavy again.

"Tired," she whispered softly.

The boy nodded, laying her hands back on the bed. As Regina closed her eyes, he began to stroke her hair. His fingertips brushed against her forehead, trailing across her ears and against her neck.

"Stay with me?" she asked, feeling warm and secure.

"Yes, my love."

Regina smiled. Then she drifted off to sleep.

*

Tap.

Tap. Tap.

Natalie blinked wearily. She rubbed her eyes and threw aside the cover on her bed. Faint rays of light peeked through the closed curtains on her window. The sun was rising.

Tap. Tap.

Click.

Natalie turned on her light. Someone was tapping lightly at her door.

A thrill of excitement ran through her body. Someone wasn't just tapping—she was *lightly* tapping.

It couldn't be—could it?

Natalie jumped out of bed and opened the door.

A golem stood in the doorway, hand still poised in the air for another light tap. The golem had painted black hair tied in a sculpted bun behind her head. She wore a blue apron and carried a blue bucket. Her white eyes shone brightly.

Natalie's heart sank. She knew it couldn't have been...but for a brief moment...

"Hello, Miss Bliss. My name is Anita. I am your new housekeeper. I wanted to introduce myself because I will be cleaning your suite now."

Natalie held out her hand. "It's nice to meet you, Anita."

Anita looked at Natalie's hand and held it carefully. "It is nice to meet you too. You knew my sister, Florentina."

Natalie's heart skipped a beat at the name. "Yes! I knew Florentina. She was a wonderful golem—a wonderful person."

"She was a great leader and a mighty warrior." Anita still hadn't let go of Natalie's hand. "I asked Abbess Persephone if I could honor my sister's memory by taking her place as housekeeper. Abbess Persephone told me that Florentina was a mighty housekeeper."

"Yes, she was." Natalie pulled her hand gently away from Anita's grasp. The golem dropped her hand by her side. "She was very dedicated, and she paid close attention to detail. Very close attention."

"That is good to hear. That is fitting for a golem. It is our Purpose to always do our job well. I will continue the same level of cleanliness that Florentina provided for you. I will be a mighty housekeeper like my sister."

"Oh, thank you." Natalie put on a pair of slippers to warm her cold feet. "So you'll be...cleaning every day as well?"

"I will clean every day to keep the dust and stains away."

"Oh," Natalie tried to keep from grimacing, "good."

"I shall start by cleaning your sheets." Anita reached down to take Natalie's cover, but the red-haired girl grabbed it first.

"Actually, I was thinking about using that a while longer."

"To do what?"

"To sleep." Natalie nodded at the window. "It's very early."

"The sun has risen." Anita's glowing eyes narrowed in confusion. "The day has begun. Do you sleep during the day?"

"Er, sometimes. It's been a long few days, so I thought I would catch up on my rest."

Anita nodded slowly. "Very well. Then I will clean your bathroom." She started to walk out of the bedroom. Her cleaning materials clattered noisily in the bucket.

"Actually," Natalie cleared her throat, "if you want, you could just come back later in the morning."

Anita stopped and turned around—or rather, stopped and swiveled her head around to look at Natalie.

"You could get some more rest too. If you're tired...?" Natalie finished lamely.

Anita stared at Natalie for a moment. "I am not tired. But I understand your unspoken words. If I clean your bathroom, I will make noise. That will make it hard for you to sleep. You want me to come back later so that you can sleep without interruption."

"Yes." Natalie clasped her hands together gratefully. "That would be excellent."

"Very well. I will come back at nine o'clock."

Natalie fell back onto her bed. "Nine o'clock then."

Anita was almost out the door when Natalie sprang up from her bed.

"Anita!"

"Yes, Miss Bliss?"

Natalie hesitated. "How did you know to tap lightly on the door like that?"

"Florentina told me."

Natalie sat on the edge of her bed. She stared intently at the golem. "When did she tell you? Did she know that you were going to be my new housekeeper?"

"No. But the Clay speaks, Miss Bliss."

"But..." Natalie's heart beat faster. "But Florentina's dead."

"Yes, Miss Bliss. But Florentina was my sister. She was Clay of my Clay. The Clay speaks."

"The Clay *speaks*?"

"The Clay is a Mystery, Miss Bliss."

Natalie stared down at her lap. "I don't understand."

"Yes. You do not understand. But perhaps you will understand if I use different words. Florentina is alive in our hearts, Miss Bliss."

Natalie looked up. A tear slid down her nose to fall on her clasped hands.

Anita's eyes twinkled.

"Her memory is alive in us. Hope is for the living." She walked out of the bedroom. "I will see you at nine o'clock. Good morning, Miss Bliss."

AUTHOR'S NOTE

This is the second edition of *The Undying Fire*. Some typos, sentence structure issues, confusing details, and lines of dialogue have been fixed. Certain paragraphs have been modified, deleted, or added to make chapters flow more smoothly.

One complete chapter has been added: Chapter 27, "The Gargoyle Guard." I added the chapter because Bellamy disappeared from the narrative for too long in the original version, and the reader had to assume that he delivered the spell-book to Captain Barias. The new scene ties up that plot detail and clarifies that Bellamy withdrew from Calypso for his own reasons.

I also modified the cover titles and added a dedication and an acknowledgements section.

Thanks for reading.

ACKNOWLEDGEMENTS

My mom, for sharing her love of books and making libraries my second home

My dad, for providing for my study abroad trips to Oxford, England, without which these stories would not exist

My brother, for reading my books and loving fantasy

My sister-in-law, for loving tea and teaching me to do the same

Mel Odom, for his continuing friendship and guidance

Dr. Melanie Wright, for inviting me to Oxford a second summer—the trip which inspired this book

Dr. Alan Velie, for the pub crawls in Oxford

Caleb Holt, for his constant encouragement that the artistic life is worthwhile and necessary

Alyssa Grimley, for being my brutha and writing buddy

Daniel Kordek (daekazu), for his beautiful cover illustration and titles

Adam Oxsen, for taking me to El Dolce for *gelato* and starting a friendship of artistic endeavors

Nicholas Key and Shelby Simpson, for our writing friendships and mutual encouragement

About the Author

Steven Thorn was born in Virginia, USA. He and his brother were homeschooled through high school by their mother, a former public school teacher in California and Florida.

Steven received his Bachelor's and Master's degrees in Professional Writing from the University of Oklahoma, his dad's alma mater. He is a musician and recording artist. He enjoys studying history, mythology, and religion. His other pursuits include football, soccer, tabletop games, and perfecting parallel structure. When he's not writing or doing his annual pushup, he's pondering the mysteries of the universe.

Visit his website at www.steventhethorn.com.

Read his thoughts on life, liberty, and the pursuit of happiness on his blog: steventhethorn.blogspot.com.

You can also follow him on:

facebook.com/steventhethorn
instagram.com/steventhethorn
twitter.com/steventhethorn
youtube.com/steventhethorn

Made in the USA
Coppell, TX
18 June 2020